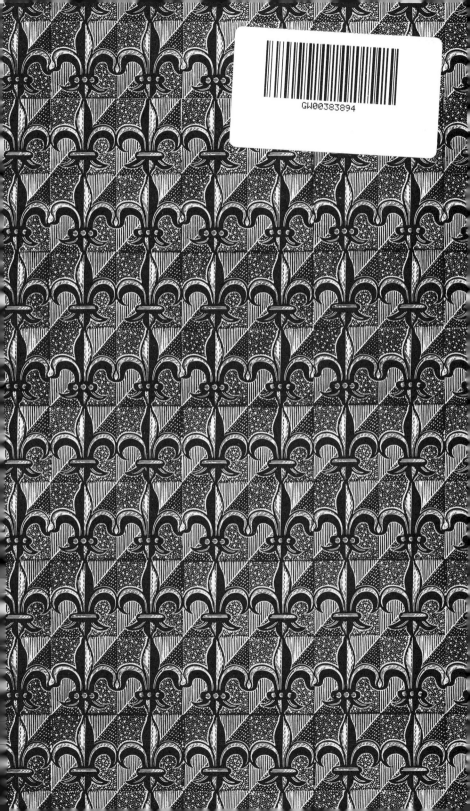

LOVE AS A
FOREIGN
LANGUAGE

By the same author

OUR MOTHER'S HOUSE
A SENTENCE OF LIFE
MAUNDY
A WOMAN OF CHARACTER
SLEEPING DOGS LIE
LOST AND FOUND
BLOOD FOR BLOOD
ONLY YESTERDAY

LOVE AS A FOREIGN LANGUAGE

a novel
by

JULIAN GLOAG

SINCLAIR-STEVENSON

First published in Great Britain by
Sinclair-Stevenson Limited
7/8 Kendrick Mews
London SW7 3HG, England

Copyright © 1991 by Julian Gloag

British Library Cataloguing in Publication Data
A CIP catalogue record for this book is available from the British Library
ISBN: 1 85619 097 8

Typeset by Phoenix Photosetting, Chatham, Kent
Printed and bound in Great Britain by
Butler & Tanner Ltd

FOR
M. V. W.

WE all love to instruct, though we can teach only what is not worth knowing.

Jane Austen, *Pride and Prejudice*

Find Someone in the Room Who:

> *Has more than two children*
> *Is working as a teacher now*
> *Has lived in more than two countries*
> *Knows what a modal is*
> *Has lived in Paris for five years*
> *Isn't afraid of grammar*
> *Speaks three or more languages*
> *Is a man*
> *Was not born in Britain*
> *Knows what 'realia' are*
> *Has worked for more than ten years*

THE STUDENTS stand up and move out of the circle with pencils and paper and smiles. The questions are a model of impersonal tact. It would be a lot more interesting to know Who: has been married more than twice, takes tranquillisers, has false teeth, dyes their hair, is under thirty, oversexed, anorexic, alcoholic . . . But this is an exercise in Breaking the Ice – not rocking the boat or melting the heart.

–Hey, you're a man.
–More or less.
–What's your name?
–Walter Waller.

−Walter − right. Let's see now − have you lived here for five years?

−Yes, but you're only allowed to have me once, I think. My turn. Are you a woman?

−But that's not a question.

−No? Okay − yes, what's a modal?

−I guess it's some kind of a verb − like 'could' or 'should' or 'might', stuff like that.

−Terrific. What's your name?

−Linda.

−You weren't born in Britain − you're American, aren't you?

−Yes, but you can only have me once. And she grins.

They go back to their seats and Adam, the slightly sweaty instructor, asks them all to identify themselves. Then, rapidly:

−Harriet, who did you find with more than two children?

−Janet − there. She points, and Janet, with a horsey face but magnificent dark eyes and eyebrows, blushes.

−And Janet, who did you find who . . .

Besides Walter, there is only one male student, Fred − in his twenties, but with a quiet ill-nourished air that suggests he's already been teaching for some time. Linda is the sole American and there is one Irishwoman, Kathy, exquisitely boned. The rest are Brits, nearly all middle-aged and most of them with the serious exhausted look of mothers bracing themselves for yet more labour. Walter is by far the oldest person in the room, twice as old as one or two, a fish out of −

−Walter?

−Hello?

−How many people can you name?

−Well . . . He takes a breath and runs them off − Kathy, Harriet, Phyllis, Linda, Janet, Fred, Sylvia, Julia, Gillian, Caroline, Sarah, Naomi − faultlessly until he comes to the last.
−I'm sorry, I've forgotten your −

−Connie.

−Good, well done. Thirteen women, two men − you'll all remember them I expect, ha-ha. (Despite the suggestive

snuffle, Adam is obviously attempting to be amiable.)
–Anyone else want to have a go?

   –I'm hopeless at names –
   –I always forget names –
   –I can never put a name to a face –

A small chorus of silver English voices disclaim any such simple accomplishment.

–No one? Perhaps later then. One thing I want to emphasise right at the start is that this course will be conducted in British English and *not* American English or any other odd variety. Last year we had one American student who *failed* the course simply because he was incapable of writing ordinary British English. That said, we can move on . . .

Adam is a small man with heavy glasses and thick lips and the kind of intelligent ugliness that must have often got him beaten up as a boy; but now he has a beer belly and a comradely smile and is fearlessly in charge. –What would we have been likely to find in a language class twenty-five years ago?

Walter glances at Linda, red-haired, foxy, a little grim now, and then at Kathy – Irish, another odd variety.

– . . . we call it *register*. What might be another word for that? Anyone? Well, what's wrong with this sentence: Would your Majesty be so gracious as to get off your arse and shut the bloody door?

–Damned impertinence, says Walter not loudly, but he is heard.

–Right. What's another word for impertinence? How about inappropriateness? So now we have . . .

It's very hot in the classroom. He was foolish to have had wine at lunch. Overwhelmed with all this Englishness, Walter begins to nod.

It is the end of the first class of TEFL (pronounced 'teffle') and the group dissolves quickly – reeled in to hearth and home and husband – leaving Walter alone with the unknown Connie on the pavement outside the language school.

–Do you go this way too? she says, as he lights a cigarette and falls into step with her.

–Same general direction . . . I'm sorry I forgot your name.

–That's alright, she says with a quick smile. –I expect I'm pretty forgettable.

This is a far more ludicrous pronouncement than any made in that afternoon's classroom. She has large brilliant brown eyes, even white teeth, advertisement-perfect features and, when not smiling, an oddly immobile look as though waiting for the camera to flash or a bus to come. How could he possibly have missed her out?

–Not at all, he says in his best English voice. –What did you think of the class?

–I can't bear the stuffiness in that place. She walks with a quick, limber stride. –I didn't understand a word.

–It's all balls really, isn't it?

–What?

–Bollocks.

–Oh yes. She gives him a sidelong smile. –You're smoking. I gave up smoking three years ago – forty a day, but the real thing, Gauloises. I can't stand the smell now. Oh don't worry, it's alright in the open air. But it made a battle with the weight – I let it go, then had to lose a stone . . . I don't know a thing about English really. I never got a degree or anything like that. I have to buy food. Where do you . . .?

–I go down here. I live in the Fifteenth – not far. I'll walk home.

They stand on the corner for a moment, a hint in the air, a smile.

–Goodbye.

–Goodbye – till next week . . .

It is a pellucid afternoon in late September, too warm to be truly autumnal. He saunters slowly, past Rodin's garden, which is still predominantly green, and cuts across into the long avenue. Here the leaves have begun to turn. Every so

4

often he looks behind him at the great dome of the Invalides, mauve as a shadow in the declining light. Eventually he tries walking backwards to keep it constantly in sight – and catches a heel in one of the hoops guarding the central grass and comes down with a thump on his bloody arse. He laughs and a woman wheeling a baby in a pushchair looks away and pushes a little faster.

Not long ago such a fall would have shaken him, but recently he's taken to early morning swims in the local pool and daily exercises (How to Flatten your Stomach) – fitting himself for the ordeal of teffle perhaps. He swings easily to his feet, proving to the baby-pusher that's he's not some alien old drunk.

In the square where he lives the newly planted maple trees have not yet shed a leaf; the pigeons rise and swirl around the Wallace fountain, then settle again. Someone has dumped an old armchair – but tomorrow it will be gone.

He picks up the afternoon mail from his box and takes the creaking elevator to the fifth floor – no, *lift*. He must unlearn these transatlantic oddities and try to recapture the English of his childhood. In the apartment he examines the letters. They look uninteresting and he shoves them unopened under the sleeping china cat on the mantelpiece. He pours himself a glass of Gewürztraminer from the fridge, tastes it, tips it down the sink and mixes a martini.

He washes his hands, then sits down to type up the afternoon's notes. From his white worktable by the window, he has a comforting view of the top of the Eiffel Tower. He puts a fresh sheet of paper into the machine and types: *Teaching of English as a Foreign Language (First Class)*. He takes a swallow of martini and feels a satisfying shiver at the back of his neck. He is going to take this course seriously.

The weather has turned brisker, cold enough for a coat, and as Walter walks across the esplanade the wind rattles the lanyards of the serried flagpoles like the clacking of Roman geese.

He is last into the classroom and finds an empty seat between Harriet and Phyllis, with Connie and Kathy and Janet opposite – ensconced in a nest of birds. They exchange fluttering smiles. On his yellow pad, Walter writes the name of the teacher, Emma, and today's subject, Nouns and Noun Phrases.

Emma is thin and has a serious hang-dog look, but she has a switch-on radiant smile which she uses at once while explaining how rotten she is at names – lamentably true. She seems to have a store of names in her memory bank (few of them belonging to members of the class) which she uses at random, then, –Oh sorry, switch-on smile and wrong again next time.

She starts the class with handouts: the teffle calendar for the year; the aims of peer teaching; the peer-teaching calendar; assigned tutorial groups; a list of everyone's name, address and phone number. Each time she gives only two or three copies to Walter's group and each time has to be asked for more. She can't count either.

As if to deny it, she leads them quickly into countable and uncountable nouns. There is a list. There is a list for everything. But everyone surreptitiously prefers the list of names and addresses – countable concrete people (smiles and whispers) are a lot more interesting than abstract uncountable nouns (truth and beauty). Only Connie and Walter actually live in Paris (the rest dwell in the outer darkness of the suburbs), although *she* is in the Seventh, chic and bleakly affluent, while *he*. . . She wears a platinum wedding ring, but her hands on the desk have the rough look of laundry and washing-up, and not much time in the boudoir.

He casts his eyes down and, as instructed, reads the sentence: *All these five red country houses on the hill are for sale* . . .

Warmth and torpor of nouns have turned them all languid; though it is the English Language School, no draughty halls of England here. They remove sweaters, jackets, cardigans. Not Walter; he is wearing an old black and white shirt with a hole in the armpit and, if he took his sweater off, he has the feeling a hundred female fingers would flash with instant needles to sew him up.

–And country – what is 'country'? A noun modifier – that's right.

Walter lifts his head. –Isn't it an adjective in this case?

–No, it's fulfilling an adjectival function, but it's not an adjective.

–Why can't it be called an adjective when it's used as an adjective – and a noun when it's used as a noun?

–Well, because 'country' is not mainly or normally used as an adjective. (The switch-on smile is losing electric current.)

–I don't know – country man, country clothes, country town, country produce, country air, country bus – isn't that all normal enough?

Harriet jumps in with a smile. –The point is that if a word can be used as a noun *and* an adjective, then it's a noun. If it can *only* be used as an adjective, then it's an adjective. Take 'red' for instance – 'red' can't be the head.

–The head?

–What you Brits call the toilet, says Linda from somewhere at the back of the class.

Emma bravely surmounts the sniggers. –She means 'red' can't be used as a noun.

–But we say, 'Philby was a red'.

–Yes, but we don't mean by that he was literally red in colour.

–Originally we did – not Philby maybe, but didn't the Bolsheviks wear red stars and what-not?

–Originally perhaps, but that isn't what it means now.

–You mean that for one briefish moment 'red' was a noun and then by some process of grammatical inevitability reverted to being an adjective again?

–Oh dear. No, that's not it at all.

–I don't get it. Another voice from the back of the class. –Isn't it a kind of ellipsis?

–I don't think so. Emma's blink rate is now quite high. –I

don't know. Perhaps we shouldn't spend too much time on . . .

Walter catches a smile from Connie. His head is full of porridge.

Later, walking home (to her home) in the exhilarating autumn chill, she tells him that Linda was so upset by Adam's crack about American English that she nearly quit the course.

–Well, I wouldn't cry. She reminds me of my second wife.

–Was she American?

–Yes.

–Oh. She pauses for a moment. –How old do you think she is?

–Linda? Twenty-nine.

–Really? I should have said older – but I'm useless at guessing people's ages . . . How old do you think I am?

–Thirty-seven – thirty-eight?

–That's nice. I'm forty. How old are you?

–Me? Oh . . . His tongue is thick in his mouth. –Well, in fact, I'm sixty.

–Old enough to be my father! Her laugh rings out. –You don't look it.

He touches her arm. –Look, he says and points to a towering cloud over the Seine caught pink in the descending sun. –French clouds.

–What's so French about them? She smiles as they stride off.

–You've never seen clouds like that in England, have you?

–I don't know. Haven't I? I haven't been in England for years – not properly, not for more than a few days. Do you go often?

–Not now, not since my children grew up, I don't.

She sighs. –I'd love to go in the holidays sometimes, but my children are a bit of a handful – nine and seven and always quarrelling – and my husband . . . well, he's French, of course. She looks at him; her dark eyes startlingly intense amid

8

the mild perfection of her face. –What do you think of the course really?

–Today was pretty soporific. Emma doesn't help much.

–No – all those 'I don't knows'. Like some sort of mechanical toy that keeps running down.

–A clockwork mouse. But who's got the key?

–Not me. Honestly, Walter, I don't see my way through any of it. It's not what I expected. With two children I haven't got much time – and this is such a large slice of it. I'm not sure I should go on. It's like what you said today – I'm not getting it. I feel swamped.

They begin to move again, but more slowly. –Maybe it's a bit like psychoanalysis – or a love affair – you *are* swamped at the start, but that's natural and you have to accept it and just let yourself float, you can't claim control, otherwise nothing will come of it.

Connie frowns, concentrating. –Yes, that's how I learnt French – just lived it. I've been perfectly bilingual for years, even the French think I'm French. She laughs. –Well, here we are.

They halt on the corner of the large placid square where she lives; it has a garden with grass and gravelled walks and green benches and trees and a church along one side – quite different from Walter's busy café- and shop-lined *place*.

–You don't look French.

–Don't I? I got a credit in their translation course – so I must be some good, mustn't I? Of course, I failed the exam the first year round, but that was because I was pregnant . . .

–But you're not pregnant now?

–Oh no . . . but I'm not well educated at all, you know. I'm sure all the others have degrees. I expect you have too, haven't you?

–Yes, but that doesn't mean much – I can't remember anything.

–What do you do?

–Do? I – er . . . Off-balance, he flubs the return. –I used to be in publishing.

9

–No, I mean now.

–Well, I do a bit of translating and any hacking that comes my way – the odd book review, articles for airline magazines – 'Apple-blossom Time in Old Normandy', that kind of crap.

–I thought you might be a writer – I'm quite good at professions.

–But I'm not – I just told you.

–Well, you look like one.

–My God! he says in mock horror.

Her expression softens. –Have you been in psychoanalysis?

–Well, yes – a long time ago.

She smiles and unexpectedly holds out her hand. He feels the roughness of her skin – a dry, decisive handshake. But what has she decided?

The early-morning swimmers never exchange a word. They stand silent in line until the doors open, show their passes and scatter to cubicles to change. Haste is essential, for only the first few can claim a channel in the long narrow pool – a right respected by all but a few capped and goggled musclemen who keep their heads down and force the less athletic to give way. Walter, sedate in a spidery breaststroke, gives one a passing kick and bland apologies – désolé!

The solitary exercises he performs at the side of the pool do not attract attention. In the book, the movements are illustrated with happy girls and grinning guys. But there are no smiles here. No one plays and the clock is set five minutes fast to hurry you away. The showers are segregated by sex and heavily chlorinated. Only the hair-dryer fixed to the wall is shared.

In the apartment he puts the kettle on to boil, then changes out of his yellow tracksuit. After he has shaved, he clips the stray hairs from the tops of his ears and examines his countenance in the bathroom mirror, searching for some literary trace but finding only a poached and melancholy look and the dull thumbprints of age under the eyes.

He takes his tea into the sitting room and drinks it in front of the open window. It is full daylight now and in the pavilion opposite the metal shutters have all been folded back. The two old men (one fat, one thin) who inhabit the house never go out but are sometimes to be seen lifting the corner of a net curtain and peering out at the untended garden. In the calm of the morning, the ragged bushes and the lone chestnut tree are alive with birds and a cat stalks tranquilly along the mossy top of the wall. Soon their housekeeper and her black and white mongrel appear on the top step. Tall and thin, in baggy trousers and an old beige raincoat, her face raddled with chainsmoking, she lights a cigarette as the dog prances into the garden with a flurry of barks against the world.

Walter steps back and shuts the window abruptly and sits down at his work table. He is translating a thin trilogy of adolescence, the last volume of which by some typical whim the English publisher wishes to bring out first. If it does well, he might get the commission for the other two. *Fleur-Marie-Fleur* is set on a summer's beach in Brittany, complete with rock pools and seaweed and shaded caves. He met the author when she won a prize, a pretty lady dressed up in frills for the occasion, but the backs of her hands were grimy and her fingernails black. Just so, the work strikes him sometimes as charmingly delicate, other times as puppyish and grubby.

He picks up the phone to call Connie.

Today is going to be a delicacy day.

–A pretty damned fruitless quest. We ought to have phoned first.

–I did, she says, racing her little red Renault out of the rue de Rivoli into Concorde. –But I got that wretched French girl who doesn't know anything but always says, *'Oui, Madame, on a tout ici.'*

The sun shines, the day is brilliant, with just a hint of crispness overriding the traffic fumes. None of the books they'd wanted had been in stock at Smith's (snatched by more eager students perhaps). Yet, on the other hand, they'd had fifteen minutes not walking or moving, but murmuring quietly together in bookstore calm over textbooks unsuitable, inscrutable, intractable . . .

–It's kind of appropriate, isn't it, that the top authority on all this stuff is called Quirk?

She gives him a quick glance – a mistake. She has to brake hard as the lights change, and Walter is jolted forward, caught by the seatbelt and flung back like a sack of carrots.

–Sorry. Are you all right? Am I driving too fast?

–No no – I'm okay. You're doing fine.

– It's just that I don't want to be late picking Tom up from school – I've got to rush him off to the dentist. He kept me up all night with this tooth of his; of course it was fine in the morning, but I'm not risking another night like that.

Walter touches her arm. They are stopped behind a bus and in the back seat are a couple kissing. The young man is wearing steel-rimmed glasses and his head is turned almost right round – he kisses, then draws back to stare at the girl with the utmost concentration.

–He looks as though he's studying some rare manuscript. Connie laughs. –Or the menu.

The bus moves off with a heave of its great body and the little red Renault whisks down a sidestreet, turns right, left, right again and pulls up in front of a school.

–Walter, I've decided I've absolutely got to go to England. My father's not well and I haven't been for over a year and it's getting ridiculous – so I'm going over for a long weekend at the end of Toussaint. Would you be interested in a place in the car?

–You're driving?

–Yes.

–With your children?

–Good heavens no, I'll have had them for ten days, won't I? That's the whole point – to get away on my own. I'm not offering you a free ride, I can't do that, but . . .

–Sure. Fine – it's about time I went too. We can stock up on teffle books. Where are you going – London?

–London first, then just outside Eastbourne. Is that awkward for you?

–No, suits me fine. My brother's place isn't far from Eastbourne, you could pick me up there. We could share the driving.

–Oh no, I'm not insured for that. Besides, I don't really like being driven by people I don't know.

–I'm quite responsible, you know.

–Are you really? She looks at him with unblinking gravity. –We'll have to leave Paris at about four in the morning.

–That's okay with me. Look, I'm sorry, how do I open this door?

–Just pull. Like this.

She leans across him and clicks the concealed handle. For a moment she does not move, they are so close he can feel the breath from her lips.

In the street a little wind stirs the leaves and lets them settle.

–Well . . .

They are out of the car.

–I must run. Till next week.

–Next week . . .

October is the handsomest time of the year and Sunday the busiest morning of the week in Walter's square. The young maples still guard their dark green leaves but the branches aren't big enough for birds; the pigeons that cluster at the foot of the Wallace fountain are kept in a constant flap by early shoppers criss-crossing with bread or croissants.

Walter strolls among the old ladies with felt hats and little dogs and buys a dozen oysters from the *écailler* in front of the *tabac*. He halts for a moment to admire the display of game next door – guinea-fowl and red-legged pheasant, partridge

13

and quail, hare, rabbit, ducks and does, and a boar hanging head down, dripping deep crimson blood from its left ear onto the pavement.

A little girl touches the gore with her fingertip.

−*Mais, Sandrine, qu'est-ce que tu fais?*

Outside the *boulangerie*, he hands a couple of cigarettes to the pale young bearded beggar, hunched against the brisk air, and lights one for him. The young man shudders as he takes the first drag − he has fine eyes and cherry red lips − and sighs and bobs his head in thanks and shuffles away.

At the polished copper counter of the Floréal, Walter drinks a ten-o'clock beer and smokes his first cigarette of the day. Now and again he exchanges a word or two with Monsieur Laigle, his upstairs neighbour, over a heavily marked-up *Paris-Turf* − but this is too serious a business for idle chatter. Monsieur Laigle, grey and ancient, lives in a maid's room on the sixth floor with his equally grey and ancient dog, and is faultlessly courteous; he pins impossible hopes on the *tiercé* − rescue from debts and dying and desuetude.

Walter orders another beer.

−Today we're going to talk about verb forms and tenses. But before we start, did anyone try the exercise in Konkomba I gave you at the end of the last class? Adam perches on the edge of the desk informally half-arsed; his lower lip still glistens and occasionally sprays, but his clothes have taken a turn for the better (a buttoned shirt, and shoes and socks). −Well, how did you find it − easy, difficult?

There is a general modest murmur.

−It seemed fairly simple − like a crossword puzzle, Walter says. He turns up the Word Class Sheet on which he's worked it out.

−Right − well, perhaps you'd go up to the blackboard and explain it to us.

–Me? Okay – sure. He walks round and picks up the chalk.
–Now . . . He pauses, staring at his plan.

–Well, what's an axe?

–An axe? He has no axe – only numbers: *kibaa, libaa, mulee, bulee* – or are they numbers? –I think I must have the wrong sheet . . .

–Anyone?

–*Lilal.*

–Good. Could you write it up?

Walter dutifully scrawls it on the board.

–A hill? A spear? A knife? A year?

–*Lidzool, ngbalim, nudzum, bugmu* . . .

A white mist descends upon his head veiling all but the pigeon shit and chicken toes on the blackboard. He wields the chalk mechanically, understanding nothing. Konkomba, Bariba, Esperanto, English, French merge into a soft dyslexic fog . . .

He is back at last, staring dazedly at the freckles on Connie's arm – uncountable freckles but each a sudden island of meaning in the flesh.

–Now. There are only two tenses in the English language – the past simple and the present simple.

Her hand rests on a page of 'time-line drawings': a fixed period around Now, an Infinite period, a point in the Past.

–Everything in the simple past is *factual*, conveying *remoteness* . . .

. . . *kipipeek kigbalik npipeem mugmu* . . . Chimborazo Cotopaxi Popocatapetl . . .

–That's the one I like, she says.

–What? He blinks slowly back from remotest Konkombaland to her finger pointing to a heading on the facing page: –The Dummy Auxiliary. . .

–Oh yes, he says, –that's me alright.

Waiting on the edge of the square, bag in hand, he whistles softly. Soon he begins to sing –Standing on the corner, watching all the girls go by – standing on the corner, giving all the girls the eye . . . Only it's four-thirty on a cold morning and there are no girls or anyone else abroad. His hair is newly cut, and under his overcoat he is wearing a suit and tie. The chill penetrates to every part of his body, laying an icy hand on his naked head, nipping the tips of the ears, freezing the feet, shrivelling the testicles. The cold container only defines more strictly the warmth of the contained.

He is waiting for a forty-year-old married woman with two children to come and carry him off to England. Yet is she not still a girl – a pure, sweet English girl trapped in an alien container?

The little red Renault zips up the street and stops in front of him.

–Am I late?

–Dead on time. He throws his bag onto the back seat and gets in. There is a second's hesitation – no kiss, no touch. A quick taut smile, and a long breath.

–Right – which way?

–Left at the lights, up Vaugirard, Saint-Michel, Châtelet, then straight on . . .

–Did you sleep?

–A bit – not enough. The children . . .

–What?

–Don't like me going much – at least, Tom doesn't. It's silly, really – after all, it's only five days, yet it feels like, I don't know – a wonderful gift, an adventure . . .

–A voyage into the unknown.

She gives him a look as they speed past the gilded gates of the Palais de Justice. –The unknown? What's that?

–England . . . home and beauty.

–Oh yes. Yes, that must be it.

–Must be what?

–Must be why I didn't sleep . . . much.

And they smile, racing through the empty heart of Paris, not another car on the road and all the lights in their favour.

Theirs is the only vehicle waiting for the boat – a queue of one. Delicate mauve clouds brush the pale gold sky, drawing the eye upwards from the blind blocks of flats surrounding the port to the basilica crowning Boulogne. They have talked without ceasing for four hours, drunk the tea in her thermos and eaten an entire bagful of madeleines.

–You'd better have this back, Walter says, holding out her passport.

–Oh hang on to it, would you – they'll have to inspect it again at Folkestone. You've got the boarding passes?

–Yes – and the tickets entitling us to a free cup of tea. Constance Verity Thompson. Why your maiden name?

–I wasn't going to change *that* on my passport. It's bad enough having to go about being introduced as Madame Henri Mantel. I hate that – just tagging along as a sort of extra.

–A negative tag.

–If that – *une quantité négligeable*. I never really wanted to get married at all. Are you cold?

–No. Why did you then?

–Pressure – not that *he* minded one way or another. But the baby was coming and there was all that business about paternity. And his parents couldn't understand and *my* parents couldn't understand, and the gynaecologist was so bloody rude about it – *Mademoiselle*, he kept calling me with a nasty little sneer. So in the end I gave way, what does it matter, I thought – but of course it did, does. I know I was weak and I hate being weak.

–You don't strike me as weak.

–I don't? Really? She smiles, pleased. She opens her bag and takes out a folder of photos. –Would you like to see my children? Here, look, that's Sarah on her eighth birthday.

A large-eyed pouting child in a white frilly container.

–And that's Tom – he was six then . . . A small boy with an almost manic look of animal alertness, stiffly holding his sister's hand – and behind them a tall, balding man with a discontented downturn of the mouth – the three of them grouped against a black and white timbered farmhouse wall.

17

–That's Henri – my husband – in the yellow sweater. He always wears yellow sweaters. And this is the family house in Normandy.

–Nice place.

–It's horrible – God how I hate it! And this is me at home, a typical Sunday breakfast. She laughs and points across the table – muesli, a milk jug, Marmite, surprised children grinning – to a figure in a flowered bathrobe, shoulders slack, face covered, head bowed. –A rotten night, I suppose . . .

He gives back the photo, shocked with desire and dismay.

–I think the man wants us to move.

–What? Oh yes. Walter winds down the window and hands over the boarding passes. The official, who'd issued them ten minutes before, now gravely inspects them, nods and unchains the way for the car to pass.

–What does your husband do?

–I hate that question. If you must know, he's a banker – in venture capital. Does that mean anything to you?

–Oh I think so.

–What? I've never really understood.

–It's a form of financial vampirism, isn't it? You do the work, I'll take the profits.

–That doesn't sound quite right. She laughs as they swish slowly over the ramp into the hollow entrails of the ship.

The motorists' lounge is all dark pannelling, crimson and royal blue plush, mirrors and sharp bright lights. There is no tea, no coffee – nobody in sight at all.

–It looks like the inside of a doll's house – it smells funny.

–That's authentic enough. Lounges on liners always used to smell like this – as though they're just about to give up their dead. Let's get out of here and try the bar.

–Shouldn't we look at the sea first?

–Do you want to?

–Well – I'll leave it to you.

–Tea first – then the sea.

–How lovely not to have to make the decisions. She smiles happily. Her face is clear of care and more beautiful than ever in class (choose for me, make my choices for me, just for a few hours, like a prayer . . .).

–I had a nightmare a few days ago, she says, stirring her sugarless tea. –Perhaps I shouldn't tell you . . . I haven't told anyone . . .

The ship lifts a little. Walter sits still.

–I was at the top of the Eiffel Tower with the children – which is quite unlikely because I can't stand heights. Henri was somewhere behind me – at least I think he was – and suddenly he fell off. All I saw of him actually was a flash of yellow sweater going past. I rushed for the stairs – I don't know why I didn't think of the lift – and started running down. They seemed endless, but I wasn't a bit afraid – I felt I was sort of floating, round and round and round, like being just a tiny bit drunk but perfectly safe and lovely . . .

–That doesn't sound very nightmarish.

–The nightmare was when I got to the bottom – the whole place was filled with firemen and ambulances and police and flashing lights. And I knew he was dead. And then I woke up. It was awful. I felt as though I'd killed him.

–But you hadn't.

–Well, it was my dream, wasn't it? I mean, it was me who set him up. So it was really me that pushed him . . .

–Why? He might have decided just to jump off – lots of people do.

–Henri wouldn't.

–Why not?

–He never takes risks.

–A true venture capitalist. Walter drinks some now tepid tea. –Anyway, maybe the yellow sweater acted as a kind of parachute and he just gently floated down – like you.

She leans forward earnestly. –But then what about all the ambulances and fire engines at the foot of the tower?

−Maybe all that was there for you, not him. The ambulance to take you to hospital to heal your wounds, the firemen to put out the dangerous flames, the police to −

−What 'dangerous' flames?

−We are talking about sex, aren't we?

−Oh. Are we? She blushes. She carefully drinks her tea, as though it might unexpectedly make her drunk. −Are you clever?

−Am I . . . ? I don't think so. I used to be − in that half-baked kind of way publishers have. But not any more. Why?

−When were you a publisher?

−In New York − a long time ago.

−I don't know very much about you, do I? Except that you have two children and you had an American wife − two wives.

−Actually, three.

Connie laughs − a rich, unconstrained sound. Another couple in the bar − middle-aged, frowsy, the man drinking beer at nine o'clock in the morning − turn and stare.

−Are we moving?

−We've been moving for quarter of an hour.

−It doesn't notice.

−You mean you don't notice it.

−That's what I said.

−No you didn't. You said, 'It doesn't notice'. You can't say that.

−Why not? People do.

−People beat their wives and kick their dogs.

−That's not the same thing at all.

−Abuse, misuse − not so very different.

−But what have I said wrong?

−You've credited the ship with the capacity to observe its own motion.

−Have I? Well − alright. But you know what I meant, so what does it matter?

−If you don't think the distinction between use and misuse matters, before long you won't even remember the distinction. That's how the language gets degraded and −

–Oh come on! The mistake I made – if it *is* a mistake – it's a very fine point and if –

–But language is precisely *about* fine points – that's the very heart of it.

–I thought the point was to *communicate*. Isn't that what teffle's all about?

–God help us, I'm beginning to think so – but to communicate what? The quickest way to the public lavatory?

–Well, if you need a lavatory, it might be convenient to –

–I don't need a lavatory! Who needs a lavatory? Let's do it in the road. For God's sakes!

–You're getting all worked up.

–Am I? Sorry.

–Oh no – I like it. But can we go up on deck now? I'm starting to feel a bit sickish.

The sea is calm and a milk-white mist conceals the coast of France so the ship glides in a great pale cavern of its own. The tip of the stern is blocked off by rows of circular plastic life-rafts; but they stand as close to it as they can, at the rail, almost touching but not touching.

–What happened to the children?

–What children?

–Your children – in your dream.

–They just sort of faded out . . .

Her voice is small, and both of them are almost whispering. Walter clears his throat.

–Have you noticed there aren't any gulls today?

–Are there usually?

–Lots – wheeling and squealing.

–Perhaps it's their day of rest . . . She moves her hand a fraction on the rail and their fingers touch.

–Your hands are cold.

–Walter –

Suddenly the loudspeaker blares. –This is a ship's

announcement about safety precautions. In the case of an emergency, an alarm will . . .

Instinctively they've drawn apart – now they look at each other and laugh. The loudspeaker voice is both stentorian and finicky in its enunciation, as though it were shouting at mental patients on the moon.

–. . . you will proceed at once to your muster station. If you are already assembled at your muster station, you should remain at your muster station. Members of the crew will . . .

The announcement is made in English, then in French, then German. (How many Germans cross by ferry at dawn on a weekday in November? But perhaps it's all done to frighten away the seagulls.) Then abruptly it stops and the silence returns tenfold – they can hear the whispering of the water against the ship's side and the soft flap of the ensign in the small breeze of passage.

She says, –It sounded best in French, didn't it?.

–Well, the French take more naturally to formality than we do.

–Don't they just! Do you know, Henri still *vouvoi*'s his father.

–Where's that – in Normandy?

–Normandy, Paris – it's all the same. Though it's worse in Normandy – we're all together there, there's no getting away.

–In that house?

–The house and the grange and even the *four au pain* – it's like a military encampment. Aunts and brothers and sisters and grandchildren – and the old man rules them with a rod of iron. And they're all so *rusé*, sly and snide and snobbish and . . . Oh, I'm not going to talk about all that. Who cares?

A solitary gull appears from nowhere and settles on the stern rail with a melancholy cry.

–I'm sorry – I upset you. Are you alright?

–Oh yes. A bit queasy perhaps. She gives him a wan smile. –I really prefer the hovercraft, it's much quicker.

–But basically unstable – a strong gust of wind could flip it over on its back before you'd sipped your gin and tonic.

–But it seems so much safer. For the children anyway. Look at this rail – Tom could slide under there and tumble overboard in a second; just the sort of thing he would do – he's always been naughty. That's why I've never taken them on the boat – it scares me stiff.

They look at the sea, now black with malice.

–It would swallow him up, she says. –He'd sink like a stone.

–Would you jump in after him?

–He'd be gone. Look how fast we're going – he'd be a hundred yards away. I'd never reach him . . . What would you do?

–I'd jump. It wouldn't do much good – I'm a lousy swimmer. But how could I live with the creature I'd be if I didn't jump? I'd probably drown, but it's supposed to be a pleasant death, and I'm not all that valuable.

–It's funny you say that. I had a friend once who said just the opposite. She felt that if anyone had to die, she'd rather it were her two children – and they were young at the time – and not her. Of course, she didn't have a husband, so I suppose that made a difference, but her theory was that the children would be so utterly miserable and helpless without her, they'd be better off dead. But *she* could live without *them* – however miserable she was – and perhaps have other children. I don't know. I . . . Walter – I'm sorry . . . could we . . . it's getting to me.

She stands with her hand on her heart, motionless, staring at the colourless green wake that stretches out across the Channel.

–Maybe the best thing to do would be to scream.

–Scream?

–Scream and people would come running. Do you know how to scream?

–I suppose so – yes. She turns a little and looks at him.

–No, but I mean really scream. I remember once going to a dinner party with Leonore and –

–Leonore?

–Number three. Anyone, the subject got on to rape – it

usually did sooner or later with Leonore – and suddenly a little old lady said in a sprightly voice, 'Well, you have to know how to scream.' And she told us this story of how her father had taught her to scream – he was a woodcutter and when she was quite small he took her into the forest once a week to practise until she got it right. 'Do it,' I said. 'Alright,' she said – and she threw back her head and let out the most blood-curdling yell I've ever heard. It had us all transfixed and the cat ran mewing under the sofa, I remember. Want to try?

–I don't know – what, now?

–Come on – why not?

She takes a breath and gives a small squeak – and they laugh.

–Again. She manages something approaching a scream.

–Still sounds like a seagull. Come on – you're running, he's after you, you're at the end of your tether, you're being attacked – scream!

But she does nothing of the sort. She looks at him. –Am I being attacked?

He puts his hands on her upper arms and kisses her.

–Connie . . .

–No – don't . . . She pushes him gently away. –There's nothing I can do about it.

–Well . . .

–I'm married.

–Yes, but –

–I've got two children.

–Yes . . . Look.

–Look?

–We're coming in – the white cliffs of Dover. See?

–Yes, she says. –But it's Folkestone.

–How long have you been away?

–About thirty-seven years.

The customs officer bends down and gives him a closer look.

24

–We live in France, Connie says brightly.

–I see. And what is the purpose of your visit?

–To see family and friends.

–And how long will you be staying?

–Four nights.

–And do you have any alcohol, cigarettes, cigars?

–A litre of gin for my parents.

–Right then. He hands back the passports and smiles. –Have a nice trip.

–That was easy. Now – where do I go?

–Left here, then round to the right. He must think we look respectable.

–I am respectable.

Walter laughs. –We could stay in Folkestone for the day.

–Why? Is it nice?

–Absolutely unspoiled – a bit seedy and not smart at all. I never heard of anyone having a dirty weekend in Folkestone.

–Oh God – a dirty weekend!

–You've got to get used to it – you're in Benny Hill country now. Maybe we should stop here and fill her up.

–Right. She turns into the petrol station and stops, but doesn't immediately get out. –Have you really been away from England for thirty-seven years?

–Longer, if you count the years I spent in the States during the war.

–You were in America in the war? But you were only a child.

–An adolescent. An acned teenager – a transatlantic evacuee.

–But you are . . . English?

–Oh yes. I am. Well, actually I'm American too – I took out citizenship after I'd lived there for a while.

–Before or after you were psychoanalysed?

–It was a perfectly rational decision – I never expected to live in France.

–No, nor did I. But – then when Adam made that snotty crack about Americans, you . . .

–There was no point in upsetting him . . . one of those moments when it's best to sit back and avoid injury.

–You don't have an American accent.

–It wore off. Does it disappoint you – my being sort of quasi-American?

–No, of course not. Why should it? Anyway you seem perfectly English to me. Now – petrol. Will you do it or shall I? You do it.

They are out of the car. Walter punches the four-star button and lifts the handle. As he puts the nozzle into the tank, a gout of petrol sloshes over the mudguard.

–You're not very good, are you?

–Clumsy, you mean?

–Yes.

–But I'm not afraid of heights.

–You pig. She laughs. –Don't watch me – watch what you're doing . . . You know, all that lot up in Normandy – the family – they think Benny Hill's hilarious, they always watch him.

–Yes, well – the French don't have much sense of humour.

–No, they don't, do they? That's enough. Here, catch this. She tosses him the petrol cap. –I'll go and pay.

And away she strides to the office.

It's a brilliant day now. In the little harbour the boats – blue and green and red – sit like toys in a toy shop.

He too could walk away – there's time. The *Hengist* is still at the dock. He could board it and be gone in half an hour. He could leap into the following sea and sink like a stone and no one would scream.

Instead, he gets into the car and buckles up the safety belt.

Connie halts to let a blue van come in from the left. The driver gives her a grin and a wave, and she lets another car go too.

–Aren't you overdoing the courtesy bit?

She smiles, sitting up very straight. –I'm doing it on purpose. They see it's a French car and they'll think how nice and polite the French are.

26

–Don't you believe it. They're thinking, 'What a dishy French bint.'

She laughs and whisks past a long line of traffic on the inside. –It's fun being taken for French when you're not, don't you think?

–Nobody ever takes me for French – anyway, that little manoeuvre's lost you all the credit you gained.

–I can't stand the way they just hang around.

–It's called lane discipline.

–I've never been good at discipline. Oh look at that. Arsehole!

He stares at her in astonishment. *–Arsehole?*

–Well, did you see what he did?

–No, no, no. Keep going straight – we don't want the Dartford Tunnel.

–Are you sure? It says London.

–Absolutely sure.

–Well – okay.

–You don't sound convinced.

–You weren't very good in Boulogne, were you?

–I don't know Boulogne. But I got you out of Paris alright, didn't I?

–I admit that, yes. So where are we now?

–Er, let's see – Bexley?

–Bexley!

–Sonny Tufts!

–Sunny what? What does that mean?

–That's going to be hard to explain if you don't know.

–No, I don't. But the question is – do you know how to get us to Chelsea?

–Sure, of course – I used to live in Chelsea.

–I'm hungry. Can we have some lunch somewhere?

–Great idea. We could stop at Putney – there's a good pub by the river, or used to be. You don't mind a pub?

–Not as long as they have food. I shan't have to drink, shall I?

–It's not compulsory. Do you want to hear about Sonny Tufts?

–Yes. I want to hear about everything.

Connie has eaten her chilli voraciously, bread, butter and jam roly-poly with custard. Walter has managed no more than a few sticky mouthfuls of rice.

–That was marvellous. Now all I want is a bath.

–Not part of the facilities here, I think.

–I'll have one at Viv's. I said I'd be there about three – do we have time to get the teffle books?

–It would be pushing it. But I'll get them, I've got the list.

–Alright, but you don't want to cart them all the way down to your brother's place – why don't you pop back to Viv's and we can dump them in the boot?

–Good idea. I'll do that. Do you mind if I smoke?

–Not as long as it doesn't blow in my face.

As he lights the cigarette, she watches him intently – as though he were engaged in an altogether different type of ritual. They are sitting in the window and outside on the river an elderly eight is paddling lightly into the boathouse for a few pints before lunch. The pub is beginning to fill up now, but the room is large and airy and not noisy. The cigarette smoke floats in a sleek layer just above their heads and the sunlight glows amber in the remains of Walter's bitter.

–Aren't you going to finish your beer?

–I've had enough. What about you – are you sure you don't want something?

–No thanks. You're very good about not insisting. When I gave up wine last summer, you'd have thought I was advocating, I don't know, child-beating or kicking the dog. She laughs. –No, but seriously, the whole family behaved as though I was deliberately insulting them. I was anti-social, they said. But what's wrong with being abstemious?

–It can make other people feel a bit gross – our virtues insult their vices. You don't drink, you don't smoke . . .

–No. And I don't gossip and backbite. And I don't have little snogging sessions with Marc and Jean-Pierre on the side.

–Why not?

–I believe if you're married, you're married. Why should you want anything more?

–You're setting rather a high standard, aren't you?

–Am I? You mean – oh, because I have no vices. Is that it? I used to have vices.

–A naughty little girl?

–Oh no, I was as good as gold as a child. We used to live in Penge. What's the matter – have I said something funny?

–No . . . yes. I mean . . . He takes a deep breath to choke down his laughter. –Endearing – adorable . . .

–Walter, you mustn't say that to me. I'm definitely not adorable. Penge wasn't so bad, you know. It was childhood I hated. She smiles, a little shyly. –I suppose it does have its funny side.

–Yes, he says, looking her straight in the eyes, stuprate with secret lust.

After Connie has dropped him in front of Viv's neat Chelsea house, Walter strides purposely off in a vague, high-wire haze. Daunted by the thought of buses, he hails a cab in the King's Road.

–Where to, Guv?

–What? Oh – Dillon's bookshop. It's just off –

–You don't have to tell me. Here, don't I know you?

–I doubt it.

–I do though. You famous?

–Good God no.

–Yeah, they all say that. But I seen you alright. You on telly then?

–No.

–Yes you are.

–I am not on telly. I have never been on – well, that's not quite true. I was once on a –

–There, see – I knew it. Now who are you?

–on a book programme on Channel 13 in New York twenty-five years ago, but I very much doubt that you could –

–Robin Day – that's who you are. Yeah – you just taken your glasses off, haven't you? What you got – contact lenses?

–Listen, I am not Robin Day, I have never met Robin Day – whoever he is – I –

–Come on – who you kidding? I can spot a celebrity a mile away. I had your friend David Frost in the back a couple of weeks ago, a nice bloke he is, he told me –

–David Frost is no friend of mine. I don't know David Frost. I don't want to know David Frost.

–Professional jealousy, eh? I know – dog eat dog in your line of work, ain't it? You people ought to be ashamed – all smiles up there on the box and then –

–Listen, will you shut the hell up and drive!

–'ere, if you're going to go on like that, mate, you can get out of my ruddy cab.

–Right. I will. Pull up.

The taxi stops with a jerk that sends Walter sprawling. He climbs out, trembling with absurd rage, spilling pound coins on the sidewalk.

–Keep your bleeding money. You rich bastards are all alike, aren't you? Just because you're famous, you think you can shout the odds at an ordinary bloke minding his own business. I tell you, if you wasn't such a fucking feeble-looking old sod, I'd get out of this 'ere cab and knock a bit of respect into your fat gut – Sir Robin or no Sir Robin. What you –

–Stick Sir Robin up your ass. Piss off. Drop dead.

–'ere! The driver rears up and starts to open the door.

And Walter turns and runs . . .

Later, as he mounts the immaculately scrubbed steps with a plastic sack full of teffle textbooks, the door of number 49 bursts open and a large beige lady with a pale face confronts him. –Hello – what can I do for you?

–Oh – I . . . my name's Walter and I've come –

–Oh, Connie's friend. She grins. –You're a bit early, aren't you? No matter. I'm Viv.

–How do you do. Things went a big quicker than I expected. I could come back later if –

–Of course not. I've got to rush off to one of those awful parent-teacher things, but you come in. Connie's upstairs having a bath. Make yourself a cup of tea if you like. The kitchen's the second door on the left. Or if you'd rather, the drinks are on the table in the sitting room.

–Tea would be fine.

–Good. Now why did I assume you were French? She gives him a quick once-over from head to scuffed toe. –Well, I must fly. See you later perhaps.

The door slams and he is alone in the parquet hall. He hangs his coat on a hook under the stairs where there is a neat row of Wellington boots – green, red, yellow, blue. The kitchen is large and comfortably farmhouse: oak cabinets and counters, a big scrubbed deal table, a butcher's block, a high-chair and a solid pine school desk next to a chintz-covered sofa under the window. There is a big Dufy-like lithograph on the only bare wall – French bandsmen with drums and trumpets and red-striped trousers.

He plugs in the electric kettle but, though dusk is beginning to fall, doesn't switch on the lights. The house is peculiarly quiet, with that special quiet of absent owners. Walter drifts into a gloaming reverie of other houses, other times: just up the road in Chelsea, on the Connecticut River, in the Auvergne – dry sherry, Bloody Marys, *un petit blanc* . . . And far far back in Pleasantville, Phoebe playing the piano, limpid notes on a summer's evening from another world . . .

–Oh my God!

–Connie.

—Walter! What are *you* doing here?

—I'm making tea. I've given you a shock.

She's in a terrycloth bathrobe, her feet bare, her hair dampened down. But even in the half-dark, a gleam of light catches her eyes from somewhere.

The bowels of the kettle begin to stir.

—I – I thought you were . . . Her voice quivers. She is close, open.

—A robber? A thief in the night . . . He puts his hands on her back, holds her. —It's alright.

—No, she whispers, no, it's not. The bathrobe falls apart. —No, it's not fair . . .

They tumble together on the sofa.

The kettle sings, Connie cries out in the twilight, the band plays on . . .

—That was shit. That was awful. You bloody bastard.

She jumps up and is gone in a swirl of white and brisk soft footfalls on the stairs.

Walter stays still. Soon he gets up and makes the tea.

The high has held for four entranced days and the fifth morning is just as glorious, the sky a lofty blue, the sun twinkling the sea on their right as they beetle along the South Coast in the scarlet car.

—It won't take us anything like three hours to get to Folkestone, do you think? Connie is in a merry mood, bright with recaptured energy, all nightmares erased.

—Not unless we hit a lot of Sunday traffic. And it's too early for that.

—Yes. But Daddy was worried, the poor old dear. She laughs. —When you rang last night he thought you were Henri.

She laughs a lot – the awkward teffle laugh, the rich resonant laugh, the easy laugh like now – yet there are no marks of laughter on her face, few marks at all. At forty, she seems strangely unsullied by time.

32

–Yes, he says, –I gathered that. He tried to speak French to me.

–Poor Daddy, he rather prides himself on his French, but when he actually has to talk he gets a bit tongue-tied. And Henri's English is of the I-zink-eet-ees-vairy-nize variety. Makes communication a bit difficult – but, otherwise, they get on very well. I rang the children last night – they sounded so sweet and subdued. Can we stay up till you get home, *Maman?* I said we'd be back about eight – do you think that's a bit optimistic?

–What? Oh no . . . about right. He unwinds the window a little – it's suddenly stuffy in the car. –You don't mind?

–I suppose if the weather changed . . . She is wearing a red sweater and dark tartan trousers and her cheeks are as soft as down. –It's not going to be rough or anything, is it?

–Not until we get to France, at any rate. He reaches for a cigarette, then stops. You're looking particularly –

–What?

–Healthy.

–Alright. I thought you were going to say 'pretty'.

–I changed my mind.

–Don't *ever* call me pretty or beautiful, do you understand? I hate all that.

–Right, Connie.

–I learnt some lovely new words – 'dinky', 'nimby' – do you know what 'dinky' means?

–Something about double income?

–Double income no kids yet. What bliss! And nimby?

–Not in my bed yet?

She gives him a sharp glance. –Not in my back yard. What have you got in that plastic bag that keeps clinking – whisky?

–No, sherry. And Bovril and Rose's limejuice, Gentlemen's Relish, Lyons Red Label tea, mint jelly and bloater paste. What about you – what's in the cardboard box?

–Farmhouse cheddar, Marmite, golden syrup, mint chunks, Wagon Wheels, chocolate animals for the children's stockings – oh and custard powder.

They burst out laughing.

–Connie, really – custard powder. Don't tell me they like custard!

–Of course they do. What's wrong with custard?

–Dog's vomit.

–Well, what about bloater paste? I'm surprised you haven't got pickled onions.

–Oh, but I have – I forgot. They'd go nicely with your cheddar – except I don't like cheddar.

–The only thing I'd take off you is the limejuice. Where are we now?

–Hastings?

–But you're supposed to know. Oh look, Bexhill Royal Hotel – it must be Bexhill.

He thinks, I am dying of love and I am driving through Bexhill-on-Sea.

–I didn't think about teffle once, did you?

–No, but it's about time we did . . . we've got to get that essay in before Christmas. What do you know about gerunds?

–Nothing in the world – I was hoping you'd tell me.

–You must remember something – you're a lot closer to your schooldays than I am.

–Walter, I told you, I'm barely educated. At the convent school I was at they didn't teach us anything worth knowing – I got out as soon as I could.

–You're a Catholic?

–I was. I gave it up when I was fifteen. I got so pissed off with the nuns. I just said to my parents, I'm not going to mass any more, and I didn't. And after a bit they stopped going too. She sighs. –All the same, I had Sarah and Tom baptised.

–Why – is Henri especially devout?

–You must be joking. He doesn't believe in anything. But that doesn't matter to the French, does it? I say, 'How can you

34

call yourself a Catholic if you go on doing things the Church says you mustn't?' 'But I was *born* a Catholic,' he says. It seems so pointless. What are you?

–I'm not anything either. My parents were extremely pious atheists. Of course, I had the usual doses of the Church of England at various boarding schools, but –

–What's that like?

–The Church of England? Lovely to listen to, but unspeakably dreary in practice. Nowadays they've revised the words to make them as stale as the faith – the communicative approach to religion, as it were.

–Didn't you *ever* believe anything?

–Nope. The nearest I ever got to faith was with my American family in the war – they were Quakers. But then there's something so essentially decent about Quakerism, it's hard to think of it as a religion.

–Are you never serious?

–Not if I can possibly avoid it.

The motorists' lounge is off limits to motorists.

–Sorry, mate, reserved for the Orient Express this sailing.

–That is simply *not* satisfactory. An elderly Englishman of the blazered and flannelled variety. –Your company has some very serious questions to answer – very serious. I shall not take this lying down. (Clearly nothing agreeable has ever come his way lying down.)

–Look, I just work here.

–I shall be writing to the management.

–You do that, cocky – write to the bleeding Queen for all I care.

Walter and Connie retreat with the other motorists to the bar, where cocky is now sipping gin and tonic as though it were castor oil.

–No really, I'm alright, just a bit dizzy. It used to be far worse – I'd get a terrible pain and I couldn't do anything for hours. When I was working, they'd send me home in a taxi. But the funny thing is, since Tom all that's changed. All I get now is this vagueness.

–What about driving?

–Oh don't worry, it'll be gone by then. As soon as it comes, I'm okay. She shivers.

–You should have a drink – a stabiliser.

–What's that?

–Port and brandy, half and half.

–I don't like port.

–Champagne then.

–Champagne – well, I would like a glass. But we'd have to get a bottle, wouldn't we? It'll be expensive.

–Isn't that what money's for – to spend?

She stares at him with glum solemnity and for a moment he thinks she's about to burst into tears, but instead she gives an odd little explosive laugh. –I'll pay half.

–You can pay for what you drink.

Even the first taste of Clicquot chases the pallor from her face. –A client of Henri's sends him a dozen Krug every Christmas. We don't drink really – there's a whole cupboardful of undrunk whisky and brandy – but sometimes it would be nice to have a bottle of champagne. But it sits there in the *cave*, you know, and I think, what's it for, why are we keeping it?

–For a rainy day?

–But champagne won't keep out the rain. He earns plenty of money, I think – he's always investing it on good tips and deals he's been let in on on the ground floor. But why are we saving? Why can't we use it now? I need it to buy the children shoes and have their teeth seen to, let alone holidays. I don't care about the rest of it – I don't want jewellery and smart clothes and lavish gifts. He's finally got *that* message. We went to a family party not long ago and I wore little earrings I'd made in star shapes out of old rose silk, and they all said, '*Mais* Connie – what about the rubies Henri gave you?' I loathe those rubies. I don't want to show off somebody else's money. I want to

36

earn my own money. Yes – just a little – half a glass.

He pours the champagne gently, the ship is steady, the voyagers quiet.

BOUCHONS BOUCHONS BOUCHONS – the van on the hard shoulder flashes the electric warning and the traffic slows abruptly to a dawdle on the rain-slick autoroute.

–Where are we now?

–Beauvais, somewhere like that.

–How far from Paris?

–Eighty kilometres maybe.

–Oh God, if this keeps up all the way, we –

–It won't. There's probably been an accident, but once we're past that, it'll be okay.

–We won't be back till ten. I know it. The children will be in fits.

–Nonsense, they'll be thrilled to stay up that much later. But if you're really worried, we can always stop and phone.

–Why did this have to happen? Oh if only I hadn't been to England!

–It wasn't exactly your fault.

–What kind of shit is that? Of course it was my fault. She doesn't look at him, stares straight ahead through the glistening windshield.

Walter eases his seat-belt. –Connie–you're not proposing to *tell* him, are you?

–Of course I am. I don't lie.

–I see. I'm sorry, I've got to have a cigarette.

–Just keep the bloody smoke away from me.

He lights the cigarette and opens the window a crack. The night is getting chilly. In front of them the rear lights of the cars stretch in a ruby necklace for miles. Somewhere up there ahead are crushed bodies and mangled metal.

–Why? You don't *want* to hurt him, do you?

–I *have* hurt him, haven't I?

–Not if you don't tell him.

–That's nonsense. I've hurt our relationship – there's no way out of that. I'm not going to live a lie.

–You think he'll know anyway – whether you tell him or not?

–I . . . No, perhaps not. But I know, don't I? How *could* I? God, I don't know!

–But why make it *his* problem? You don't want his money – do you think he wants your shit?

–Is that what it is – shit?

–Isn't that what you're saying? If he cares, you're going to wound him. If he doesn't care – you're just doing yourself in the eye.

–Well he cares.

–What did he say when you told him you were driving off to England with me?

–He didn't say anything. Why should he? He never does say much. You make it all sound so – oh shit! As the car in front moves, Connie puts her foot hard on the accelerator and the Renault jerks and stalls. And suddenly a pair of ambulances and a police car sweep up the hard shoulder, hee-hawing like demented donkeys. –Oh God, it *is* an accident. I can't bear accidents.

–If my wife – if *any* of my wives – had driven off to England with a strange man, I would have been, well, just a little anxious – unless he'd been gay or –

–Old enough to be her father.

–Never trust fathers. He pitches his cigarette out of the car and winds the window shut. Is that what you told Henri?

–What?

–Just some fucking feeble old sod?

–I didn't tell him anything. Why should I? It's none of his business. He trusts me. And anyway, I don't care about you.

–Well I care about you.

–That's not my fault. I didn't ask you to. I haven't done anything to you.

–Of course not. I accept that. It's my business.

–Yes, it is. Connie changes gear smoothly as the traffic gathers speed. –It's not your fault either. I know that. You can't help what you feel. . . They are fast approaching the group of yellow and blue flashing lights that mark the accident; Connie grips the wheel more tightly and sets her jaw.

–Don't worry. You can look. It's just a truck overturned. There's no blood on the road.

–'Constance, my dear, there's something I want to say to you.' Poor Mummy – although I didn't think 'poor Mummy' then of course. She was standing by the bed with a bundle of clean sheets in her arms. I was, what? – sixteen, seventeen? – and I had a formal date that night, a dance or something. 'I just want to tell you,' she said, 'that the first time it is not really very pleasant.' She held those sheets tight against her like some sort of armour and it took me a moment to catch on. I ought to have laughed. After all, I'd being going to bed with Mario for months, but –

–Mario?

–He was Portuguese. He had a car. But I was so angry I couldn't think of anything to say. And then I said, 'Mummy, why do you take half an hour to make the bed when you could do it in five minutes?' And *she* said, 'Because I'd rather spend half an hour making the bed thinking about Proust than five minutes making the bed thinking about making the bed.' Mummy's a great reader . . .

–'Well,' I said, 'we're ordinary people with an ordinary problem – a marriage cracking up – so let's do the ordinary, sensible thing.' Poor Leonore dressed for it like a funeral – black suit, black hat, spiked heels to repel boarders, everything but a veil. The marriage counsellor turned out to be a man which didn't help matters –

–Why not?

–Leonore didn't much care for men by this time.

–But I thought she had a lover?

–She did, but he was about sixty-five and had everything under the sun wrong with him – emphysema, some sort of kidney condition, no soles to his feet.

–No soles to his feet?

–He had them of course once, but he'd worn them out. Connie laughs. –How can you wear them out?

–In his case by playing squash, I believe – he'd been some sort of champion, and all that starting and stopping and braking and skidding had worn the bones down to wafers.

–What happens when you have no soles?

–I gather it makes it painful to stand up for long.

–So he had to lie down a lot? Oh dear, I shouldn't laugh, she says, laughing a full rich laugh.

–Oddly enough he died of a heart attack the following year.

–*Walter!* She tries to straighten her face. –And what did the marriage counsellor say?

–He said, 'Normally, Madame, if one has a lover that makes the relationship with the husband easier – *plus gentil.*'

–And what did she say to that?

–She nearly hit him with her handbag.

–I think Leonore sounds rather nice . . . We need some petrol.

–I used to buy a bottle of vodka on the Friday night and drink vodka and lime all weekend till I'd finished the bottle in a kind of floating haze. I just drank and smoked and wept and slept – I didn't even look out of the window. I didn't go out. If I'd gone out, a gust of wind would have blown me away.

–Petrol station coming up.

With a quick glance over her shoulder, Connie slips neatly into the slow lane. –Of course it wore off in the end.

–Hold on – there's somebody shouting and waving.

–Damn – what now? Connie slows to a halt at the exit. –Did you pay?

–Yes. It's a woman.

–Shall I back up?

–No, she's coming after us.

–Madame, Madame!

Connie rolls down the window. –Can I help you?

–It is not I who need help. The woman is a little breathless, but has a hard face and a neat head protected by a large umbrella. –You have forgotten your petrol cap.

–Have I? *Merde*. How kind of you. May I have it? Connie holds out her hand and the woman recoils.

–I have not got it!

–I don't understand – where is it?

–Where you left it, of course – on the petrol pump.

–You didn't bring it?

–Why should I bring it? I am not your lackey. It is not my fault.

–You mean you ran all this way just to bring me the bad news?

–It is not up to me to correct your foolishness, Madame.

Connie slams the car into reverse. –*Quelle conne!*

–I'll get it.

–No you won't. She races the car backwards in a dead straight line, leaving the Samaritan stiff and smug under her umbrella. –It might be my sister-in-law. They're always stirring it up, aren't they? Snotty little superior bitch. It's just sadism – why do they have to do it? Why can't they be decent and kind?

–Why can't a woman be more like a man?

–Well, I'm not going to be so very late after all, am I? Are we close?

–Not far. Left here – a bit further. This is it.

41

–Here? I'll park in this driveway, it won't matter for a minute. I'll unlock the boot.

She leaps out bright and agile, all traces of menstrual dizziness long gone, and hands him his case and the plastic bag and holds up her cheek to be kissed – and then the other cheek.

–See you on Tuesday – don't forget it's your turn to peer-teach.

–Connie . . .

But she is back in the car, and he – bowed with the burden of Bovril and bloater paste.

–Thanks for the ride.

She looks up at him for a moment, letting the motor idle. –Was it worth it? she says with a smile.

He watches the rear lights vanish round the corner, then crosses the street and punches the code to release the front door. As Connie drives home to the arms of her loved ones and the ancient lift jolts Walter slowly upward, he consoles himself with the thought that no true Frenchman would screw his bloodied spouse.

–Right. What did everybody think of Walter's performance?

–I thought he was good.

–He didn't use the blackboard very well.

–The article was dull, but he was interesting.

–He seemed very self-confident – I mean, he seemed to know what he was talking about.

–But did you *learn* anything?

–I think we would have done – if he'd gone on longer.

–Oh yes, he explained the vocabulary very well – all about fund-raising, which is very dull really.

–He was genial.

Adam stands up with his notes; he's wearing a curious pink and white garment, a cross between a shirt and an anorak, yellowish under the arms. –Good. He was interesting – adequately informative – seemed to know what he was doing – and was confident. That's important – nervousness very quickly communicates itself to students and makes class management that much more difficult. He was also extremely bossy and directive. Adam gave his loose-lipped smile. –He began by saying 'Right' in a loud voice – told you what you were going to do, told you to do it, flung down the papers for handing round. A regular Adolf Hitler. I'm not saying there's anything wrong with that. If it works, it works. And he got away with it because he *was* genial, amusing – not threatening.

–So like Adolf Hitler.

–And that *acc*ent, says Linda, smiling snakily. –Where did you get that wonderful *acc*ent?

–The blackboard technique was not too good. He wrote it all out clearly at the beginning, but then didn't use it. And at one point he was rather indecisive.

Walter murmurs, –Neville Chamberlain?

–Anyone spot that?

Walter looks round at his peers, who sit silent like so many pickled onions in a jar (for a moment, even Connie's amazing eyes remind him only of pickled walnuts). Peer solidarity. Class comradeship. Total boredom.

–Right then . . .

It is dark and raining lightly, and they walk fast in a rhythm that allows shoulder and elbow to touch without jolt or recoil. As they come up to the café on the corner, he says, –Do you have time for a coffee or something?

–No, I have to rush home and cook pheasant – somebody sent Henri a brace last week – another banker, of course. So we've invited them over for dinner, his wife's a lawyer, I think – I've only ever met them once. Plain roast, I thought, with roast potatoes and lentils – avocado and shrimp to start, and then –

–Connie?

–What?

43

–Did you tell Henri?

–No.

–Why not?

They have reached the edge of the square and she stops and stands facing him, shielding her head from the rain with her folder of notes. –I thought about what you said. What happened – whosoever fault it was, it wasn't *his*, was it? It had nothing to do with him. It just happened. An accident – like a pet guinea-pig dying or . . . no, don't laugh, Walter, please. You know what I mean. We just have to forget about it.

–Alright – we'll forget all about it. Will you have lunch with me?

–Promise?

–Promise.

–In that case, yes. She sneezes. –When?

–Thursday? Have you got a cold?

–It's just my sinus acting up. And ever since Sunday I've had this migraine, and yesterday I put my back out . . . No, Thursday's no good – the only day I can manage is Friday.

–Friday then. You sound a bit of a wreck – oughtn't you to be in bed?

She watches him for a moment, then shakes her head. –I'm used to it – these things always come in batches.

They wait in the rain, reluctant, too awkward for kiss or handshake.

–Well then . . . goodnight.

–Goodnight. Till Friday. Connie . . .

–Yes?

–Take care.

She gives him a smile, then crosses the road and enters her house. Walter shivers and turns up his collar.

–Butterflying?

–Like a butterfly, as opposed to – to a bee. Bees make a beeline for something – I mean, they know where they're going and what the point of it all is and they're not going to be deflected – like the French, it's only when they buzz off you can get a word in edgewise. Bees are logical and *dirigiste* and –

–And hard-working.

–Well, that too, I admit. But you shouldn't have to work hard at pleasure . . . or even at getting a living. Butterflies don't. They hover and potter – let themselves be wafted from flower to flower. They don't have to drain a topic or a blossom before fluttering off to something else attractive in the garden. Yet they're just as well nourished as bees – *and* they don't sting.

–But it's not going to get them anywhere, is it? Connie eats the steamed-shrimp ravioli quickly and neatly. –They're trapped in the garden.

–Maybe. But what's wrong with that? It could be the garden of Eden.

She laughs. She has come straight from the doctor – sinus, backache, headaches – but no one on earth could look healthier.

–I don't want to be trapped anywhere.

–Well, you are – trapped in a Chinese restaurant.

She's wearing a dark skirt and a mauve cashmere sweater and there's a touch of shadow on her eyelids and powder on her cheeks. Dressed up for the doctor, perhaps.

–You haven't done very well, she says, as the waitress removes the little wooden steam boxes. –You're alright, are you? I've got Sarah at home with flu.

–I never get these things. I haven't been ill for years. In fact he's felt shaky for the last two days, but he manages to pour the tea almost without a tremor. –How did the pheasant dinner go?

–It was awful! Oh the food was alright – delicious, and my soufflé was perfect. But this couple! I told you she was a lawyer. I suppose that's why she talked so much – she just went on and on about secretaries – why secretaries? I don't know – how idle and useless and incompetent they were. No interruptions allowed, and then when she stopped, her husband went sort of 'Hee-hee, what can you expect, *chérie*? Secretaries are only there to be laid.'

–An experienced man.

–I doubt it. You should have seen him. He reminded me of Adam – our teffle Adam. Like the slimy toads in *Alice*.

–The slithy toves.

–Slithy toves? Well, you know what I mean. It would make you feel sick to touch him. Or her. By the end I could cheerfully have poured the champagne over their heads. Oh look, my imperial chicken's got peanuts in it. I can't eat peanuts, they make my throat swell up.

–Pick them out.

–I shall. And you know what? When they'd gone, Henri turned round to me and said, 'They were charming, weren't they?'

–Irony?

–Oh no. She laughs.

–So you poured the champagne over his head?

–I should have done, shouldn't I? His precious Krug. I was a really good secretary, you know. The first year we lived together, I earned more than he did. Has he just conveniently forgotten all that?

–Why conveniently? Have some of my beansprouts.

–Thanks. Well, because he likes to think my taking this course is completely frivolous and absurd – *une folie*. Anyway, the thing that really got up my nose was that they didn't even compliment me on the meal.

Walter sips his tea – with any luck, she will eat all of his food as well as hers. –I thought you didn't care for compliments.

–Well, I don't – normally . . . But sometimes, you know, I think – when I'm all dressed up with my make-up on and my earrings – I think sometimes it would be nice if Henri said, 'How lovely you're looking tonight, darling . . .' But if he did, I'd probably hit him.

And her merry laugh rings out.

The cold smites him directly he steps out of the door, freezing the sweat on his forehead and making his knees tremble, and a hard, sharp wind strikes right through to the pyjamas under his clothes as he hobbles across to the pharmacy on the corner of the square. He is possessed by a French craving for pills, capsules, ampules, syrups, suppositories. He's feeling his age – not only his own age but the age of everyone in line at the pharmacy, all added together and dumped on his hunched shoulders. He's lucky and gets the *petite blonde* assistant who is sympathetic, almost tender, and loads him with 332 francs' worth of medication and instructions beyond comprehension.

Outside, as he leans for a moment or two against the Wallace fountain, he's approached by the doe-eyed, mute beggar. In lieu of cigarettes, Walter gives him ten francs. The young man holds the coin in the palm of his hand as though he knows nothing of money. He hasn't even a shirt under his ancient jacket and, as he finally turns away, Walter sees he is shoeless – his bare feet black with grime. In Paris, dirt is the only protest left perhaps. . .

Walter pulls himself together and walks the few yards to his front door, past the huge bus-stop poster of Isabel Adjani's anxious brow and clean white breasts and the butcher's bloody display of dead meat.

In the hall, Madame Mouchet is rattling the gate of the lift.

–Ah, Monsieur Valaire. Someone has not properly closed the door above.

–What a scandal! Walter is pleased to get her favourite word in first. Madame Mouchet is a small cock-sparrow of a woman, not unattractive, a widow or just possibly a divorcée.

–You're right. It is scandalous. There is no discipline any more. Without a doubt it is Monsieur Bailly again. Rattle-rattle. –I pity his poor children with a father like that. You don't look well, Monsieur.

–Just a touch of the *grippe*.

–It is everywhere now. This year it is particularly virulent. And she cascades into a detailed discourse about the different types of flu – Singapore, Sechuan, Peking (–All from Asia, naturally!) – and their respective virulence, the body's inability to produce antibodies to cope with type 'A' . . .

–Rather like AIDS, Walter says. –Except that's from Africa.

–*Afrique* – *voilà!* Madame Mouchet gives a triumphant cackle. –I shall go and fetch the lift. You, in your state, must wait here.

Walter waits, clinging to the grille. The cords of the lift descend slowly like strings of licorice and in a moment she is there, opening the cage door for him.

–But Madame, I shouldn't like to infect you.

She laughs. –*Mon cher Monsieur, I* have been vaccinated. And to his dismay she does not get off at her floor but accompanies him all the way to the fifth.

–Thank you, Madame. You are very kind. I can't thank you enough, he babbles at his own front door, appalled at the prospect of her pushing her way in.

–*De rien*, she says. He need not have worried – she is only seeing him home. –And your children – they are well?

–Yes – yes, thank you. They are very well.

–And where are they now?

–Amy's in America and Charles, well, I think Charles is still in India. At least he was when I last heard.

–India! She purses her small mouth – what fell disease might not strike him down in India?

–Connie! You . . .

–Yes, I came. Is it alright? I rang you and rang you but . . . Walter, you look awful.

–I've had the *grippe*. How did you get in?

–I'm not in yet, am I?

Walter steps back to let her enter. –Connie . . .

–You gave me the code before we went to England – don't you remember? In case you overslept. What did you do – unplug the phone?

48

–Yes – yes I did. He shuts the door and leans back against it, weak with convalescent astonishment, near suddenly to tears. –But . . . you were worried?

She hands him her coat – heavy, thick, pine-needle green. – I thought you might be dead.

He clears his throat. –New coat.

She laughs. – New? I've had it for years – an old friend. Henri's been hinting I might like a mink for Christmas.

–A mink? But I thought . . .

–And you're right. Are you going to cling on to that coat forever? Think how many decent holidays and hours of baby-sitting that would buy! But a mink is an investment.

Walter laughs and throws the coat on a chair and leads her into the sitting room. –You're the investment – the mink is the improvement.

–Me in a mink! I tried on a rabbit-skin coat once – I looked like a whore. Oh Walter, what a lot of books! There must be miles of them. She goes to the wall of bookshelves and runs her hand along the spines, then smells her fingers.

–Yards – that's the way you measure books – in yards.

–And you have read them all?

–Most of them – not all of them – but most.

–And you'll read them again?

–I don't know. Maybe not.

–Then why keep them?

–Old friends.

–Comforting, you mean?

–Yes, but not just comforting. All that sweat of soul – that love – that passion . . . not all of them of course, but –

–But it's dead.

–Oh, no – it's alive – forever – exciting –

–Is it? Is it really – exciting? She stares at him with an intense concentration he's never seen in her.

–More than that. It's words – it's language – it's all the difference between heaven and –

Abruptly the dog in the garden bursts out barking. Connie goes to the window and looks down. –Why, it's a Jack Russell.

–Is it? He comes and stands beside her.

–Well, sort of. The legs are too long. Mongrel-ish. What a racket – does it do that a lot?

–Yes – it's anti-people. It can see through the glass door at the back when anyone is waiting for the elevator or starts up the stairs – and it goes off into one of those fits. If there aren't enough real people around, it sees imaginary ones and barks at them. Or –

–I'm not imaginary. She turns, not smiling. –You haven't kissed me yet.

He kisses her cheek, her neck, her lips. Outside in the drab afternoon the dog barks with furious rage. They stand together – kissing like butterflies.

She touches his cheek. –You haven't shaved. She takes his hand. –Come on.

In the bedroom, she says, –You've got a single bed.

–I'm a single person.

–But don't you . . .?

–I don't encourage it.

Her eyes are alive, alight as she unbuttons his shirt. –You encouraged me. Her fingers are quick and deft from thousands of mother hours undressing and dressing infants. And her hands are not rough – how could he have thought that? Her hands are soft as silk.

And her body is white as milk.

–Connie?

–Walter – don't ask me questions.

–Why?

–Because I'll have to think of the answers.

–I was only going to ask about the class I missed.

–Oral Skills Practice?

And they laugh, laugh until they are breathless and aching in the muscles of laughter, the muscles of love . . .

And then, astonished, they make love again.

–I must be off – I've got to pick Tom up from school. Yet she lingers, although dressed and ready (a couple of quick strokes with the brush, no make-up), moves round the room, touching, looking. –'*Vue de pais proche de la Rivière de la Montagne de Richmond.*' Richmond – is that near Putney?

–Up river a bit.

–It's beautiful.

–It's not like that now – a gasometer on the skyline – but pretty enough, I suppose.

–And this girl and this grumpy-looking little boy – is that you?

–That was my uncle – the girl is my mother. Ninety-five years ago or thereabouts.

–She's beautiful. She glances from the photo to Walter and back again. –You look like her. Abruptly she turns away. –This is nice. She caresses the china cat.

–I thought you didn't like cats.

–This one's alright – it won't scratch. Where did you get it?

–Phoebe Parrott left it me in her will.

–Phoebe? Not another wife?

–The Parrots were the people I was evacuated to in the war. Phoebe had a baby grand piano and the cat used to sit on top. She was a pianist and sometimes she'd sit and play me English songs and airs – at least when I first came – she guessed how homesick I was. And I'd lean on the piano and stroke the cat and try not to cry. Soppy, my mother would have said.

–Soppy . . . I really must go. But her hand still rests on the cat's head. –I was late picking him up once. I had an accident, nothing much – just some idiot woman started through the lights, then stopped and I ran into the back of her and banged my head on the steering wheel which knocked me half-dizzy. But I had to deal with her – a bit like the woman at the petrol pump – and then the *directrice* at the school who shouted at me till I explained and even then turned up her nose. Why *are* they all so hateful?

–The French don't like each other much – you should know that by now.

–And when I rang Henri, he said, 'How could you be so stupid as to run into the back of another car?'

Walter lifts her hand from the cat and turns it over. –What's this red patch on your thumb?

–Beetroot juice – my skin stains dreadfully. Why, did you think I'd drawn blood?

He holds her for a minute. –I'll come down with you.

–No, please. I'd rather you didn't. She casts a last look round. –What a nice sunny room.

–There's no sun today.

–So there isn't. It must be all those bright books then.

–No books in your house?

–Hundreds – Henri's a great reader, history, biography, that sort of thing – but they're French books – all cold pale old bones on the bookshelf. Walter . . .

–Connie . . . He helps her on with her coat and she ties the belt hard. –Tomorrow?

–No – I can't manage that. I've got Sarah sick at home and –

–Monday then?

–Walter, I'll call you . . . She kisses him briefly and is gone.

In a minute the dog in the garden breaks into a flurry of farewell barking.

The Champ de Mars has its usual Sunday-afternoon quota of tiny dogs and sedate ladies and children chasing pigeons, and lost-looking Americans eager for an answering smile. Two young Spaniards are kicking a ball with their heels to keep it as long as possible in the air. A well-dressed man feeds grain to a multitude of sparrows who perch on his arms and thighs and shoulders. The Eiffel Tower spreads its legs comfortably over the tourists.

Although it's a warm windless winter afternoon, Walter wears an overcoat and scarf and a tweed cap and carries a stick against any latent shakiness in the knees. He walks slowly along the river towards the museum. On the far bank a Ferris wheel put up for Christmas is brightly lit although the day hasn't yet begun to darken; he pauses to watch it turn, brilliant but empty. In the forecourt of the museum a bearded clarinettist in a green anorak is accompanying a tape of a Weber concerto. Walter leans against the bronze hippopotamus and listens, smiling. The fulsome Romanticism of the music and the absurd charade of the musician are a perfectly comical combination, and Walter laughs out loud. To atone for this lapse in manners, he places a fifty-franc bill on the crimson velvet of the instrument case.

For a few moments his laughter has lightened him, emptying his mind, and he takes a roundabout route, gently rambling until, as it might have been by accident, he finds himself in Connie's square. There is no one in the central garden, not even a pigeon, as he stands on the gravel watching, surrounded by green bushes with shiny leaves. There is a smell of rain past or rain to come, an opalescence in the grey calm of the afternoon. Walter recognises them instinctively as soon as they enter the square – the man in a yellow sweater hand-in-hand with a small boy half-running to keep up. They pass by close enough on the other side for him to see the boy's bright brown eyes – Connie's eyes – and the sullen superior tucked-in look of the husband in the photo. No smile, no word spoken between them, they slip into the house as though going, not home, but to a rendez-vous with a dentist.

Walter feels a flush of heat in his whole body and he turns away quickly. One glimpse . . . but one glimpse is enough to guess too much . . . the flip of the great reader's pages in the marital bed, the sighs at the cries of the children in the night, the yawn-smothered sexual congress. Secretaries are for screwing – Henri'd agreed to that, he even went so far as to marry one, *une petite anglaise*, harmless, no threat there.

He strides home, slamming the stick into the pavement, until the sweat prickles his head under the cap. But by the time the lift carries him to the fifth floor he is shivering with returning chill.

–I've given up making my Christmas puddings for this, she says, kissing his neck, his shoulder, his jowl and cheek with insect lightness.

He touches her stomach with his fingertips.

–Don't! She pulls it in. –I've been eating too many chocolates.

–It doesn't notice.

–You make me laugh . . . She holds him tight. –Do you always make them laugh? I shouldn't ask that, should I?

–Why not? I'll tell you anything you want to know.

–Anything?

–Yes. Yes, I will, he says, shaken at such young man's temerity in an old man's mouth.

She is silent, her breath soft in his ear. –And will you make me cry?

–Bound to, some day. And you'll make me cry too.

–Will I? She gently bites his earlobe.

–I expect so. But not yet.

–Not yet. She props herself on one elbow. –Perhaps never?

He smiles. –Perhaps never.

She puts her hand on his chest and nimbly springs out of bed. –Come on.

She's slim, small-breasted, long-legged, with a low-slung ass. She has hardly any pubic hair ('I lost it all when Tom was born'). It reminds him of – what was her name? Lyceum 5-7826 – who covered herself with Estée Lauder and wanted to play Scrabble all day.

–You're not very well equipped, are you? she calls from the bathroom.

He goes to the door and watches her squatting in the tiny bathtub. –Thanks.

–I mean . . . you *know* what I mean – no double bed, no bidet . . . She twists the showerhead and sprays him.

He smiles, letting the water wash down him like sweet refreshing rain. –No French letters?

–French letters! Really!

–Doesn't Henri use them?

She stands up and turns off the shower. –Don't be ridiculous. I've got a coil.

–We're all supposed to use condoms these days.

She is drying herself vigorously, suddenly holds still. –You think Henri screws around?

–I don't know the man.

–Well, he doesn't! She throws the towel on the floor and steps on it as she gets out of the tub. Her eyes are large and dark and glittering. –If he did, I'd – I'd . . .

–Don't fret, it's coming. There it is, see – reflected in the shop window.

–I can't bear to be late. I haven't got a ticket.

It's colder today and the sky over the Fifteenth is flocked like cheap wallpaper, betokening a hard winter maybe.

He inserts two yellow tickets into the slot and the machine instantly bites them.

–Don't pat me.

–I'm not patting you, goddamnit, I'm hanging on to you.

They sit on the double seat by the exit door, shoulder, hip and thigh together. –Where do we get out?

–La Tour Maubourg.

–You're sure?

–Look, I may be half senile, but I –

–Not bad for sixty. She smiles and takes his hand.

–We can hold hands?

–Until we get off.

–And then we split – you go your way and I go mine and we get to the school from different –

–Oh, I don't care!

–Maybe you should.

–Yes, of course I should. I do. She squeezes his hand hard. –I do. I do. I won't!

He leans forward and presses the bell. The bus stops and they get out, the only descending passengers.

55

–I'm leaking.

–What?

–I'm leaking – you.

He laughs and after a moment she laughs too.

From the esplanade the sky is different – white and grey strips of cloud topped with gold above the Grand Palais. But, after all, this is a superior neighbourhood. The little trees are all bare and immaculate, as though every leaf had been picked by hand.

–Walter – I don't want to go to this class.

–Nor do I much. It's the Clockwork Mouse – bound to be boring. But I think we should.

–I want to go back.

–Come, he says, –come on.

–Oh, alright then . . . If you kiss me.

So he turns her to him and they kiss there in the vast *place* surrounded by solemnity and flagstaffs.

After two hours, somnolence is heavy on the air and, beside him, Connie is almost asleep – a sinus snuffle could be a snore. But Emma's clockwork mechanism is working well today and the general lassitude only seems to make her more skittish. The subject around which she cavorts in a puddle-grey dress with a frilled white collar, is Teaching Beginners and is being explained in something closely resembling Konkomba.

–The controlled situational framework is very important because it allows for several different exponents of the same function. For example . . .

Connie gives a definite snort and Walter nudges her knee under the desk. On his yellow pad there is a single verbatim quote – 'Really I'm a lower-level person.' He pushes it toward her. She looks at it blankly then laughs.

Emma stops. –Sorry?

Connie, –Nothing.

–Sorry. Now in a minute we're going to look at the hand-outs, but first . . .

And all this is costing 5,800 francs or – he works it out on his pad – roughly $950 or £530 sterling. With which he could buy ninety-six bottles of Gilbey's gin, eighty-three bottles of Johnnie Walker Red Label, 282 large jars of Bovril, nine return flights to London, twenty-eight non-alcoholic Chinese meals with Connie, a winter week in Dubrovnik for two, 1,920 average-priced condoms, thirty-one and a half . . . But no no – this is an investment for the future, the provision of income against the infirmity of years, rainy days, the creepback of senility in the lively parts. Pay attention, learn to be a lower-level person – what now?

–Page three – no, sorry, page five. Has everyone found it? This is a good example of the discourse chain. . .

He reads:

A.   *Would you like to come to the cinema tonight?*
B.   *I'm sorry, I can't. I'm washing my hair tonight.*
A.   *Oh well, what about going to a disco tomorrow?*
B.   *I'm sorry, I'm afraid I'm busy tomorrow.*
A.   *Would you like to go to a party on Friday?*
B.   *O.K. That'd be nice.*
A.   *Shall we meet in front of the Post Office?*
B.   *O.K. Fine. Bye then.*
A.   *Bye.*

–Of course, if this is not very interesting to the student, you can write your own discourse chain. Does anyone in the class have any other ideas. Yes – Valerie? Oh, sorry – Phyllis.

Walter starts a fresh sheet on the pad and writes:

Would you like to come home and make love after class? and shoves it to Connie. She writes back:

I'm sorry, I can't. I'm making the dinner tonight. You rat!
How about tomorrow then?
I'm afraid I'm busy on Wednesdays – as if you didn't know!
When can you come then, for Chrissake?
I think I could manage Friday.
Shall we meet in bed?
O.K. That would be very nice.

–No Christmas presents. I mean it – please, Walter.

Almost at the corner of her square, they dawdle, halt half-hidden by an overhanging porch.

–Okay. No presents.

–You do understand, don't you? It's just that . . . I have to hang on somehow. I have to – have to, don't I? It would topple me. I . . .

–I do understand. He touches her cheek.

–Not here, we're too close – no, I can't. If you gave me . . . Then she pulls him close into the shadow and they kiss, a quick, wrenching kiss. –Friday, she says, – and is gone.

–Friday . . .

Outside the Bon Marché a small Salvation Army silver band is playing Christmas carols; a pure, tranquil music – no raucous blare of 'Jingle Bells' or Santa Claus's ho-ho-hoing. 'Come All Ye Faithful.' But the faithful are in short supply; because of a transport strike, millions are locked in the suburbs and Paris is enchantingly empty. And the shopkeepers are obliged to put on unaccustomed smiles for the thin smattering of customers.

Walter lays a two-franc piece on the tambourine, preferring to give real money to the beggars with their cardboard placards – *J'ai faim*. In the rue de Sèvres, modestly adorned with Christmas lights, he sees just such a one cross-legged, hunch-shouldered on the pavement with an enormous dog beside him: *Nous avons faim*. He hesitates, but passes by, keeping his money close – Charity giveth not to dogs.

As he shuts the front door behind him, he's in that queer state of soul and body – like the day after a touch-and-go operation – where the past is hazy with undifferentiated childhood bliss and the future is unthinkable. He turns on the lights everywhere except in the bedroom which he leaves dark with the door shut. He makes a cup of bitterly strong coffee, drinks it and sits down to learn about the gerund:

> . . . the permanent tendency in language is towards the correct
> and logical, not from it . . . all gerunds ought to be made
> distinguishable from participles . . . the distinction is a useful
> one and . . .

What the hell is a participle? He rakes back in his mind but can
turn up nothing but old pebbles of boyhood perplexity. Mr
Stagg, the Greek master, *This boy appears to be incapable of
mastering the most elementary grammatical principles*; Mr
Bullock, the headmaster, *He must learn to labour at the dull
things*. How ill those full-blooded surnames befitted their
bearers. Well, they were all dead now.

Perhaps if he took vitamin pills or chewed seaweed, his
brain would clear. Instead, he fetches a glass and the Scotch
bottle and turns to a later authority:

> . . . by avoiding the binary distinction of gerund and participle,
> we seek to represent more satisfactorily the complexity of the
> different participial expressions as we move along the gradient
> to the most verbal end . . .

Walter feels himself washed with the waters of melancholy.
Verbal End – a sister station to those last stops marked on an
incomprehensible subway map – Flatbush, Flushing, Far
Rockaway – destinations better dreamt of than arrived at. He
pours the Scotch, eyes it sadly, lifts the glass to his lips – and
the phone rings.

Could it be . . .? Not a chance – Connie will be in the
kitchen, Henri in history, the kids in an uproar. He hesitates,
puts down the glass, answers.

–What? Yes. From Boston? Yes, I'll take it. Amy? Amy,
angel . . . you're coming? It's a definite? When?

–You're really pleased, aren't you?
–I am pleased, yes. I only saw her for a couple of weeks in
the summer, you see.

–You don't have to apologise. Connie sits in the small black rocking chair, but doesn't rock. What'll you do over Christmas?

–We'll go to England, I expect – to brother Edward's. Amy likes all the traditional stuff, and she'll want to show off Hal. Hal's her beau – Halston Makepeace – she's bringing him along too.

–It'll be a bit of a tight squeeze in that little cottage, won't it?

–Where you picked me up, you mean? That's just one of the estate cottages – Edward and Margot live in the big house, but it seemed pointless to open it up for me when they were away.

–They must be rich.

–Rich-ish. Edward did very well at the bar indeed, but somehow just missed getting onto the bench which has made him rather bitter – despite the splendid house and a young wife and a Roller and a flat in town, everything that money can buy.

–Did it buy him the wife?

–I often wonder what else she can see in him. The truth is he's a crashing old bore. But he's fond of Amy and for some reason she's fond of him – so there must be some good in him somewhere.

–And what does Edward think about you?

–He thinks I'm a layabout.

–Well, you are, aren't you?

Walter smiles and holds out his hand, and she takes it and comes to her feet with a tilt of the rocker and they stand loosely together.

–Bed?

She shakes her head. –No. I've just got my period.

–Feeling vague?

She smiles – a small, tefflish smile. –That's before – and only for an hour or two.

–Okay, come on then.

–But . . .

–You don't think I'm afraid of a bit of blood, do you?

–I feel heavy. I'd like to lie here forever. I don't want to leave.

–Stay then.

–I can't. I've got my role to play.

–Your what? Covering her with his body, he moves a little so he can see her face.

–My role – mother, spouse, housewife, cook, cleaning woman, laundress, social secretary . . . When we first lived together, I used to sing going up the stairs.

–And now?

–I haven't sung for – for years, it seems like. But when you don't get any response – oh forget singing – even to just talking, and when can I stop talking? –it's killing somehow. There was one weekend – not so very long ago – when Henri didn't say one word to me – he just sat reading his damned history books and he wouldn't speak. There was I chattering away – and nothing. Nothing. By Sunday afternoon I'd had it. I started shouting and screaming and then I ran out of the house and slammed the door and went and sat on a bench in the park for two hours and wept. And when I went back, he looked up at me over his book and said, 'All the time you were gone your daughter lay on the couch with a cushion over her head . . . You should think what you are doing to your children when you behave in that way'. Not his daughter or our daughter – *my* daughter . . .

–*Une mauvaise mère.*

–Yes – the bad mother – that's me. It made me . . . She gives a a little helpless laugh. –It did make me wild, but then . . . Slowly the touch of angry red in her cheeks fades.

–And you think he just let her lie there – didn't try to comfort her at all?

He probably told her not to be such an idiot – if he said anything at all. He's not very good at giving comfort – if I'm anything to go by. Besides, there's . . . Walter, could I have a cigarette?

–Of course.

When he comes back with the cigarettes and an ashtray, she is sitting up in bed with her arms round her knees, hunched forward with concentration.

61

–Thanks. She inhales the smoke and lets it drift slowly out of her mouth. –What I was saying, you see . . . there's a sort of jealousy thing going on too. He didn't like it when I breast-fed Sarah – he felt my breasts belonged to him. He used to go out of the room. He seemed to regard her as an intrusion – and it wasn't just him either. The family did too. I was over the moon when Sarah was born, you know – I whisked her up and popped round to my sisters-in-law – there are three of them, if you can imagine – just to show her off. I thought they'd want to admire her, but instead they were faintly horrified. What's this strange object in our house? What did they think – she was going to shit all over the parquet de Versailles?

–And all that surprised you . . .

–Yes it did – perhaps it shouldn't have done, should it? I suppose I was naive. But I thought I knew it all, you see – I was so plunged in the life, I spoke the language perfectly, I thought in it, I *was* French. Insofar as I thought about it at all. I just assumed we were all human beings. And then to discover . . .

–That the French weren't human?

She shakes her head. –I didn't think it was them – not then. I thought it was me, I began to think there was something wrong with me. Here I was in a lovely large apartment, not having to work, no worries, no hassles, with all the time in the world to devote to my beautiful new baby – and yet I was getting up in the middle of the night and shutting myself in the kitchen and sobbing for hours. I think that must have affected Sarah, don't you? And then right at the beginning I'd decided to talk English to her . . . I thought it would be easier, more natural . . . But it wasn't, you know. The English words didn't sound right somehow – they stuck in my mouth and I felt it all false and artificial. It was strange – like I was acting the part of the mother, but hadn't been given the right lines.

Connie stubs out her cigarette with care. –And if *I* felt that, what about *her*? We never have got on. I can hardly remember a day when I haven't shouted at her – of course, she's sullen and stubborn and difficult, but that's no excuse really, is it? Even the day after we came back from England, when they said how delicious the dinner was – and I expect it was after the kind of thing Henri had been dishing up – I told them never to congratulate me on something I *had* to do. And I tell Sarah how frightful it is being a wife and a mother and a housewife and – and . . .

And she bursts into tears and Walter takes her and holds her. –It's alright, my darling, it's alright. No role play here.

–No – oh no . . . I'm not used to this. I . . .

He rocks her gently as a child and kisses her cheeks wet with tears and dries them. –Connie, Connie . . .

Her face softens. –You called me 'darling', she whispers, a tremulous accusation.

–So I did.

–I can't . . . You said you'd make me weep. Oh Walter . . . She pulls him tight to her so as to hide her face. –Tell me to go – make me go!

–I am going to sneeze. What am I going to do? All together.

–You are going to sneeze.

It's the last class before Christmas and Connie is doing her peer teaching. Outside, there are wafers of ice on the puddles and the buildings are white with the bold light of winter. But in the classroom it is spifflicatingly hot; any comparable French gathering would be thick with beloved body odours, but here all is clean, decent and Anglo-Saxon and the air is scented with nothing more tempting than shampoo.

–Janet – what are you going to do tonight?

–Tonight I am going to wash my hair. Janet's fierce face blushes modestly at the laughter.

–What is Janet going to do tonight? Everyone.

–She is going to wash her hair.

–Very good! Connie today is brilliant with youth and her exhilaration is catching. Could it be that she's a natural teacher?

–And now – will Fred and Walter come up here please?

As they go to the head of the class, they grin at one another, but Walter is uneasy. In the Bloomingdale's sweater and matching socks Amy has brought him from New York, he is conscious of looking uncharacteristically natty. Fred might have selected his clothes blindfold from an Oxfam shop, but he is less than half Walter's age and has a gentle Devon accent which Connie much admires. Is she going to ask them to do battle?

But no. She puts a basket on the table and takes out three packets of *langues-de-chat* and two bottles of champagne.

–Now, what are Walter and Fred going to do? Well? They are going to open the champagne. Together!

–They are going to open the champagne!

Walter laughs and strips away the foil and twists off the cork. It's the Krug – she has robbed Henri's cellar.

The class is invested with seasonal smiles and all the chatter is of the holidays. Linda is off to the States, Kathy to Ireland and the English wives are away to England, dragging alien husbands behind them. Except of course for Connie – stuck in Paris. But for the moment, she is merry.

Walter lifts his styrofoam cup and raises his voice. –Let's drink a toast . . . to the best peer-teacher of the year!

The café is as anonymous as a cheap motel – globe lights, beige tiles, fake wooden tables, orange plastic *banquettes*. The one touch of character is the *patron* with a speech impediment who keeps pressing them to eat apple tart as plastic as the café itself.

–And what's he like? Connie stirs a lump of sugar into her hot chocolate.

–Hal? Oh . . . Walter tries to concentrate, but it's their last moment together for . . . –He's okay, I guess – good-looking, rich, polite, calls me 'Sir' all the time. He's very serious – a graduate law student. He'll get on a treat with Edward. And Margot too – anything male under thirty on two legs has great appeal for Margot. She's at the susceptible age.

–Like me, you mean?

–Not like you at *all*!

She smiles, a furry line from the chocolate on her upper lip.
–When are you going?

–Tomorrow.

–Oh. Suddenly the smile is gone. –And you're going to be
away for – how long?

–Through New Year's, I imagine. It depends on Amy,
really, but in any case she and Hal are flying back on the fourth.

She takes his hand across the table. –Nice, long, bony
fingers . . . Two weeks!

–What's this? He touches a grey patch on the inside of her
thumb.

–It's from peeling the potatoes – I can't get it out. It's such a
long time – Christmas, the New Year . . . She grips him tight
as though he might suddenly let go or disappear there and
then. –I remember when I was little I had – diphtheria, I think,
though they never told me. I had to be isolated in this hospital;
in a large hospital I suppose there would have been lots of
other children, but this was a little local hospital and I was the
only one. I remember being in a white-flannel nightie in a
white bed in this small white room with white nurses flitting
in and out – nuns? And I had to eat sort of white food –
arrowroot, I suppose, and rice pudding. No one was allowed
to visit me – not even my parents. Of course, I didn't understand why – why I was there or even where I was or anything
at all. I was only four – five perhaps. And I thought and
thought and finally I decided I must be dead and the nurses
were angels and I was in heaven forever. And the funny thing
is, it didn't bother me a bit. I thought on the whole it was quite
nice. Why? Why are you smiling? I talk too much, don't I?

–The talking cure.

–Cure – it's more like a disease, I think. I should love to be
calm and quiet. Isn't that what your Quakers do, you told me
– sit in silence and only speak when they really have something
to say?

–When the spirit moves them.

65

–How do you tell – when it's the spirit, I mean, and not just a compulsive need to chatter?

–Well, as far as I recall, a lot of the Friends couldn't tell the difference – there was a great deal of banal burbling. Maybe the spirit wasn't often in good form.

–But sometimes?

–Yes – I suppose – sometimes.

–Did it ever happen to you?

–Once – at least I thought it did.

–What was it like?

He stubs out his cigarette and straightens the empty cup in the saucer. –There was an odd sort of creeping feeling at the back of my neck – and my head felt very light all of a sudden, and my chest tightened as though I were being filled with something too big for my body, floating me, expanding me . . . gently pushing me to get up . . . But I didn't.

–Why not?

–I thought it might be just indigestion. No – that's not true. But I was what – fifteen? – spotty, shy, a foreigner . . . But I'm sorry I didn't. I'd like to have heard what I was going to say. Maybe I'd have been endowed with the gift of tongues or . . .

Connie is staring intently, but through him, beyond the plastic café to some other place, an alternative interlanguage country – a white heaven, a Meeting house, a sceptred isle . . . She sighs slowly and gives a little shudder. –What's the time? I've got to go.

Outside, she fits grey woollen mittens carefully over her fingers. She takes his arm. It's bitter cold now. They walk, distracted, without a word, their lively breath as white as the moving spirit on the night air, their footsteps slow, stopping, beginning again, treading the water of dreams.

–There, he says at last, –you see? Silence.

–How long – two minutes?

–Four, at least. You can.

–Oh I know I *can* – heaven knows I've had enough practice at home. When I'm not shouting at the children. Dead silence.

They stand arrested, close; passers-by skirt them briskly, a car's headlights gleam in her eyes. She looks up, looks round. –Where are we? We've come miles out of the way.

–Not far – a couple of hundred yards.

–Is that all? Oh – yes. But we must hurry. She drops his arms.

Quick now, quick they walk, pace for pace, their feet clacking on the pavement, until they reach the corner of the square. This is where they always part – in the leafless square under the naked trees. But now it's too dangerous for kiss or touch or even a firm handshake.

–Happy Christmas, Walter.

–Happy Christmas, Connie.

On the other side of the road, she turns abruptly. –Walter?

–Yes?

–Give my love to England.

The benign mantle of New Year warmth has spread from England to France; no need of cap or gloves as he sets out from the house for the early morning tryst set in telephone whispers the evening before. For a moment he's touched by the doubt he's spent all night trying to stifle – a tremor of dismay that the scene is set for bad tidings. But as he walks through the little passage onto the dusty ground of the Champ de Mars, his heart lifts. The city is pale blue and softly golden in the sun's haze, open as young lilies on an ancient field.

She is already there, straight as a sentinel, staring down to the Eiffel Tower, hands thrust into the pockets of an old suede jacket. Suddenly, stopped still, watching her, Walter has an impulse to flee – an importunate dove has clambered on his shoulder saying, Arise, leave me now, never let us meet, eternal distance now command thy feet.

And then she turns, slowly, and looks at him. The dove flies up forgotten, and he goes to her and they open their arms without a word and hold each other.

The park is empty – too early for dogs or children, too early even for the birdman; only pigeons occupy the space, potter and peck. He touches her springing hair, the nape of her neck, an earlobe. Her cheek against his is soft as a sparrow's breast. She smells of Palmolive soap. She is warm and quiet.

At last they kiss – a kiss of familiar love more ravishing than any passion. They draw an astonished breath, she smooths back his hair, puts her hand to his cheek. Bewilderment has gone and vanished, the look in her eyes now is of wonderful tranquillity.

–I thought here because . . .

They glance round – there is no one in sight. Here, in this field so proudly dedicated to war, the world has been cleared for them, the rough places have been made plain.

–You were right.

–I've got all day.

–All day!

They smile dizzily.

–I brought the car, but we don't have to . . .

–No, we'll walk.

–Good – I don't want to have to stare at the road. Where?

–Home.

–Home . . .

And they moved off slowly, hand in hand, hardly speaking – starting and stopping and beginning again. And smiling and looking.

–She took one look at me and said, 'Daddy, you're different, you're in love, aren't you?'

–Is that why she went out and bought this peachy bed?

–I guess so. A Christmas present. But I expect Hal paid – he's a great organiser. When I got back from teffle that afternoon, there it was – and the whole place covered in holly and mistletoe.

–We won't move all day.

68

–Difficult to do without moving.

–Moving from here, I mean, lunkhead. She takes hold of his hair and rocks his head against the pillow. –Let's stay in bed forever.

–A lifetime's snogging.

–Snogging! She crouches, leaning over him, her face broad and merry.

–Caressing fondly – according to our fine Brighton expert on contemporary idiom.

–Arsehole. Do I caress you fondly? She touches him with quick light feather touches. He touches her. –Do I – do I?

He brings her breast down to his mouth.

–Oh, she says, oh, in suddenly unmeasured bliss.

–It's like sand, isn't it, these sheets all sunny and warm? She's awake and soft.

–Mmm, he murmurs from the half after-doze of love and daze of sunlight falling on their nakedness. And we're pale bathers hoping for a tan.

–I don't know – I don't like too much sun.

–Or heights?

–Or heights.

–Or peanuts or presents or fine clothes or compliments?

–Maybe I could get to like them . . . But I like being in bed.

–Being in bed? He laughs.

She kisses his neck. –Making love, she whispers.

–Loving . . .?

She's silent, running her fingers over his face, his eyes, his mouth.

–And the Frog – what's he like?

–What?

–Henri – is he good at all this?

–Walter! She sits up abruptly.

–What's wrong?

–Wrong? She gives him a straight, rebuking gaze, slips into

69

a prim voice. –You don't talk about people you've been to bed with when you're in bed with someone else.

–Why not?

–Because. Because . . . oh what am I going to do with you? He pulls her gently down. –You can tell me you love me. Silence. Silent breathing. Heart beating.

–I – I can't . . . I'm sorry, I . . . I don't understand why but . . . Do you mind? She rubs the curly white hairs on his chest, blows on them softly as they spring up and sprout.

–Because of the vodka-and-lime man?

She moves back to look at him. –You remember then?

–Is it? Because of him?

She closes her eyes for a moment and her whole body trembles as though trying to throw off a great weight of water. And then she is looking at him, face to face on the pillow.

–I said it so often it didn't mean anything. I wrote it to him every day. I used to call him up all the time – day and night. To see if he was there – and he wasn't patient, you know, he was never patient. And if he wasn't there . . . it was far worse. I'd go round and wait outside his house – and wait for hours and walk up and down and count the bricks and rehearse what I was going to say, but I'd only ever one thing to say. And he'd come back and maybe he'd let me in, maybe not. And I'd get down on my knees and plead – and say it and say it and say it – and sometimes I knelt down, there in the street and . . . and . . .

And she is crying in his arms, fragile and wan and weeping.

–I don't want that, Walter. We're not like that, are we?

–No. No, we're not like that. And he strokes her back until the tremors pass in slowly dying ripples.

–I'm not going to break my heart.

–No, of course not, Connie, he promises.

She sits up to look at him. –I refuse to break my heart.

–Yes, he says, shutting his eyes against the brightness of hers.

–I refuse! You understand?

–Yes, he murmurs, exhausted with love, effete, enervated with the effort of sanity. –Of course I do.

–No I wasn't upset really. I don't know why – perhaps I'm used to it. I just sat there like a vegetable.

–Tomato? Mushroom? He switches on the bedside lamp.

She sits cross-legged, holding a mug of tea in both hands, considering. –More like a turnip, I suppose.

–White with an angry mauve top?

She laughs. –No, I wasn't angry either – oh, maybe a bit cross. I mean, it was so obvious everyone else had their little Christmas tasks, but I hadn't been asked to do anything. And then I'd brought them all presents – only token presents – but that didn't go down well at all. I might have been handing them dead rats, the way they sniffed at them. I'd got English diaries for Henri's two older nephews – after all, they are studying English – and one of them actually handed his back to me.

–What did you do?

–I popped it on the log fire. Nobody noticed – or anyway they pretended not to. The steam of the tea has added an artificial rosiness to her cheeks and there are droplets of moisture on her forehead. –Why are they so difficult about presents? What is it they feel – that they'll have to give a better one back? I don't understand.

–Well, isn't that a bit of a problem for you?

–Me? But I love giving.

–And receiving?

–Don't you think I'd have been pleased if any one of them had given me something? A box of pencils, a woolly scarf – anything. She finishes her tea and hands him the empty mug.

–But not jewellery and furs.

–That's not the same thing. Those aren't gifts, are they? She uncrosses her legs and, lifting one knee, scratches the sole of her foot. –They're good-conduct medals. Shit, I don't need merit awards for being a good wife. And I don't want gratitude – fuck gratitude – what I need is a decent housekeeping allowance.

–Payment for services rendered.

–Well, why not? God knows, I do enough.

He laughs suddenly. –You look like Iris with your leg cocked up like that.

71

–Who's Iris? she says suspiciously.

–Rodin's Iris – not mine. The mother of Eros, among other things.

She throws herself on him. –I'm going to beat you up.

–No – hold it. He slides her off him and pulls her up by the hand. –Come with me. He leads her into the sitting room, still decorative with Amy's greenery and glistening globules of mistletoe and white holly berries. –Here.

–Walter – what is it? It's not . . .

–It's not a diamond tiara, no.

She takes the thin flat box and holds it as a solemn child holds a peach from the garden wall. She unwraps it carefully, opens it, unfolds white layers of tissue paper to the bright splash of scarlet underneath. –Gloves! Red leather gloves! She lifts them out of the box and slips them on. –Oh, they're cold.

–Silk-lined – they're only cold at first. Your skin's too soft for wool.

She puts them to her cheek, sniffs at them, then turns her hands this way and that. –My silk-lined gloves! She whirls round on the balls of her feet, circling three times – stops in front of him with a brilliant smile and, taking his face between her gloved hands, kisses him on the lips.

–It's okay then?

–They're beautiful. But I've nothing to give you.

–So what?

–So let's go back to bed. She laughs. –No, wait – you go. I shan't be a tick.

She comes two minutes later, in her red-gloved hands carrying the glove box filled with mistletoe berries. She flings them over his outstretched body.

–There! She stands triumphant. –A thousand kisses!

–Am I fat? She asks as they soap each other under the shower. –I think I'm fat.

–Look down – as long as you can see your private parts without leaning forward, you're not fat.

–Oh ho-ho – that's all very well for people who stick out. She gives him a swift tug and hops out of the shower and starts to dry herself with rapid, zestful rasps of the towel. –I could go on forever. Perhaps that's what I ought to have been.

–What?

–A prostitute. Why not? At least it would be my money. I could buy myself presents. I'd be independent. Of course, the parts wouldn't be so private any longer. She sighs. –Oh well – it's too late now.

He dries her back and the nape of her neck. –Not really. There's an old whore who parades up the side of the Dôme who must be sixty if she's a day – white-haired and most respectable looking.

She glances at herself in the mirror and ruffles her hair. –How odd – who'd want an old woman?

–Who'd want an old man?

She touches his crowfoot wattles and smiles. –A nice old man – who wouldn't? She takes the towel from his hand and dries him gently. –Walter . . . have you ever been with a prostitute?

Dawn. Why this one particularly? A rosy dawn, the garbage trucks grinding below, but up there clarity and fine air pricked by the Chrysler Building's sword. Down here, a lone whore, awkward in pink party pumps, tired to death, part of the litter lifting and settling in the early breeze.

–You looking for me, honey?

–How much?

–Fifty dollars?

–Come *on*!

–I'll give you a good time, hon – thirty?

She's a big yallerish girl . . . he looks at her closely – girl? Forty, give or take a day or two. A worn-out middle-aged

73

junkie whore, scavenging for a last trick at an hour when even the bag ladies and the winos are buried in sleep and the young ladies have ceased to pace their apartments up and down and have fallen exhausted into doze – wives and lovers and ex-wives, homeless at home. The daybreak has cracked her make-up, cracks her smile.

–Thirty? Okay? Where d'you live – you got a place round here, hon?

–Hold it. He must have smiled and she'd taken it as assent. –What's your name?

–Rose.

Rose. That did it. –Okay, Rose. Not my place – I can't go home. Where do you live?

–I don't live nowhere. Listen –

–That's it then – sorry, Rose.

But she has her hand on his arm, her eyes urgent and appealing – fine black eyes. –Listen, I know a place just up the street – for a quickie?

He hesitates. –Twenty then.

–Twenty-five.

–Okay – twenty-five.

She takes his arm and guides him confidently; from her fingers on his sleeve he can feel the relief energising her body, quickening her step. –What's your name?

–Wally.

–Wally – where you from then, Wally?

–New York.

–With that accent? You gotta be kidding.

–England, originally.

–Hey, no kidding? That's a great place, England. I had a good friend come from England, he was a real nice guy, he used to . . .

He knows the street, knows the old redbrick tenement she takes him to, half boarded-up and empty except for a handful of ancient statutory tenants battling the landlord. Six storeys to the top. He clings to the iron railing – he's trembling with the night's recirculating liquor and the awful fragility of the dawn.

—Now where?

—Why right here, honey. She gestures at the flight of stone steps leading up to the roof as though it were a bridal couch of silk and down. And she poses herself on the fifth step, hoists up her skirt and spreads her thighs wide. No artifice, no panties. And suddenly he is cock-high and suffocated with lust.

Between the open legs of Rose on the stony steps, her pink slippers against his biceps, her cheap powder dusting his lapel, he surrenders. As he looks up at the open door to the roof and the oblong of the rosy dawn beyond, he floats easily and limberly, rising lifting uplifted and spun through the opening to the effulgent sky . . .

—Oh boy — you sure needed that, honey . . .

—It sounds pretty squalid. She is ready to go, in her grey overcoat and red boots and red gloves, but she doesn't go.

—Why do you say that?

—Well, it was a bit one-sided, wasn't it? I mean, all that rosy-fingered dawn stuff — but what did she get out of it?

—The price of a fix. It's what she wanted.

—Oh shit. What is it — a symbol of maleness, all your wives and mistresses and prostitutes — something to boast about?

—Nobody boasts about whores.

—You were! So bloody squalid and —

—I was telling you because you asked.

—*Squalid* — and so fucking sad . . .

—Connie . . .

He touches her, but she shrugs him off.

—I don't want to be sad! I don't want to be a mistress or a whore or a wife or *une petite amie*!

—You're not a —

—What am I then? What am I doing here?

—We're lovers, we —

75

–Lovers? She stares at them in the tall mirror garlanded with yew and holly and ivy – side by side, not touching, ghostly in the late afternoon light. –Oh God, she says to the glass, –I'm *jealous* . . .

–You don't need to –

–I know, I know – but I do – I am . . .

–It was a hell of a long time ago.

–So she's old – older than you are even – haggard, sad, pathetic . . .

–Most likely dead.

–Dead. She turns her head and looks at him in the flesh. –But *you* remember her.

–Yes.

–You may be the only person in the world who does.

–Yes.

–Can I come tomorrow?

–Yes.

> *Words strain, crack and sometimes*
> *break under the burden,*
> *under the tension, slip, slide, perish,*
> *decay with imprecision, will not stay*
> *in place, will not stay still. . .*

Adam points to the blackboard. –Does anyone know who wrote that? Yes? T.S. Eliot – that's right.

–An American, says Linda in her most drawly accent.

–Well, in a way – originally. Adam licks his lips. –Words strain, crack and sometimes break . . . What do we make of that? Walter?

–Typical writer's moan.

Adam titters. –Alright. Words. Lexis. Masses of words. A basic communicative vocabulary threshold is five hundred words. Five *thousand* words gives anyone a reasonable fluency. But what about the *educated* native speaker? How many words do you think he has in his vocabulary – his passive receptive vocabulary – words he is familiar with or at least understands?

–Ten thousand?

–Oh more, more.

–Twenty thousand?

–Far more.

–Fifty thousand.

–A hundred thousand!

–More more more.

–Two hundred thousand?

–Yes yes – two hundred thousand words.

–Holy shit! says Linda softly in the limpid silence.

–Well, now I think it's time for the break . . .

–It was your lesson plan that let you down. She flips back the pages of Walter's essay mutilated with red scars: *I don't understand this . . . Useless . . . This would never work in the classroom . . .*

–Lesson plan, lesson plan – how the hell can you plan something you've never done? It's like asking a nun to plan an orgy. He dips a lump of sugar into his cognac and crunches it angrily. –There must be something more to it than that.

–Maybe. He doesn't like you much.

–Well I don't like him!

–No, sweetie, you made that pretty obvious this afternoon.

–I suppose I did. It's just that I can't stand those ludicrously dogmatic statements – 'There is no such thing as a synonym'! For God's sakes.

–But why did it have to be dick and cock and pecker and prick?

–It's what came into my head.

–I just hope you won't live to regret it.

–It's not the things one does one lives to regret – it's the things one doesn't do.

–Like not going to college, you mean?

–Not shooting the dog in the garden.

–Or pouring soup into Henri's lap.

And they laugh, suddenly merry.

The *patron* hopefully cocks an eye at them, but Walter shakes his head. –You didn't want apple pie, did you?

–No. Walter . . .

–What?

Two or three men at the counter leave in a puff of noise, and a white-faced young woman in a purple coat at another table gets up and goes down to the toilets. All at once the café is nearly empty; its brown plastic surfaces and orange globe lights and fake leather *banquettes* have the anonymous melancholy of an unoccupied railway compartment.

–Walter. We're going away in February.

–You – aaah . . . All the blood in his body floods into the centre, crushing his chest.

–Oh no no – I mean, just for the February vacation – only ten days. We –

–Ten days? He lifts his glass, stares at it, puts it down.

–It's just to ski. Henri has these friends who've offered –

–Bankers, he murmurs – heart murmurs, heavy with blood.

–They're all bankers or lawyers, yes. Anyway, they've offered us this chalet, they usually go themselves but he's been posted to Dubai – I only heard last night. She stubs out her cigarette. –Walter?

–What? Oh – sorry. I'm with you. Skiing, he says brightly. –I didn't know you skiid.

–Don't be like that, darling. I can't bear it. I'm supposed to be the cheerful one.

–You want to go . . .

–Of course not. I hate all that sort of thing. I dread it. But it *is* only ten days – and you were away a fortnight at Christmas. It'll be gone before you can say dummy auxiliary. What's time anyway?

–The second most used noun in the language. You called me 'darling'.

–Did I? Oh . . . well . . . She takes his hand and spreads it

78

flat on the table. The blush fades from her cheek and she is left solemn and pale and still. –You never know – something might happen . . . Then she raises her face and smiles.

The dome of the Invalides is no longer a dome, but an immense circular metal cabin surmounted by a bandaged thumb – a cock in a condom, a prick in a thimble.

Walter turns his back on it and looks down the avenue in the damp and dour evening light – the naked and unmoving trees are as stark as the bars on a row of prison cells. The clipped central strip of forbidden grass is guarded by iron hoops to trip the old, the blind, the infant, the innocent. How ugly, charmless and denatured Paris is – as disciplined as the regiments of the dead emperor in his monstrous sarcophagus, as rigid as bureaucracy, as harsh as police, cruel careless remote arrogant unloving clean, a city of light that brings not a single candle to those that dwell in darkness or sleep on the gratings of the Métro. *J'ai faim . . . Je m'en fou!*

A cat treads across the sodden lawn, stopping every now and again to shake a damp paw delicately. When it reaches the gravel on the other side it moves more surely – as though to a known refuge – and Walter follows at a distance. But even cats aren't safe from the iron of *la discipline*.

–He borrowed this airgun from a friend and –

–A banker?

–No, Maurice is an accountant. Anyway, it worked.

–You mean – he shot them?

–It's very light, you know, it's only pellets, it couldn't have –

–Done them any harm?

–It frightened them off – and they were such a nuisance yowling all night.

–Just smashed a nose, put out an eye, tore the odd arsehole.

–Walter!

–What a hideous bloody thing to do. You don't maim

79

animals merely because they annoy you. Do you? Can you? Come on, Connie.

She stared at him for a long moment. –He's quite good with Sarah's hamster.

And then they laughed and it was alright. But it wasn't really all right.

–It doesn't help to be told to pull yourself together, does it?

Connie has come straight over from dropping Tom at his school. She dumps her plastic sack on the dining-room table, but delays taking off her coat and gloves, moves about the apartment, not settling, casually touching him (–Oh, what's this? Is it for me or is it just the morning?), poking about.

–I can't stand all this leftover greenery – look, it's getting brown round the edges. Let's take it down – it's miles past twelfth night . . .

Together they pull down the mistletoe and yew, the holly and the ivy, and stuff it into big black garbage sacks and tie the tops. As Walter takes the sacks down to the rubbish room, Connie vacuums energetically, sucking up each last needle, leaf and berry. At last it's all done and the hoover's whine dies.

And now she sits perched on the footstool, holding her knees tight to her chest, a thin shine on her forehead, a droop to the mouth, a fresh scent of sweat on the air.

–Well, it doesn't, does it? Help, I mean.

–Something happened. This morning? He lights a cigarette to cool a tingle of dread.

–Nothing happened, no. Nothing ever happens in that house. I just felt heavy, droopy – almost impossible to get up. Of course, it has to do with my body, I know that.

–Nothing else?

–Women are always at the mercy of their bodies. Oh I'm not complaining. It's a fact of life. I'm glad we are – at least we're in touch with ourselves, we can't escape. Not like you.

Walter smiles. –Men aren't exactly immune to their own bodies.

–Oh, that. I'm not talking about the odd bit of lust. I mean, day in day out knowing you're an animal, feeling the change, the rhythm – movement. Sometimes I don't see the point of men.

–Procreation?

–Children, you mean. Children are alright. But they grow up, don't they? (Suddenly fierce.) They grow up and go away. And then – what's happened to your life?

–It bumbles on, unless –

–But what's *happened* to it? It's *gone* – vanished – used up in endless rounds of meals and washing behind the ears and sniffles and whooping cough and laundry and homework and doctors and dentists and whines and tears and slaps and to-ing and fro-ing and broken sleep and mizzling in the night and getting up in the morning and boredom, boredom and silence and on and on and on till we're sixty and rich and retired and useless and old and hopeless and half-dead and nothing to do but rock and nod and doze and remember . . . I don't *want* to remember!

–One's not always half dead at sixty . . .

–No, that's not good enough. No, Walter, don't touch me. That's okay for you. Men live. You've lived. You've had your life, you –

–I'm *still* alive.

–Yes you are – that's why I – that's what I like about you. But don't you see, *my* life's stealing by, *my* life's being stolen away. I might as well be in a *convent* – with all these evasions and cruelties and duties and penance and meanness and hurt. Why should I hurt all the time? Why *should* I? Why should I have to fight every day so's just not to be crushed, not to vanish – oh if only I could vanish! – so's just to survive? I want joy and life and happiness – no, I don't care about happiness – I want to be me, I want self-fulfilment and – and . . .

–Eternal life?

–Why not? Eternal life! If it's life at all, it's eternal, isn't it? One moment can be eternity, can't it?

She touches her cheeks, her forehead, looks at her hands. –Phew, I stink. She jumps up. I'm going to take a shower and change . . . may I?

–Change?

–That's what I brought in the plastic bag – a change of clothes. She pauses, notices him for the first time this morning. –Why do you listen to me? Why do you listen to all this shit?

–Well, for one thing, I don't want you to vanish.

She smiles, suddenly, brilliantly. –I'm not going to vanish. I'm going to–

–Wash your hair.

–Yes – and scrape off all this muck. And then . . .

Desultorily towelling her hair, she contemplates the special shelves of Waller-King books. In his old black and gold bathrobe, she has a tigerish air – though whether guarding her cubs or about to spring on her prey, he cannot tell.

–I'm going to put on the rice. Are you hungry?

–What? Oh yes – starving. Are these all yours?

–I published them, yes. Chili alright?

–Fine. How many – how many books?

–A hundred and seventy-four. Seven years' worth.

–Seven years . . .

She reaches out to take a book, and he turns away to the kitchen. For nearly a decade those volumes have sat in the same place on the shelf, undusted memories, and to see her touch one, open it, makes him uneasy. As he measures a cupful of rice, his hand wobbles and a few grains scatter on the floor. The kitchen tiles are cold to his knees as he bends to sweep up the rice . . . he stays for a long moment, kneeling, his mind blankly counting the grains . . . Then he gets up and brusquely busies himself with warming and stirring. He chills the glasses, polishes the forks and the silver pepper pot, and sets the table and opens the wine. When the rice is drained and set to steam and the gas turned low under the chili, he fills two glasses and carries them in.

Cross-legged on the sofa, she looks up from the book on her knees, taking a moment to focus.

He hands her a glass. —We can eat whenever we want.

She holds the glass as though it were an unfamiliar object – a candlestick perhaps or a piece of chalk. —I thought you said you were only a publisher?

—What have you got there?

She raises the book to show him. —*Happy Childhoods.*

—Oh yes – well, that's an anthology. I did edit *that* . . . a dead loss – totally mistimed; no one was interested in happy childhoods in the fall of '68 – Vietnam, Nixon, Abbie Hoffman, Black Power, the Weathermen . . . Bobby dead, everybody decent dead – or ruined . . .

—But you didn't just edit it – you wrote a piece: 'Rural Free Delivery' by Walter Waller.

—Yes. He sniffs the flowery scent of the wine, but doesn't drink.

—But it's American. Pleasantville – that's where you were sent in the war, isn't it? It's not really your *child*hood . . .

—I was twelve. I was homesick a bit at first, but on the whole those four years were the happiest I can remember . . .

—Truly?

—There's no point in writing anything that isn't true.

—But it sounds so sad.

—Does it? Maybe that's because I wrote it the year Phoebe died – 1967.

—And I was nineteen . . . She raises her glass and sips the wine. What's this? It's nice.

—Gerwürtztraminer. He takes a gulp and sits down beside her on the sofa.

—It's funny, happiness and sadness are all together somehow, aren't they – all mixed up, I mean. She drinks some more, breathes in the bouquet. —I remember once when I was, I don't know, eight or nine, sitting in the living room on a Sunday morning after mass and looking out of the window, not paying any particular attention, just looking. Then everyone went into the dining room for lunch, but I didn't move, I just sat there, I don't know why. I was sad, terribly sad, and it was raining and it was all very green – the grass, the trees, the shrubs, so green and wet and – and, well just sad. But I wanted to be there, I didn't want to move . . . I can't explain it, it was as if . . . I don't know.

She leans forward and the book folds shut in her lap and she puts her hand in his. –What you wrote about that house – the bacon and waffles and coffee, and the wisteria and woodsmoke and the dusty smell of the trunks of the apple trees – and that was all – happy . . . I know, I understand all that somehow. Although the window was closed because it was cold out and rainy, yet I could smell the garden, I'm sure I could – and I longed for it with a kind of insufferable longing . . . insufferable?

–Ineffable.

–Of course, if I'd been older, I'd say it must have been sex . . . animal desire. She gives a sudden painful smile and a curt laugh. –And now we don't even have a garden.

–And there aren't any smells left in Paris, either.

She looks at him in surprise. –Aren't there?

–Just the stink of cars and the odd touch of stale body odour on the Métro.

And they laugh and he touches her hair, dry and springy now, and they kiss.

–Who was King?

–King was Paula – my number two wife.

–Was she beautiful?

–Beautiful and cruel.

–What happened?

–I made a fool of myself – tried to behave like a gentleman. I gave her even unto half my kingdom – all of my kingdom, as it turned out in the end . . . my Wallerdom. He laughs. –The bitch bit off my arms at the elbows . . .

Connie looks at him, intently, thoughtful. –Don't you ever recover?

84

–Recover? Recover what? Recover *that*? No of course not. He picks the book from her lap and takes it over to the shelf and slips it into its place. –Who'd want to, anyway?

He turns, leaning his back against the bookcase, now helpless for words or . . .

–Come on, let's eat. She is beside him, arm in arm.

–Yes.

–And we can play dominoes.

–Dominoes, he says. –Great idea . . .

But they play Woodland Families instead.

–Can I have Mr Owl, please?

–Mr Owl. Yes – there you are.

–And Miss Owl? And Master Owl? There – family! She lays the Owls down with a flourish. I always liked the Owls. Now what? Ah – can I have Mr Badger, please?

–Nope – too early for badgers. I want, let's see – Miss Mole.

–You don't say 'I want' – you say, 'May I have Miss Mole, please?'

–May I have Miss Mole, please?

–No, I'm sorry, you can't – she's washing her hair tonight.

–How about this afternoon then?

She eyes him primly. – Keep your thoughts on your cards, ducky. And I'd like *Mrs* Mole, please.

–Mrs Mole? You don't really want Mrs Mole, do you? I'm very fond of Mrs Mole. Oh hell – there you are!

–Family! You'll have to buck up, you know – I'm winning. How many cards have you got? Four? In that case, may I please have Master Frog? – I'm sure you've got him.

And he has – and everything else she wants too, and she takes the game by eight families to three.

–That was easy, she says gleefully.

He smiles at her in victory. –Well done.

–You were really rather pathetic . . . You didn't let me win, did you?

—Of course not. Why would I do that?

—I think you might, Walter – yes, I think you well might. But please don't.

—I didn't.

—Well, I believe you. You must try to do better in future. She laughs. –I'd forgotten what fun it is. Next time I'm in England I must buy a pack for the children.

'Children.' The word falls awkwardly among the animal families placid on the blue tablecloth. Connie picks up the cards and examines them, then starts to shuffle the pack slowly. Walter lights a cigarette with a kitchen match. Outside, the dog breaks into a paroxysm of yelps.

Walter blows out the match. –That goddamn dog.

—Listen to this: 'If children's errors are not erroneous then neither can be the errors made by learners of a second language because they are not wilful.' What do you think that means?

—I don't know. Do I look awful?

—Not exactly in your plate. She sat through the entire class without looking or listening or speaking; he's never seen her so stony-faced, so bleak and depleted.

—I think I'd like some apple tart.

When it comes, she eats it with a kind of detached efficiency, as though she were already on some cold Alpine peak.

—Is it okay? It looks like plastic.

—It tastes like plastic. Oh God . . . She puts down her fork and shuts her eyes for a moment. –I hardly slept the whole weekend, what with Tom and his earache . . . it just got worse and worse and by Sunday he was really in agony with his throat as well as his ear . . . it was heart-rending to see him. But all I thought was – if it goes on like this, we won't have to go away after all. I thought, if he dies, I won't ever have to . . . Walter – I wished him dead . . .

He lights two cigarettes and hands one to her. –But he's better now?

86

–Yes, he started to perk up yesterday, but that makes it worse somehow – he's more active and moany and wants his Mummy all the time. And that makes Sarah jealous and impossible.

She inhales the cigarette smoke deeply and holds it for a long time before letting it go. –When she got back from school last night, she was impossible from the moment she set foot in the door. Wouldn't do this, didn't want that, started pinching and poking poor Tom and stole his bedroom slippers and swore they were hers – though they're miles too small for her. Finally I got her quietened down and fed and in bed – and Henri comes in and says, 'Have you been a good little girl today?' 'Oh yes, Papa.' 'And have you done your homework?' 'Oh yes, Papa', as if butter wouldn't melt in her mouth. So I lost my temper and slapped her and told her she was a two-faced little bitch.

She watches the smoke writhe slowly in the airless café. –Why am I always wrong? – even when I'm right, I'm wrong. Did you ever slap your children?

–I don't think I ever did, no. Though Charles and I nearly came to blows once or twice.

–That's different. Sarah can't slap me back, can she? What sort of an example am I to her – and to Tom, for that matter? You know, last summer in Normandy there was this neighbour's dog, an English sheepdog, and she played with it all the time – morning noon and night and she didn't want to do anything else. It was a simple affection she could give – give and take. A sort of absolute trust where nothing else mattered – a kind of shining look of love. She never looks at me that way, she never will, I know that. And I can understand it – why should she ever want to be like me? I tell her how boring and awful it is to be a mother, how wretched and soul-destroying, how desperately hard I work and run run run all the time . . .

–Maybe she won't want children. Maybe she'll turn out to be a dog lady.

–A dog lady – you make it sound so nice . . . She sighs and looks down at his hand and touches it with her fingers. –I often think, if only we were in England, it would all be different. I'd be at home – I'd be a person.

–Connie, the England you knew isn't there any more – and even if it were, you wouldn't be part of it. There's no country people like us can call home – home has gone beyond recall.

–No . . . no! That's not true, that can't be true . . .

–But it is. You can't wind time backwards – and home is time past; and even if you could turn it back enough, home is the womb, darkness, dependence, dissolution – hell, not heaven.

–I don't want heaven, just less hell. She puts out her cigarette with quick short jabs, then looks up and makes a moue. –It's some kind of desperate irony, really. I left England to get away from men, you know – that's why I left, but . . .

–But the wily Gaul snuck up and took you by surprise?

She smiles but says nothing. –Well, didn't he? Why are you looking so smug?

–Oh Walter, you are a dear. Do you really think it happens like that?

–Well, doesn't it? I mean – what do you mean?

–Women are sort of wide-eyed maidens – and men run after them and capture them and carry them off . . . is that what you think?

–Put like that – no. But men usually make the running, don't they?

–Of course they think they do, but . . . She reaches for his untouched cognac and takes a delicate sip.

–But what?

–Look, it's good for the male ego, isn't it – all this conquering-hero stuff? But women have a choice too – after all, who asked the shining knight to slay the dragon in the first place? Her eyes glimmer with amusement. –Who captured who and carried him off to England?

He stares at her in amazement. –You're saying that you – that you had designs on me?

–Designs? That's a bit strong. I just wanted to see what

would happen. Of course I knew you fancied me – but you were a bit slow, weren't you?

–I was? He reaches for the cigarettes, but there are none left in the packet.

–You didn't notice me at the mingle, did you? I was the one whose name you couldn't remember – remember?

–Yes. He scrunches the empty packet in his hand, then smooths it out.

– So I decided you ought to be taught to take notice.

He looks at her sitting straight as a queen, gleaming, on top of the world – and he laughs. Some world.

On the morning of her depature he risks a quick early phone call, but can hardly get out '*bon voyage*' before the line is interrupted with piping childish giggles. And anyway, the words have a sour taste of hypocrisy in his mouth – how can he possibly wish her a *bon voyage* with anyone but himself?

He turns to translating *Fleur-Marie-Fleur*, but that too seems sour – a grubby day, the Brittany beach soiled with a thin scum of nostalgia and littered with the sentimental debris of an ideal summer that never was. The real day, when he goes out, is deceptively touched with spring. The Champ de Mars blossoms with an early crop of tourists and the children left behind in Paris disport themselves with glad cries in the playground. Old lady Eiffel straddles a single ice-cream van and high above her clitoral tip a con trail whitely streaks the upper atmosphere. Connie's plane maybe – to snow and Alps and sunshine. She will be in the mountains, but her heart is surely here on the level ground, the old battlefield turned to peace and promise.

He buys *The Times* at the corner kiosk and walks back past the Ecole Militaire, hardly noticing where he is – beach, mountains, Paris, Manhattan, England, anywhere, nowhere . . . He passes through the courtyard, absent-mindedly cutting the prattling ladies – aware just a little too late of their greetings.

As he enters the downstairs hall, the dog is in full throat behind the glass doors – *rrr-errr-errugh-errugh* . . .

–Oh, bow-wow to you, says Walter in shallow exasperation as the elevator gently jolts him upwards. –'Wuff-wuff, yap-yap . . . Sliding the gate back, turning . . . –Connie!

–Hello. She smiles – uncertain teffle smile. –I didn't go after all.

–Connie . . . He takes her hands in his and glances vaguely round the landing. But what about . . ?

–It's alright – *they've* gone.

–Gone? Where? He's bewildered with smiles.

–To Chamonix, of course. I drove them all to the airport and saw them off. I waited till the plane had flown away – and then I came back, came here and . . . Oh Walter, we've got ten days, ten whole . . . And suddenly the tears brim over and pour down her face. –Days . . ., she wails.

He takes her in his arms there on the doormat, but can't still the trembling of her body. –Hush, my love my honey, hush, my darling . . .

–They've *gone*!

–And I've got you.

–I sent them away, don't you understand? She pulls back to look at him, thrusts a desperate hand under his shirt. –How can you possibly want me? How could you . . . ?

–I've brought you tea. Come on, I know you're not asleep.

He strokes her neck until she opens her eyes.

–How could anyone stay asleep with all that noise you make in the bathroom?

–You mean my singing?

–Oh is that what it was? She sits up and takes the mug. –Tea, how wonderful.

–Scrub me, Mama, with a boogie beat, he says, sliding in beside her.

–Is that an old Quaker hymn? Here, what are you doing?

–Watching you drink tea. Quakers don't sing hymns.

–Just as well if you're anything to go by. We're not going to stay in bed all day, are we?

–No.

–We're going to *do* things, aren't we?

–Yes.

–What are we going to do?

–We're going to go to the Musée d'Orsay.

–The *museum*?

–Haven't you ever been? He kisses her ear.

–Of course I haven't – we never go anywhere. Ummm, you smell all clean and after-shavish.

–Don't touch.

–Why not?

–Finish your tea first.

–Alright, but then I'm going to scrub you with a boogie bat.

–*Beat.*

–And I'll beat you too.

–*La salle des pas perdus* – how lovely. But why?

–I don't really know.

They stand on one of the twin pinnacles at the east end of the museum, look across to the great station clock above the entrance and the five levels of pedestrians moving in ghostly patterns behind the opaque glass.

–Well, you *ought* to know, she says firmly. –It's the sort of thing you usually do know – the sort of thing you like knowing.

–Useless, in other words?

–But interesting. I'd like to know whose footsteps were lost – and why. Wouldn't you?

–Yes, but as we don't know, there's not much point in –

–Oh come on, haven't you got any imagination?

–Not a great deal, as a matter of fact.

–Walter, that's not true . . . She looks at him with sudden

seriousness. −Or is it? Perhaps it is . . . maybe that's why you are always being surprised. Maybe that's why you had so many wives . . .

He laughs. −How do you work that one out?

−You can't understand anyone if you don't have imagination − women, men, even children. You may have all the experience in the world, but . . .

−But it's all useless knowledge?

She pauses, then says slowly, −You think I say knowledge is useless because I don't know anything, don't you?

−No − in fact, I agree with you, most of what we learn is −

−Walter, I *know* I don't know anything . . . and sometimes it feels like − like a great hole. It makes me boring, at least for the French it does − I know that. I've thought about it, and it seems to me knowledge is like love − it's no earthly good unless you can use it, unless it can be made to work. Otherwise, it's just frivolous . . . and I haven't got time to be frivolous, don't you see?

He nods, unable to speak, and looks away out over the lofty concourse where trains steamed in from distant places, and purposeful passengers trod and lovers departed and spouses waited and porters trundled luggage amongst dogs and eager children. Theirs were the lost footsteps, replaced now by frivolous stone statuary.

She puts her hand on his where he grasps the rail tight. −You don't have to understand me, Walter.

He looks at her small, grave smile, and his heart is pierced with her beauty.

−I don't *want* to be understood, she says vehemently.

−Well no . . . who does?

−Children do . . . or imagine they do. But I think it would be terrible.

−Terrible.

−A sort of cage, like childhood − a trap . . .

−Yes, maybe − a trap.

92

–You sound like a parrot.

He manages a smile. –I feel like a parrot – a bit unsteady on my perch.

The old lady in black walks slowly away on the snow-covered path between the beech hedge and the stone-gold wall. The snow blossoms delicately on the overhanging fruit trees and whitens the roof of the church and the tower that rises amongst the winter elms to the calm grey clouds above.

A little apart from the crowd admiring the summer agonies of Van Gogh, Connie and Walter stand hand in hand, invested with Sisley's snowy silence. In the depths of the nineteenth century there the church clock strikes the solemn half-hour.

It's the empty time of the afternoon and they drink hot chocolate in a café which is almost empty too. It has clouded over, so they sit inside next to the window on cane chairs at a marble-topped table. A fly is perched serenely on a lump of sugar and at the counter the young waiter softly hums and strums an imaginary guitar.

–It's funny – before I met you I hadn't been in a café for simply ages. Not really since Sarah was born – that's when I gave up smoking too.

She has bought herself a packet of Gauloises and the raw tobacco smell acts like the scent of memory.

–And you hadn't taken a bus.

–Hardly – nor even the Métro.

–None of the ordinary things.

–None of the ordinary *pleasant* things. Do you think . . . ? Let's have a cognac.

She calls out to the waiter, douses her cigarette in the tin ashtray and immediately lights another.

–I don't mind telling you now, she says when the waiter has

come and gone. Yet she delays a little. The fly buzzes off, and she dips the sugar into the cognac and crunches it with her even white teeth.

—It was all quite easy really – once I'd got my nerve up. I arranged the whole thing with Marie and her mother over the weekend. They're absolutely strapped and Marie never goes anywhere in the vacations – so of course she was delighted with the idea of a free holiday. I didn't offer to pay her anything – I knew Henri would have kicked at that – but of course I lobbed her five hundred francs at the airport when his back was turned. Tom and Sarah were thrilled – I've been such a cow lately, they were delighted at the idea of getting away from Mummy for a bit. And they adore Marie, she's wonderful with them . . . So there it was, Henry went a bit white and tight-lipped when I broke the news, but short of cancelling the entire trip – which had all been paid for, so that was pretty unthinkable – there was absolutely nothing he could do. There was a lot of the what-sort-of-a-mother-are-you stuff, but otherwise it was the same as usual, only a bit more so.

—Which is what?

—Silent warfare. She drinks the brandy in one fell swoop. —When I'm angry I scrub the kitchen floor. When he's angry he buries himself in his wretched history books. I expect it'll be much nicer not talking to Marie than not talking to me. She laughs – the old rich Connie laugh. –Walter, you know what I want to do now?

—I could make a guess.

—But you'd be wrong. I want to go on the Métro.

The train gives its warning cry and the doors slot shut. They were the only people on the platform and they are the only ones in the carriage.

—Why did we have to come all the way to Passy to –

—Because this is where you get the best view. Wait – now . . . look left.

94

But as the train swishes out of the station onto the open bridge, she glances to her right. −Oh look − what's that funny little statue down at the end there? It looks like the Statue of Liberty.

−That's what it is − one of Bartholdi's try-outs for the big one. Tucked away out of sight in Paris of course.

And then it is gone as they slide between the apartment houses at third-floor level and draw into Bir-Hakeim.

−It doesn't stop long, does it? How close we are − you can see right into the rooms. Look, there's a man at a drawing board − and a black woman doing her washing.

−Not her washing − *his* washing.

−Oh alright − but it's exciting, isn't it? How long between stops?

−Eighty seconds.

−There you are, you do know everything! She laughs. −Exactly?

−On average − a little less on this line, I think − at least on the elevated part.

The doors open and a shabby young man makes to get in, sees them, then steps back and moves on to the next carriage.

−We frightened him away − do we look so awful?

−It's not that − he was going to give us a spiel about his starving wife and kids, but we're not enough of an audience.

There's a warning moan − the doors shut, then jerk open again.

−Walter. You were right.

−About what?

−About what you guessed.

He smiles. −Only four more stops.

She pulls his head down and kisses him on the mouth. She whispers, −Eighty seconds is a long time.

−Connie!

−I'm not wearing anything under my skirt, it'd be easy to −

−Absolutely not!

−I bet lots of people do.

−Not me.

−Walter − I love you.

The train impatiently repeats its plaintive cry . . .

−Good grief, Connie!

. . . and the doors close.

Connie wanders in from the sitting room as Walter loosens the ice in the ice tray. −She's just shuttered them all in − and it's hardly even dark yet.

−Just squeeze those for me, will you? He points to the limes and a juicer on the countertop. −Who − what? he drops the ice-cubes into the blender. −Now, where did I put the powdered sugar?

−The old housekeeper in the villa − the shutters − five that we can see and there must be more at the back. Bang-bang-bang − I'm surprised you didn't hear. She caught me staring down at her − gave me a really sharp look.

−Ah, here we are. Bugger, it's all stuck together. He raps the jar hard against the sink to loosen the sugar. −Haven't you squeezed those limes yet?

−They're so perfect, it seems a shame to cut them up. She rolls the waxy green fruit in her hand and touches it to her cheek.

−Don't start getting soppy about a couple of limes, he says, sprinkling powdered sugar on the ice.

−Soppy! Oh-ho! She picks up the knife and boldly slices them in half and squeezes them with a rapid circular twist. −There.

−Thanks.

Connie lights a Gauloise, watching him pour in the juice and two measures of rum and then an extra slosh for luck. −You know what you ought to do? I've had an idea.

−About what? He fits the hat on the blender.

−About the dog, of course. Every time it has one of those fits, you just ring her up and . . .

Her words are lost in the furious clatter of breaking ice as Walter switches on the blender. He fetches two cocktail glasses from the freezer, turns off the blender, and fills them with a foaming swoop. –Now try this.

–Wonderful.

–You haven't tasted it yet.

–I meant the peace and quiet. What is it?

–A frozen daiquiri.

–It's all froth.

–Froth with a bite – drink it while it's still creamy. Here's mud in your eye.

–Mud! She grins and swallows half the cocktail in one go. –Aaah! And gives a convulsive shiver.

–Kind of bites you in the back of the neck, doesn't it?

–A boogie bite. She drinks the rest of it and holds out her glass. –More.

–Well, okay, but . . . you'd better sit down.

–Right. She sits down with the refilled glass. She has bathed and changed back into jeans and a white tee-shirt and looks about eighteen years old. –Now what was I saying?

–That I should ring up and complain about the dog. But it wouldn't work, you know, she'd just –

–I didn't say *complain*. You just ring her up – any time – in the middle of the night –

–The dog doesn't bark in the night.

–That's got nothing to do with it. Will you listen? You don't talk, you *bark*.

–I do?

–Bark down the *phone*!

–That'd wake her up alright, but she might figure out it was me.

Connie takes a large swig of daiquiri. –How?

–There's my accent and –

–Dog's don't have accents – they're at home anywhere.

–and then sometimes I bark out of the window – and make faces at it. She's seen me do that.

–Yes, that's what gave me the idea. You were so sweet

97

coming up in the lift, barking away. I adore all these strange little things you do.

–Like in the Métro, you mean?

–There's nothing strange about that – that's natural. Oops! A finger of ash falls into the daiquiri.

–Here, let me get you a clean glass.

–Don't be silly. No, I mean like pissing in the teapot in the morning. Oh yes, I know you do – you're too lazy to go to the toilet, I know. I know everything about you.

–Well – alright. He smiles and comes and sits down beside her. –So what? That's not so strange. Urine is sterile – and it's supposed to be quite a good thing to drink a bit of your own piss every day.

–You're not serious.

–I'm perfectly serious. The Indians do it.

–No you're not. You're not serious – you're not a *serious* man. I love that. And you're not perfect either – you don't even *try* to be perfect. What a relief. She gives the ash in her glass a quick stir with her little finger. –And anyway, suppose the old bat did guess it was you – she could never prove it.

–No, but she might think I was making overtures.

–Overtures! Connie lets out a merry peal of laughter.

–You never know. Supposing she barked back?

–A mating song? Is that how it's done? How charming. She drains the last of her drink.

–Charming? Getting involved with that old hag in a mac?

–You afraid she'd lock you up in her nice little house with the other . . . oops!

–The other old men! He laughs.

–It's alright, don't worry. I'd come and rescue me – rescue you, I mean, on my white horse and . . . Let's have another dak – whatever-it-is . . . She stands up abruptly – clings to the table. –Perhaps not. I . . . She closes her eyes. –I'm falling . . .

Walter catches her and lifts her up and she puts her arms round his neck and clings tight.

–Bed for you, he says. How light she is, he thinks.

98

She opens her eyes for a moment. –Bow-wow! Then swoons in his arms.

They drink coffee with hot milk in bowls and eat tartines of yesterday's stale bread with myrtle jelly. They wrap themselves warmly in their grey overcoats against the early morning chill and set out as the day begins to break. The streets are cool and quiet and grey too – and they walk miles, hardly talking at all, Connie's red gloves being the only touch of colour. It is Saturday and there is little traffic and few people – a concierge dragging empty garbage bins into a building, an elderly man with a coat and scarf over his pyjamas walking a dog, a crossing-sweeper in green overalls, tall, black, magnificently indifferent.

They reach the Seine at last and halt on the Petit Pont. The spring sun is a muted misty yellow, the river is without a ripple, and the whole city is still and soft and only half-awake. Even Charlemagne on his charger dreams of peace. And the Préfecture de Police, its tricolour hanging limp in the motionless air, is less ominous without its weekday queue of cowed immigrants.

–Let's have a look at the birds.

–But Walter . . . She grips his hand tight. –There aren't any birds.

–What? What do you mean? Of course there are.

–No – look. It's a flower market. We must have got the wrong day.

–Flowers . . .

–Don't look so rueful – don't you like flowers?

–Yes, but I . . .

–I know, you were expecting parrots and macaws and budgerigars. But do come – flowers and garden plants . . . She pulls him by the hand. –Aren't they lovely!

Abandoning all hope of birds, he lets himself be led into an alley of azaleas and lilies, daisies, tulips, hyacinths, tamarisk, pansies . . . there seem to be no other human beings at all.

–Listen, Connie . . .

–Oh look – have you ever seen a red hyacinth before? What is it?

–I feel a bit sickish. He blinks and takes a quick shallow breath, and the whole mass of colour – pink indigo purple mauve orange yellow tiger-gold – seems to enter his body like liquid fire. –I think it must have been the coffee.

–You do look a bit pale – you should have stuck to your tea. We'd better go and sit down.

–No no – you stay and wander around. I'll be outside – by the Wallace fountain.

–Well – alright. They are so beautiful. I shan't be long.

–Take your time . . .

He leans against the fountain, resting his head on the iron bosom of the dark green maiden and raising his face to the lemon-smooth sun. Voices come and go, floating with a gentle strange intimacy on the pool of calm around the market – Italian voices, Japanese voices, German voices – invaders' voices . . . English voices. He looks down at an English family of four – mother, father, daughter, son – amiable with English smiles, in cozy English clothes, speaking English, thinking English thoughts, pleased with English pleasures, come to Paris for a clean weekend – to see the flowers.

–Hey there, sleepy head, wake up.

–Hello . . . He turns his head and smiles at her brightness.

–Come on, I've got a surprise for you.

–You don't think it's a bit like an undertaker's?

–Nope. He smiles. –No corpse.

But Connie is not satisfied – she moves seriously from plant to plant, flower to flower, her hands behind her back, bending to sniff and examine. – I'm not sure . . .

The sitting room is afire – every bloom she bought at the market is some shade of red: scarlet, vermilion, carmine, crimson, magenta.

–Wrong colours, he says. –Funerary wreaths are all pale and pastelish – white and mauve and beige and custard – gutless colours like the Queen wears.

–Perhaps you're right . . . She turns with a smile. –You're pleased then?

–They're beautiful . . . He closes his eyes for an instant, and behind his eyelids the room swims with the reds, a whirlpool of hurtling blood.

–Better than birds?

–Much better. Birds fly away.

–Not all birds. She comes to him and pulls his body close to hers. –This bird didn't.

–No vertigo?

–None at all – isn't that marvellous? She smiles at the city spread out beneath them as white and enticing as a feast at a wedding. –I could hop out and dance on the girders without a qualm.

–We're here to eat not dance.

–And I'm as hungry as a horse. What shall I have? She casts a glance at the next table where a group of businessmen sit smilelessly under the great flywheel that winds the lift silently up and down the tower. –Not whatever they're having –

–Fish. Simple fish – they mess it up when they try to be clever.

–Who doesn't? Alright. Sole? My menu hasn't got any prices.

–Good thing too.

–Walter – is it going to cost a fortune?

–Oh well . . .

–Then we're going dutch.

–Not on your life.

–But you can't afford it.

–And you spent a fortune on flowers – and you couldn't afford that . . . what the hell, we'll soon be rich.

–We will? Not teaching . . .

–Why not?

–Teachers aren't paid much, lovie.

–It depends what you mean by 'much'. They're far better off than waiters – and a lot less useful. Twenty hours a week at a hundred francs an hour is 2,000 – times two is 4,000 francs a week and –

–What's this 'times two' business? She is alert and still.

–We could go into partnership – the Thompson-Waller School of English.

She does not answer his smile. –Partnerships aren't exactly your strong point, are they? Besides, what makes you think we're going to pass?

–Of course we're going to pass. He reaches out for her hand on the pristine tablecloth – after four days of leisure her skin is as smooth as a girl's. –They can't afford to fail people – everyone will pass, and we're just as good as the rest of them.

–Are we? She glances out of the window at the criss-crossed girders and the blue sky beyond and closes her eyes. –My head's whirling – if I don't have something to eat soon, I'm going to faint.

The hall of the Mantel apartment is as big as a small railway station and about as gloomy. There are seven doors and a single window looking onto an airshaft. Walter takes out his cigarettes, then slips them back in his pocket – there is a definite no-smoking feel to the place – no smoking, no laughing, no singing. On a rickety three-legged table there's a china vase filled with what looks like dead bracken and an old grey telephone. A pair of fake Louis Quinze chairs are obviously not for sitting on.

–That was quick, he says with relief as Connie emerges from a dark corridor with a suitcase in her hand.

–I only had to throw a few clean things into a case.

–Can we go now?

–Not yet – I've got to make a quick call. She dumps the case by the front door. –Why don't you make us some coffee? The kitchen's through the swing door there, and the coffee's next to the coffee machine, you just fill it with water and –

–Yes, I do know how these things work. You're calling Chamonix?

–I promised I would. They should be back at the chalet by now.

The kitchen is vast and all white – white tiles, white enamel, white plastic – the place where the cadavers are stripped and cleaned and laid out maybe. Cold too.

Walter measures out the coffee and fills the machine and switches it on.

–Henri – c'est moi. Comment ça va? Comment vont les enf –

Walter starts to sing softly to override the stream of a foreign language in an alien voice that floats in from the hall. –It's not a palace, nor a poorhouse – but the rent is absolutely free . . .

He opens some cupboards at random and is surprised at the neatness and order of jars and bottles, cans and boxes and cartons, ranks of glasses and mugs and cups. A place for everything and everything in its place. The coffee is comfortably bubbling.

–. . . this is my house, but it's your house if you come and live with me . . .

The acoustics in the morgue are good. He reaches down a couple of mugs and raises his voice. –With a carpet on the floor made of buttercups and . . .

The refrigerator contains butter, a carton of milk and a bottle of apple juice. He sniffs the milk; it seems alright – French milk keeps forever. He pours some into a pan and puts it on the fire.

–. . . clover. All our troubles will be over . . .

The coffee machine snorts and turns itself off.

–. . . when we build a little home. Connie, do you want . . .

He pushes open the swing door into the hall. –Connie?

She is not at the phone. There is a total silence – the dead

103

quiet of an uninhabited apartment. He opens the nearest door – a black leather couch and matching chairs, Habitat table lamps, chintz curtains, a hunting print over the mantelpiece – the *living*, a little effort at England.

The lavatory – stained toilet bowl and a cracked wooden seat.

The dining room next – oddly proportioned, too high for its size with gilt-edged panelling all the way up the walls, like a coffin set on end; more Louis Quinze. The air is breathless, melancholy, mordaunt.

–Connie – where are you?

He can't find the light switch in the dark corridor, but opens the first door he comes to – a child's room, childish drawings taped to the wall, a Snoopy pillow on the bed, a dented red fire-truck in a corner. He moves quickly. Another child's room – posters of dogs, an empty cage, a plush elephant, an unfinished game of snakes and ladders.

–Connie! Full voice now. Absolute silence.

The next bedroom is much larger and has the colourless anonymity of a spare room. But no – above the double bed is a long shelf of parchment-pale books – the famous history books. Yet no ornaments, no pictures, no trinkets, no photographs in frames. He moves further into the room and looks out of the window at a cobbled courtyard and the low leaded roof where presumably the cats congregated and were potted for the nuisance of their love cries. Love cries . . .

–*Connie!* he shouts. The grey late afternoon has turned to drizzle. What the devil had the frog bugger said to her on the phone that could make her vanish? He drops to his hands and knees and looks under the bed. He stands up, creaking, shame-faced, fear-ridden . . . There's not a single mirror in the room, not even a handglass – only the pale blind screen of a word processor. Maybe there's a mirror on the inside door of the closet . . . but Connie's not in the closet, for God's sakes.

There is one more door, the bathroom – of course. She's just gone to . . . to do what? His hand trembles on the doorknob;

104

he takes a breath. –Connie? He clears his throat. –Connie? Are you there?

He gives a little half-choked laugh to the empty bathroom. What had he expected – razor blades and bloodied wrists? He touches the washbasin, dry as a bone, looks into the toilet bowl.

–Conn – *eee*! A long wail resounding from the shining tiles. Then he is running through the apartment, back the way he came, blundering, banging the doors, calling, running round and round and round like a beaten boxer in the ring . . .

He stops at last, panting, in the dismal hall. He pulls open the front door and steps out onto the landing.

–What have you done with her, you sonofabitch! . . . *bitch bitch bitch* . . . goes echoing down the lift shaft, round the empty stairwell.

He steps back as if startled by an enemy and stumbles over the suitcase by the door. Her suitcase! –Connie, he murmurs, kneeling, clutching the case, opening it, smelling her, delving . . .

–Walter? Walter – what are you doing?

His hands full of clothes, he looks up at her standing in the open doorway, a wicker basket on her arm.

–I thought you were gone, he says.

–I just went down to the cellar to get us some wine – and you were singing away so happily . . . She puts down the basket full of bottles and kneels beside him. –Oh darling, you look awful . . . She takes him in her soft arms, touches him with her soft hands. –Oh my love, my petal, my angel, my poor sweetheart . . . She kisses him with her soft lips.

–Don't ever leave me, Connie.

She leans back a little, smiling. –Of course I shan't leave you, I . . . She lifts her head and sniffs. –What's that funny smell?

–That? Oh – that must be burnt milk. For the coffee.

She laughs. –You *are* a nincompoop.

–Yes, he says. –Yes, I am.

105

–I like this bit – what is it? I could dance to this.

–It's the rondo. Try it.

–Shall I? Why not? Can you start it again?

Walter gets up and goes over to the record player. Music, she'd said, earlier in the evening – real music . . . And he had put out the lights and lit tall red candles in the silver candlesticks and placed them on either side of the mirror above the chimneypiece. He had tried her with Prokofiev, Schumann, a Haydn trio and, watching her, he was reminded of the Sunday classical concerts he'd given Amy and Charles when they were small. But it was the Mozart that got to her finally.

–Tell me when you're ready.

–Wait, she says. She has stripped down to black tights and a tee-shirt. She moves into the centre of the room with quick arched steps, an intent tilt to her head. She is straight and restrained as a tulip in the candlelight, which lends a softer, subtler tone to azalea and lily and touch-me-not. Her body braces and her head lifts to the window where over the rooftops the tip of the Eiffel Tower glows golden. –Now!

Walter lowers the needle; the record is dusty, but the rapid notes of the horn subdue the crackling whisper of age. And instantly she is in motion – so fast she seems to flutter like the wings of a blackbird in a dust bath. And Walter smiles, remembering Charles as a little boy twirling ecstatically round and round until giddiness brought him down with a sudden plop on his ass. But Connie's speed is supple and controlled – she bows like the willow, leans like the long grass in a little wind, riffles like poplar leaves before the storm. She and her mirror image dance to each other in delight.

When it is done, she holds out her arms and he catches her to him, feeling the beat of her heart, alabaster bone, flesh thriving in sweet sweat. He kisses the nape of her neck and she turns to look up at him.

–You didn't know, did you, I could do that? I had years and years of ballet class until my back gave out . . . I'll suffer for it tomorrow . . . but I don't care.

–Oh love, oh careless love.

–Not careless. She opens her eyes wide. –Carefree. That's what I used to be – carefree . . . She sighs and shuts her eyes, and all her weight is on him and she smiles.

The linen tablecloth gleams in the sunlight and what's left of the Meursault is a pale translucent gold. From the window a grassy field stretches away to the edge of the forest which is already touched with the fine green mistiness of spring.

She says, –It reminds me a bit of the view from my grand-parents' cottage – only there were cows in the field there, black and white ones. They used to come up to the garden hedge and moon over it and snuffle. They scared me when I was little and I'd run into the house and hide under the Princess bed.

The smoke from her cigarette drifts meditatively across the table, and she picks up her wine and sips. She has drunk more of it than he has and smokes more now too, in a curious reversal of habits.

–Why princess?

–I don't know really – it was a very ordinary cottage and Granny and Grandad, well, I suppose they were ordinary too – I mean, I'm sure they never knew anyone important who might have slept in it, let alone a princess. But it was very impressive – it had a headboard and a footboard upholstered in green velvet, and it stood high off the floor on carved legs which were hidden by a green velvet skirt. It was a wonderful place to hide – all musty and warm and secret under there. But I never remember anyone sleeping in it. I certainly wasn't allowed to. It was held out as a kind of promise – one day perhaps, if you're very, *very* good, maybe you can sleep in the Princess bed.

A section of ash from her Gauloise drops onto the cloth and she smears it thoughtfully with her thumb. –It's odd, isn't it? I mean, what does being very good mean? I would try terri-fically hard – I was always washing my hands and cleaning my teeth and being polite and smiling and helpful – a regular little red hen – but it never seemed to be enough. 'Have I been good today, Granny?' 'Yes, my dear, very good.' 'Good enough to sleep in the Princess bed?' 'Oh, not quite good enough for that, my chirabee!' 'Shall I *ever* be good enough, Granny?' 'We'll see, my dear, we'll see – now run along . . .' I was always running along and trying again, but it never did any good, it was always the same . . . Why did she do it, I wonder?

Walter takes a sip of wine. –She was laying a guilt trip on you, as they say – keeping you in your place.

Connie leans forward, her eyes as bright as polished conkers, her cheeks touched with the rosiness of wine. –But why couldn't my place have been in the bed?

They are caught in a gust of laughter and Walter swallows the wine the wrong way and chokes and sprays it out over the table.

–Granny'd never had let *you* sleep in the bed! Do you want a pat on the back?

–What for? He takes a shuddering breath. –You don't get pats on the back for misbehaving.

–No – that's right . . . She stubs out her cigarette and looks carefully round the room as though searching for enemies, then out of the window at the kine-free field. –You know what? I'd get fed up after a while and stop trying – and go and sit under that beastly bed and sulk. And then one day at lunch, in front of everyone, I called Granny a silly old cow . . . She was rather like a cow – she was very fat and had some sort of sinus condition, I suppose, that made her snuffle when she ate, and she had those kind of rheumy eyes . . . 'Silly old cow!' Shock horror – but I wouldn't say I was sorry. I never did. I wasn't. And I didn't feel a bit guilty – I was bloody well fed up with guilt. So you see, it doesn't always work. She picks up her glass and drains it in one gulp. –Let's go for a walk in the woods.

–A walk? After all this food?

–Not just a walk, dickhead . . . She laughs.

–Okay, Princess.

–Why are you smiling?

–A plump old bloke in the forest tumbling in the leaves with an English beauty.

–English beauty! You make me sound like an apple.

–A pippin.

The sun falls through the branches onto their whiteness as they lie in each other's arms on the mossy bank under the beech tree. She shivers slightly.

–Cold?

–No. It's just that it's so delicious, isn't it? The air and the sky and the real ground under us – I don't see why we should ever have to wear clothes, it's so much nicer without.

–Like a French TV coffee commercial, you mean?

–Rats to you. She puts her hand against his chest. –I can hear your heart going – thump-thump, thump-thump, thump-thump.

–I shouldn't wonder. He runs his hand through her hair. Would his heart beat at all if she wasn't there to hear it?

–Breathe – breathe! There! Why do you hold your breath like that? She lifts her head up to look at him.

–I don't know. He smiles, he cannot say: Because I would expire in this intolerable joy!

–I wish you wouldn't. Listen – do you notice something?

–Everything. Not a leaf or blade or bud or a hair of your head escapes me.

–I didn't mean that. She kisses him quickly. –I mean, I can't hear a single bird, can you? Isn't that odd in a forest?

–There aren't any birds in France. Besides, you probably scared them away with all your noise.

–*My* noise! she says indignantly, then laughs her deep happy laugh. –You haven't heard anything yet. And she leaps to her feet.

–Connie! He makes a grab for her ankle, but she dances neatly out of reach and stops a few yards off. Hands on hips, she raises her head high so her breasts lift, takes two, three deep breaths, closes her eyes and lets out a great swelling contralto cry – a huge shout of bursting life that stops the forest, stops Walter's heart. And again – and again . . . Her body is slender and silver-white as a birch, laced with the pattern of branches, light and strong as the elated air, vibrant with that wild call – a cry in the wilderness, a shout in the desert, a rebel yell.

–Connie. He stands up and takes a step towards her.

–Is that as good as your woodcutter's daughter?

–Connie . . . He comes close and holds out his hand.

–What is it? Are you worried? She slips her hand into his.

–Only that the woodcutter will come and chop off my head with his axe.

–There isn't any woodcutter – that's just a fairy story, my duck.

–All the same, let's get out of here.

–I don't want to – not just yet. Do you mind? Am I being difficult? I'm not usually difficult, am I?

–Well, no . . . a bit of a handful at times perhaps.

–Am I? She looks him up and down and suddenly laughs. But *you're* the handful right now, aren't you?

–Oh, Christ. Look, we ought to –

–Bed!

–*Bed?*

–This bed – moss and grass and leaves. She puts her arms round his shoulders and leans her weight against him.

–Babes in the fucking wood, he mutters as he lets himself be pulled down onto the soft forest floor.

–Hello, what's this? He leans down and touches a thin thread of sawdust on the doormat. –Oh Jesus!

–What – what is it?

–We've been robbed.

–But that can't be – not with a *porte blindée*.

–It can if you don't double-lock it – and I don't expect I did. They drill a hole under the lock and then hook it open with a wire.

–Are you sure?

–It's a well-known technique. He pushes at the door, but it doesn't budge.

–Then – they might still be in there!

–I doubt it – but it's possible. In fact, I'd be happier if you waited downstairs. He takes out his keys.

–Wait . . . She touches his arm. –Walter, shouldn't we call the police?

–Not on your nelly. You don't call the police in a police state.

–France isn't a police state!

–You could have fooled me. I don't want my name on the blotter.

–That's paranoid. You sound just like a Frenchman.

–Well, I've never said the Frogs don't have a thing or two to teach us – realism, in this case.

–You're so fucking clever, aren't you? Don't you love anything?

–Connie!

She looks at him aghast. –I didn't mean that – I don't know why I said that. I'm sorry . . . I'm scared – aren't you?

–Frightened to death. Still it's got to be done. Get in the lift and –

–No. She shakes her head. –I'm coming in with you.

He hesitates, key in hand. –Okay – but it may be a nasty sight.

–Oh Walter . . . She throws her arms round him and hugs as tight as she can. And steps back. –Open the door – quick, quick!

They sense at once that whoever had been there has long gone, abandoning the wreckage and leaving a flat and neutral hush, as though violent action has used up the day's sound. Yet after one look in the kitchen, Walter has taken off his shoes and socks, and armed himself with a heavy wrench.

As they stand silently in the sitting room, the soil spilled from the planters is soft under their toes. The moquette is clotted with the brilliant red of trampled blooms and scattered petals. The bookshelves have been tipped forward and the books lie broken-backed in desultory heaps, their bright jackets smeared with earth. The porcelain cat is smashed to fragments on the marble hearth.

–Why? Why have they done all this? Connie says softly, as though there is something sacred about destruction.

–Looking for money. Walter clears his throat and raises his voice. –People keep money in books and china ornaments and old vases and in with the tea or rice or sugar or flour – well, you saw the kitchen.

–But the flowers – why the flowers?

–Jewellery at the bottom of the pot – gold under the bed . . . they wouldn't have needed long. You can do a lot of damage in half an hour.

–And they had all day. Oh Walter, if only we hadn't gone away . . . And it was my idea – you wanted to stay and work. It's my fault.

He smiles. –It's got nothing to do with you, my sweet. If anything it was my stupidity in . . . Connie!

She is crying, her eyes shining with tears. He throws the wrench onto the sofa and takes her in his arms.

–I've brought you bad luck, I know I have. Her cheek is warm and damp against his neck. –I bring everyone bad luck – and now you.

He strokes her hair, her shoulders, kisses her forehead. –You're the best luck that ever happened to me.

She mutters something into his shoulder.

–What?

She raises her head. –Watching, I said. They must have been watching us – watching and waiting.

–That's not likely – they just start at the top and work down. They'd reckon the February *vacances* were a good bet. If they were smart enough to case the joint, they'd have known there wasn't much to be had from a shabby old chap in an unsmart quarter.

–You're not shabby – shaggy maybe, but not shabby. She smooths his ragged eyebrows with her thumb. –Walter – I suppose it *was* a robbery. I mean, apart from the mess, what have they actually taken?

–Well – in here, the silver ashtray's gone and the carriage clock from the chimney and – oh shit, the candlesticks. I was fond of those candlesticks. What else? My typewriter. They won't get much for that . . . He runs his hand across the clean patch on the worktable where the typewriter stood; next to it, the manuscript of *Fleur-Marie-Fleur* is neatly piled, untouched. He laughs. –Well, at any rate they had a nice critical sense . . . They wouldn't touch the pictures, of course; otherwise, I'll bet they nicked everything of any value. Why, what did you think – they smashed things up for the fun of it?

–Not for the fun of it exactly. I just thought maybe . . . maybe Henri hired some people to do it. I mean, to teach us a lesson.

–Ah yes, the communicative approach. Come off it, Connie, he –

–Walter, can I have a cognac?

–There isn't any, I'm afraid, but –

–Yes there is – unless they've nicked that too – in the cupboard under the sink. I rescued it from the cellar – I thought it would be a nice surprise.

Château Dufour – a mark he's never heard of. Yes, a surprise, but not an altogether happy one. Does one seduce a man's wife, then sit down and swig his brandy? Well, after all, slaloming in the distant snows, he's not aware of any pain. And yet – yet . . .

–It's good, isn't it? Papi always gives us a bottle at Christmas.

–Connie – what you said back there . . . How would Henri know about us – you haven't told him, have you?

She stares at him in silence. At last, –No, she says; and then, dragged out of her, –But he knows – not about us – but he knows there's someone, something . . .

–Has he said so?

–Of course not – we don't talk, remember? And even if we did, he wouldn't say.

–Then how do you know?

–I . . . It's the way he looks at me . . . the way you're looking at me now. Her face fills with blood, then as quickly pales.

–You've changed, you mean?

–Of course I've changed. She smiles tentatively. –I'm nicer to him, for one thing.

–For one thing. And for another?

–Oh I don't know, Walter. It's just different, that's all.

He gets up slowly and goes over and puts his glass on the mantelpiece. The room is dim and soft with ruin in the dwindling daylight. He switches on the lamp and sees his face in the glass, showing all its age, crumpled, badly in need of ironing – and the reflection of Connie in the forlorn corner of the sofa, her head turned away.

–How is *it* different then?

–Walter . . .

–Tell me. He watches her, removed by the mirror.

–I can't. I don't have to . . . She lifts her chin. –It's – it's none of your business.

–It *is* my business – Goddamnit, can't you see that?

–No I can't. And I can't talk to your back either.

He comes round to face her. –Well?

–It's – it's like what you told me someone said once – nasty, brutish and short. She raises her glass and knocks back the brandy. There – is that what you wanted?

The faint quaver in her voice instantly dissolves his truculence. –Connie, he says, taking a step forward. –Christ! He lifts his foot and hangs on to the mantelpiece. Bloody hell!

–What – what's the matter?

–I stepped on the fucking cat – and it bit me.

–Serves you right, she says primly, but with a little grin. –Let's have a look.

He limps dramatically across the room and flops onto the sofa and hoists his foot onto her lap.

–Oh yes – it's all bloody. Here, lend me your hanky. I can't see properly.

–Ouch.

–Come on, I'm only wiping the dirt away. It's your heel – yes, I see. There's something in there. Hold on . . .

–No! Connie – Jesus! He gives a yelp of pain.

–*Voilà*! She holds up a sharp sliver of china. –The cat's claw.

–It feels like a red-hot coal.

–Yes quite – punishment for being so brutal.

–Run along and don't do it again.

–You won't be running anywhere for a bit, my duck. She smiles. –Nice foot, she says, caressing it.

–Connie – I'm sorry . . .

–I forgive you . . . Then she leans down and softly licks the wound clean.

–. . . a green hill far away, without a city wall . . . Walter sings as he lifts the brittle layer of fat from the *coq au vin*. Through the open door comes a swift pattern of French from Connie on the phone – dotted with fragments of English like raisins in a spotted dick:

–*Mais non, minou*, don't be silly, *tu sais c'est* tomorrow *nous allons nous voir* . . .

Tomorrow. He fishes the *bouquet garni* from the wine-dark liquor and sets the pot on a low fire. Everything is done that has to be done.

–. . . we may not know, we cannot tell, what pains he had to bear . . .

The kitchen is cleaner than it has ever been; the whole apartment is spick and span – the plants have been carefully repacked in their pots, the carpets swept and brushed and sponged, the shards of the cat cached in a plastic sack under the sink. Only the books have been crammed back at random into the shelves. But to the eye all is as it was – all is well.

–. . . O dearly dearly did he love, and we must love him too, and trust in his tum-tum tum tum and –

–In his what?

–Hello. Oh – his redeeming blood, I believe. Finished – all serene?

–Henri has sprained his ankle.

–Good.

She smiles faintly. –What can I do?

–Nothing.

–The potatoes?

–Steaming away.

–The vinaigrette?

–Done. Makes you feel pretty useless, doesn't it?

–Utterly. And she laughs.

–My God – taste this!

Connie sniffs the wine, sips it. –It's good. What is it?

–Gruaud-Larose 1970 it says on the label. Where in the name of all that's holy did he get this?

–Oh I don't know – a friend, I suppose.

–God give me such friends.

–They're not really friends, you know.

–What are they then?

–I don't know – sort of members of a clan.

–The Ku Klux Klan?

–I thought that was something American.

–It is, but they're bound to have branches in France.

–Walter . . .

–What?

She is silent, and pale as the claret is red.

–What is it, Connie?

–I don't think I'm going to be able to eat. It's so silly – all your lovely food, but . . .

–It doesn't matter – who needs food when we've got this marvellous wine?

–I feel sick.

–Yes, I know – I used to feel the same way when I was a kid the day before going back to school.

–But I'm not going back to school – I'm going home! She reaches out for his hand. –Oh what are we going to do?

–Get married?

–No!

–Play a game? Backgammon – Scrabble – dominoes – gin – chess – chequers . . .?

–Families.

–Happy or Woodland?

–Woodland. We made such lovely love in the woodland, didn't we? She sighs, then takes a long swallow of wine. –Do you love me?

–Yes.

–Then you'll let me have the mouses.

–Mice – not a chance.

–Mouses, she says firmly. –And the badgers and the rabbits and the shrews . . .

–But the rules –

–I don't care about the rules. Be nice, Walter – please?

–Well . . . then what about me?

–You can have the frogs.

The March afternoon is as bland as June. The esplanade is leafy, the little park bright with forsythia, a hint of candles on the chestnuts. The flagpoles are up in honour of some foreign sovereign – a green banner with a circular red centre, interspersed with tricolours. All the flags are scrupulously laundered – perhaps by the presidential hands, who knows? The French are as solicitous of their public places as they are of their private parts.

Smiling, Walter runs up the steps of the Language School. He's had no word from Connie since she left, but hardly expected to (–I'll have my hands full the first few days, what with Henri and his twisted ankle. I'll call as soon as I can, but don't ring me). In the classroom he settles into his usual place and puts his coat on the chair next to him for Connie. He lays out his yellow pad, a pencil, last week's notes, listening vaguely to the ladies recounting their February vacations in the Alps – only Linda on the other side of the room is silent and smileless. Emma enters blinking. The class begins. But Connie does not come.

Walter feels prickles of sweat all over his head. He takes a long breath and, picking up his pencil, copies what is written on the blackboard, to put out of his mind Connie in hospital, Connie white-gowned in a padded cell, Connie palely strangled on the marital bed, Connie in scarlet bloodiness on the bathroom floor, beaten, bruised, abused, dying on the parquet de Versailles (–He's not violent, he's never really hit me. Not violent then – just nasty, brutish and fucking big.) . . . Connie nestling with smiles in the bosom of the family . . .

He wipes a few shreds of chewed pencil from his lips and looks down at what he's written: *Authentic . . . Non-authentic . . . Semi-authentic . . .*

Then he rises, picks up his coat and walks out of the classroom. In the basement, he lifts the receiver and dials her number . . . and hangs up as soon as he hears the first ring. He hesitates for a moment, redials, hangs up at the ring again – again . . . again . . .

–Excuse me, are you having a difficulty? Can I assist you? French courtesy, French charm, delicate French coquetry – or just the fair openness of youth. And now a little blush. –You have a problem with the instrument?

–Er? Oh no – no, thanks very much.

–You cannot do your number?

–No no – I mean, yes, it's just that . . . here, you have it.

As he goes up the stairs he turns and catches a quick frank smile. All at once he is aware that the cat scratch on his heel has reopened and his sock is damp with blood.

Out in the street, limping a little, he takes the familiar route, past the plastic café, past the church, into the square soft with new leaves. She has her hands full, he murmurs, she has full hands, her hands are full, her soft hands are full of laundry, dishes, washing, scrubbing – harsh, rough, calloused, sore.

A youth on a skateboard skates by with dangerous nonchalance, unaware of Walter leaning against a tree across from her building. There are no lights in the windows, no bricks to count here, no way to calculate the trickle of damage, the lifeblood seeping into the left boot. He lights a cigarette, shading his face like a private detective, and waits. If she came out – to buy bread . . . fetch children . . . dance the polka – he would draw back. All he wants is to know whether she is alive.

On Friday she calls. –Walter, it's me.

–Connie!

–Listen, I can't talk long, she whispers throatily.

–Are you alright?

–Yes, but everybody else isn't. The children came back covered with spots – German measles – and it wasn't Henri's ankle but a little bone in his foot that was broken – you'd think it was his back, the way he's carrying on – and the cleaning lady's let me down again and . . . *Comment?* Her voice changes up abruptly. –*Quoi, maintenant?* Well, get him *un verre d'eau* from the *salle de bain* – I shan't be a minute. God, they're all impossible.

–But *you* – you sound peculiar.

–It's just my sinus playing up – and I'm half dead on my feet of course. But how are you?

–Me? I'm fine. I mean . . .

–I bet you thought I was dying, didn't you?

–How did you know?

She laughs softly. –Of course I knew. I just couldn't get to the – oh shit! I've got to go – somebody's just smashed something and –

–But for God's sake when are you coming?

–Soon. Very soon.

–But –

–Listen, it's all *right*. Don't worry. I'll just arrive. I must go – they're screaming their heads off . *Je viens, je viens!* Everything's going to be fine – really. I promise. Good –

For a moment the wails of the distant children (and Henri too?) seem to linger in the sitting room – then silence. Silence – and a promise. He looks around, his eyes fully open for the first time for days. There is a different look, an altered feel to the apartment; the place has been cleaned, the plants repotted, the pictures straightened, but everything functional has been removed – TV, radio, record player, typewriter, clocks, toaster, vacuum cleaner, blender, even the Remington Fuzz-away is gone . . . The thieves have stripped him of modernity, sparing only objects of unmarketable nostalgia: the leather cigarette case Lily gave him after first love under the barn wall on the leafy hill above the Croton lakes where, afterwards, crouching to pee in the bushes, she had inflamed her ass with poison ivy; the Parrots' tea-cosy which one winter morning he'd put warm on his head like a bearskin and tried a little military drill, to be softly rebuked by Phoebe, –We're not very fond of soldiers in this house, Walt.

Walt – his American semblable . . .

There is much to be done.

That afternoon he goes up to St Paul and gets pecans, pickled herring, real corned beef, bagels, smoked salmon and Heinz baked beans from a Jewish grocery. In a junk furniture depot he finds a wind-up phonograph in perfect condition complete with wooden needles, and in an antique jeweller's a matt-black pair of old jet earrings – music and beauty.

On Saturday he buys a portable typewriter and translates three pages of *Fleur-Marie-Fleur*.

On Sunday morning the glass is still high and the weather of unbroken calm. At the Floréal he drinks Gerwürtz and exchanges a word with Monsieur Laigle pondering his *tiercé* and gives a cigarette to the barefoot boy in the square where the young trees sport new sleeves of green. At home he puts on the old seventy-eights and makes a ham-and-mushroom pie as the music floats out over the garden, silencing the dog and enlivening the old gentlemen in the pavilion:

> Put that pistol down, Ma, put that pistol down,
> Pistol-packing Mama, put that pistol down . . .

On Sunday evening, at nine o'clock, she comes.

–I said that – he understands that. No visiting, no writing, no phoning. You're not in the phonebook, are you?

   –No, it's in the landlord's name, but . . .

   –But what?

   –Well, if he really wanted to find out where you were, he could have you followed from the English School.

   –Yes he could. But I'm not unreachable. Suzy knows where I am, and I've told him to call her if there's an emergency – a real emergency – and she'll let me know.

   –Suzy?

   –My English friend, the one that's married to the advertising man, a real Parisian arsehole. I trust her, at least I think I trust her – she *is* English.

   –And what's a real emergency?

They are sitting at the blue table, her baggage on the floor beside it – two suitcases, a plastic sack full of shoes, another of teffle books, and her Supermac word processor. They're drinking Famous Grouse (–Duty-free from my parents last time they came to Paris).

   –A matter of life or death.

There's a look to her face he's not seen before – so pallid that the tiny broken veins show red in her cheek, but firm, bony, shaped to purpose. Unteffled.

–It had to be a cut-off. You do see, don't you? She drinks a little Scotch, not really asking for a reply. –I can't lead two lives at once. These past few months have been killing me.

–Yes . . .

She focusses on him for a moment and lightly touches his hand. –It's not you, my sweet. It's the lies that have been killing me, the lies at home, everything in my mouth a lie – the duplicity . . . the grief. But yes, it is you in a way. I don't know – I feel like a human being again here. Oh not just *again* – because it's different. You think of me as someone, don't you? A particular person. No one else does – just as a sort of *thing* to be there, to be relied on, used, run to, put up with, blamed – oh yes, and grateful to in a kind of offhand way. A function – I'm hardly even a woman. None of that has anything to do with *me*. I look at myself sometimes and . . . No, Walter, don't laugh. It's true. Maybe this is where I started – your house is full of mirrors, did you know that? I see myself – and it's as if I'm performing some awful sort of dance where the music never stops and I have to go on and on with only me watching because everyone else is chattering among themselves and drinking champagne and making paper chains – but if the music stopped and I stopped dancing, they'd all frown and sneer and boo.

She finishes the Scotch in her glass with one swift motion. –And I have stopped – and they *are* going to boo . . .

–Do you care what they think?

–Of course I care. Wouldn't you? They'll all blame me. I know that. Even you . . .

–How can I blame you, Connie?

–A bit, Walter – only a bit, but if you didn't . . .

–If I didn't?

–If you didn't blame me just a bit, you wouldn't really love me – and it's because you love me, you make me matter to myself. Don't you understand?

–Let me get some more ice.

–No, I don't want another drink. She lights a cigarette with a Ship kitchen match. –All the way from England . . .

Walter . . . Walter – you mustn't mind, but I shall cry a lot sometimes and get all cold and go off. But I'll come back . . .

   –You're not going anywhere, are you?
   –Only during the summer vacation.
   –Oh.
   –You mind?
   –Yes.
   –I promised. You won't try to stop me going, will you?
   –No.
   She smiles a little. –Only with your deep grey eyes.
   –Connie . . . you must always do what you want.
   –And you – what about what you want?
   –Right now I want another Scotch.
   –Okay – me too.
   –By the way, he says, getting out the ice tray and breaking the cubes into a bowl, –I've got something for you.
   –*Another* present? She lights up like a Christmas child under the tree. –What is it? Oh Walter – earrings!
   –But *not* rubies.

A precise oblong of light from the window falls across the duvet over their knees, deepening the dark of the bedroom.
   –It must be a full moon.
   –That's not moonlight.
   –What do you mean, it's not moonlight? Of course it's moonlight.
   –It's not. It's a young couple opposite – they're often up at all hours – a fractious child, I think, or a Siamese cat – you can hear it crying when the window's open. Anyway, their bedroom light always falls like this . . .
   Connie pushes back the covers and hops out of bed. –Aha, she says, –come and look.
   –Must I? I'll take your word for –
   –No. Come on.

123

–Oh Lord. He sits up, heavy with whisky and love and years. It's cold.

–Oh do come!

He hobbles across to the window and clutches her shoulder.

–Now look, she says, –look up there – what's that, a fractious child?

He lifts his head to the shining silver disc in the night sky. –More like a cross old man.

She looks at him – in the moonlight, her eyes are as black as the jet at her ears – and kisses him on the lips. –And here's another one.

The tip of the Eiffel Tower is rosy grey in the morning haze.

He can hear Connie's phone voice from Amy's old room (now Connie's office), even, calm – what do they call it? – syllable-stressed. French, then; an unemotional language: coffee is offered or death announced in exactly the same tone of voice. Which is it – coffee or death? He yearns desperately to know, but makes no move.

Stoically he continues to type: . . . *expressing hope, certainty, gratitude, appreciation, expectation, desire* . . . The assigned essay: 'Functions of the Interview'. Codswallop.

–Walter – Walter! Connie dances barefoot to his table. –I've got a job!

–A job?

–Well not a *job* – but I rang up my old boss and he's going to give me some typing and translation to do – I'm going to see him tomorrow, isn't it wonderful?

She is so smiling, it's impossible not to smile. –Wonderful. Who is this generous fellow?

–It's nothing to do with generosity – I'm good, you know. Maître Bizien – he's a love and they're always desperate for competent bilingual people.

–A lawyer.

–Of course. I was his secretary for two years, so I got to

know a lot about all that legal language – and he's really nice, he really liked me.

–Liked you – I'll bet he did. A real love? *Droit de cuissage* and all that?

–Sometimes you're so vulgar, Walter. She leans over him.

–How are you getting on? Only page three – you are a slow old thing.

–Don't read it.

–What's this – 'anxiety, doubt, disappointment, despair, disaster, death' . . . ? Oh Walter! She throws back her head and her laughter peals through the room and out of the window startling the pigeons and setting the dog barking.

–Do you think I'd better Tipp-Ex that out?

–Oh dear! Perched on the radiator, arms tight across herself, she weeps with merriment.

–Look, I've got enough money to last a year or so, even without –

–Yes but I haven't. And if you –

–without earning anything at all, not even counting –

–think I'm going to depend on you, you've got another think –

–what I'll get for *Fleur-Marie-Fleur* when it's done.

–coming. How much?

–What?

–How much will you get for the translation?

–Well, if they accept it – two thousand pounds.

–Two thousand pounds! You're living in a cloud-cuckoo-land.

–Maybe cloud-cuckoo-land's not such a bad place to live.

–That's just bloody irresponsible.

–Being irresponsible is quite a responsibility, you know.

–Damn you – you always have an answer for everything, don't you? Well, just don't think I'm going to support you.

–I don't think it – I wouldn't ask!

They are shouting, red-faced and breathless, across the kitchen counter, the lunch dishes stagnant in the sink.

—We're having a row! she says, pained, astonished.

—Yes we are.

—A row about money. Why does it always have to be about money?

—I suppose – money makes the world go round.

—I don't believe that for a moment.

—No nor do I.

—Walter – sod the washing up – let's go for a walk.

—She looks as though she's just had a good shit.

And it's true, the Eiffel Tower has the smug rosy look of someone arising spread-legged after a comfortable crap. It's a good time for her – an early spring with the trees newly out, the lawns freshly mown, and the flowerbeds alternate blue and yellow lozenges on a green bosom, a benevolence as yet unspoilt by charabancs from Düsseldorf and Dortmund.

—Come on.

—No – I think – really . . . He takes a limping step.

—Oh, your foot. Why didn't you say? We could have brought the car.

—I'm against cars.

—What – my nice little red car?

—Yours – is it yours?

—Aha – I see. Yes, it *is* mine, in my name, bought with my savings. And we're not selling it to eat. Now, what do you want to do – take the bus back?

—Not yet. Let's go over to the *brasserie* on the corner.

They sit outside in the mild sun with half-closed eyes. They drink beer and Walter props his foot on the chair.

—Just like Henri. Connie sighs.

—Do you want to talk about it?

—I'm not sure . . . She lights two cigarettes and hands him one. But then she does begin to tell him, in a desultory distant tone of voice at first. –It crossed my mind to wonder if he hadn't done it on purpose so he could stay at home looking pathetic. He hates the bank – hates going to the office, and he's not faintly ambitious. They were all impossible – Sarah whining all the time and Tom scratching at his spots and Henri playing pathetic. And in the middle of it all I got my period. But if I'd waited till everything was perfect, I'd never have left. And somehow it seemed so typical there was a crisis – there always are crises and I'm always at the centre of them. I wonder if there isn't something about me that attracts crises, causes them even . . . I don't know. Like some sort of foreign body that itches and irritates and upsets the whole metabolism – so that nothing can really go right . . .

–A kind of psychological German measles.

–Yes, but German measles is natural, isn't it? I'm thinking of something unnatural – like the coil . . . God how I hate that bloody thing inside me.

–Or teffle.

–Is that unnatural? I admit it's a bit hard to swallow at times but –

–Sitting there listening to lies about the English language – hard to swallow?

–Alright, it's humiliating – I've thought that for a long time. But it can't all be nonsense.

–It's worse than nonsense – its mechanistic obfuscation pretending to be enlightenment. It's dogma rigged out as democracy. It's ignorance masquerading as logic and common sense.

–I'm not much good at common sense.

–Well, that's fine – language hasn't got anything to do with common sense.

–What has it got to do with then?

–It's what makes us human, for God's sakes – it's our past, our soul, life itself, not something invented yesterday after-noon by some bleating Brighton professor. What fucking arrogance!

She touches his hand. –You're pretty pissed-off, aren't you?

–I was trying not to show it too much. He laughs.

–No, she says seriously, –please always show it. I don't care what you do. I'll manage. I've had too many years of silent anger . . . it does something to you . . .

–Screws you up.

–Yes – like the coil . . . it has screwed me up – my body, my head. Screwed up – like a punishment. She grips his hand hard. –But what did I do wrong? What, Walter? . . . what – *what*? She cries out to the indifferent passers-by, the laconic waiter delivering beer, to the Eiffel Tower, to Fate, God, Walter, Sigmund Freud . . .

–Honey . . .

–Walter, I'm going to burst . . . I'm going to cry – I'm going to – Oh God . . . Walter! Suddenly her voice grows small.

–What – what is it?

She blushes bright red. –Walter, I've gone in my tights.

He laughs and leans over and kisses her. –That's called suiting the action to the words.

–But what . . .

–We'll get a cab. He slips a hundred-franc bill under the beer glass and they look at each other and giggle.

–Phew!

–Hello? Oh – Marion. How lovely to hear from you, how are you? Oh fine – fine . . . No, I was in the shower . . .

Walter holds the phone in one hand and a towel in the other, trying to prevent drips from his wet hair falling onto the essay assignment. He is cold and damp and naked and the threadbare towel is already sopping.

–No, she's not my cleaning lady. Yes . . . I guess you could say that . . . Connie . . . No she most certainly isn't – English as the driven snow. Yes. Yes . . . Marion dear, did you call me just to quiz me about my – what? Oh – Friday? No – of course

I'd not forgotten. Eight-thirty. Great, looking forward to it
. . . Oh I'll bet you are. Swell . . . bye.

He puts down the phone and sneezes all over 'Functions of
the Interview'.

–Who was that?

–Marion Johnson, she . . . My God!

Connie stands smiling in a mini-skirted grey and white
check suit, white blouse, white tights and shiny black pumps.
She does a quick pirouette. –You didn't think I could look
smart, did you?

–Smart? You look . . .

–What?

–Wonderful – like something from another world.
Suddenly his body is hot and he hastily knots the towel round
his waist. A world barely recalled – a brave young heady
shining world.

She gives a mock frown. –I'm not supposed to look wonderful. I'm supposed to look competent.

–Oh you do – unbelievably competent.

–Your Marion didn't think I was competent – she talked to
me as though I were an idiot child.

–Oh well, she's an academic . . . He laughs. –She's invited
us to dinner.

–When?

–Friday. You will come, won't you? She always does these
things well.

–What things?

–Dinner parties. There'll be ten of us, she says. She's a damn
fine cook.

–But she's a professor or something . . .

–That doesn't affect her cooking.

–I didn't mean that . . . But they'll all be fearfully intelligent, won't they?

–I'd be surprised – nice, amiable American academics, I
expect – quite harmless.

Connie hesitates, then nods her head. –Alright. She smiles.
–I used to love dinner parties . . . Now I must fly.

—And I must get dressed.

—Yes . . . But she puts a hand on his arm. —Walter . . . this Marion.

—She's great, you'll like her – great fun. Terrific sense of humour.

—But what's she *like*?

—Like? Oh I see. Rather like a pug dog, *une jolie laide* – a nice pettable pug . . . I mean, not the snappish kind. Terrifically decent – I've known her for donkey's years, she's . . .

—Have you been to bed with her?

—With Marion? No of course not.

—Why not?

—Why not? Because I never fancied her – she's not my type – she's . . . Connie, this is ridiculous. I've never slept with Marion – nor do I ever want to! I'm not some sort of satyr.

—Promise?

He takes a deep breath. —Promise.

—That's alright then. She laughs and pats him. —No – Walter, you're all wet . . .

—Not any longer.

And they are in one another's arms and kiss, swimming without sense of time . . .

—What is it? she murmurs, her eyes closed, the eyelids brushed with blue. —My outfit?

—You look so damned immaculate.

—English as the driven snow . . .

—You listened . . .

—Yes. She gently bites his earlobe – Walter. Can we go to England over Easter?

—England? But . . .

—But it was so horrid last time, is that what you were going to say? But it wasn't really, was it? Can we?

—Well . . . I don't see why not . . .

—Good . . . Now I really must run, sweetie. She unclasps his arms.

—Well, if you must, you must. When'll you be back?

—I shan't – I've got a million and one things to do.

He follows her out to the hall. —But I thought you were just picking up some stuff from your lawyer friend.

—Oh that won't take long. I shall be flying all over town. I'm taking the car. Do you think it's going to rain – yes, no?

—No, but listen –

—I haven't got time. See you at teffle, darling – and buck up with your essay. Bye . . .

—Hey, Connie . . . Goodbye, he calls as the door closes behind her, conscious all at once of how cold he is. He sneezes.

—Look at all my fine feathers – and you said it wouldn't rain!

They've had a long run from the car to the apartment and are both thoroughly soaked.

—You'd better get changed.

—No, I've got to rest for a moment. You go first. And she plumps down on the sofa next to her packages and closes her eyes. —It's cold. Turn up the heat, will you?

—Sure.

But when he comes back in dry clothes ten minutes later, she still has a pale, bleak look. There is a cigarette in the corner of her mouth and letters lie in her lap.

—Mail?

—Yes – I stopped in at Suzy's to pick it up. That was one of the things I had to do. She sighs and touches the sheet of handwritten squared copy-paper on her knees. I should have put it under the cat, if the cat were still there.

—From Henri?

—Yes. Do you want to read it?

—No.

—You're sensible. Bloody family. She coughs on the exhalation of smoke. —They've got to him.

—You mean he's told them?

—Of course he's bloody well told them – for all I know he tells them when I have my period. She takes a final puff and

131

stubs out the cigarette. –Shit. I don't want to be like that. No, he probably hasn't told them. He doesn't have to. They're all there – brothers and sisters and their husbands and wives and that old fart of a father – like tombstones in his bloody brain engraved with epigrams and –

–epitaphs.

–Right, epitaphs about family and duty and work and *la patrie* . . . I need a drink.

–Cognac?

–Whisky, please.

–I'll make us a grog.

–Listen, she says when he brings her the steaming tumbler, –here's something more cheerful. Viv's moved to Eaton Terrace and she says we can have their house over Easter – they're off to Wales.

–We?

–You and me. She likes you, ducky, or she wouldn't offer.

–But how does she know we . . .

–I rang her a couple of weeks ago and told her what was going on. What do you think?

–About Eaton Terrace? He must be loaded. Cheers. He sips the grog.

–Well, he is. Cheers. Oh this is good . . . the problem is, I don't think I really want to be in London – I'd rather be in the country somewhere.

–That might be arranged. Edward and Margot usually shoot off some place warm for a few weeks at this time of year. I'm sure we could stay there if I butter Margot up nicely enough.

–But she wouldn't want *me*.

–On the contrary, the danger'd be she might stay behind just to catch a glimpse of you.

–Whatever for?

–Oh – brother Walter's sex life and all that. And no, if you must know, I have not slept with Margot.

–I wasn't going to ask that. Besides, that would be incest.

–All true love is incest.

–What's that supposed to mean? She stands up and faces herself in the mirror. –God, I look a mess. She ruffles her bedraggled hair. –Would you love me if I were ugly?

–Yes, but not as much.

She laughs. –You know what? It's so nice to be with someone who actually answers when I say something silly.

They are the only smokers in the party, and at first when they light up there is a palpable unease and a slight shifting of chairs and Marion hurries off to fetch ashtrays. But the room is large and high-ceilinged and the windows are wide open, and the smoke vanishes as quickly as the offence. Two male academics move closer to Connie, their nostrils a-quiver with something other than allergy. The soft American voices are so exactly suited to the surroundings that they seem to emanate from the pale suede upholstery itself, from the perfection of pearly carpeting, the glimmer of glass and the rich white scent of unseasonable stocks. Trust Marion to find a place so –

–What? I'm sorry – I'm afraid I missed that.

–I was asking you what you did.

This woman is in a little black number; another, hefty, white-haired, in sky blue; a third in mauve, and Marion in academic dun. Connie in her new scarlet is a brave banner among old flags.

–Well, nothing much nowdays – a bit of this and that . . . But I used to be in publishing, he says, generosity overriding *ennui*.

–Publishing – in London?

–Good heavens no – in New York.

–New York! She blinks at him – why do they all blink? –But you sound so British.

–Well I am British – in a way. Maybe they go to a special Blink School – one blink for surprise, two for disbelief, three for outrage, four for disdain, five for –

133

—Who were you with in New York?

—As a matter of fact I had my own outfit. He finishes off his over-sweet *kir* and glances at Marion for another. Lucky to get *kir* at that – no gin, no whisky, no cigarettes, no music or dancing or wild wild women.

—Would I have heard of it?

—Depends how old you are. Waller-King – twenty years ago now – God knows who has it these days . . . Gulf and Western, Krups, Mitsubishi . . . Oh yes, thanks Marion, I wouldn't say no . . .

—But what did you publish?

—Anything that caught my fancy, really. I did a series of off-Broadway plays, and another of one-off novelists – that was –

—I don't understand – what does that mean?

—Writers who published one novel and then never wrote another – thirties and forties mostly – some fantastically good stuff but entirely forgotten because –

—Like who?

—Oh . . . Chester Whitehorn . . . Donald Wayne . . . Eunice Lee Caesar . . . John –

—Eunice *who*? Black frock's blink-rate shoots up and the freckles flush on her pale face.

—Eunice Lee Caesar.

—You're kidding me.

—Absolutely not.

—What was it called – her novel?

—*For There My Mother Wrapped Me Warm*. Orville Prescott said it was the best thing he'd read all year – admittedly he was reviewing it in February, but still . . . Don't tell me you haven't read it?

—My goodness, I don't read books! It takes me three months to read a sentence.

—Really? Oh – thanks, Marion. He holds the glass still for a moment, then takes a long gulp of the sickly mixture – he senses he's going to need all the alcohol he can get tonight.

—That must put you about half way through *Winnie the Pooh*.

–She's really lovely – I'm so happy for you.

Walter smiles dutifully, but he doesn't need Marion to be happy for him. He can be happy all by himself. But her purring interrogation all through dinner has put him off the food (*borscht, boeuf bourguignon, batavia, brie* – what next, *bananes flambées*, blueberry pie, brown betty?). Not so Connie, who has consumed everything with alacrity. Amidst the low-keyed chatter of conferences and colloquia, publications and papers and grants and sabbaticals, he has several times heard her real laughter from the far end of the table. Why should his heart sink while hers is high?

He helps himself to more wine and turns to his right-hand neighbour. What's her name, this beefy lady with white hair in pearls and sky blue – Claude-something – -ine or -ette? Maybe because she's connected with Art she reminds him of Paula – or maybe it's just the cold-souled blue-eyed stare.

–I guess you must get a big kick out of helping artists – a sense of real achievement, I mean.

–No, you don't understand. The foundation is not inter-ested in anything later than the nineteenth century. Perhaps I explained it badly.

–Oh – ah so. Of course, how stupid of me – naturally, they have to be dead.

–I'm sorry?

–Better dead than in debt, so to speak.

–I'm afraid I've lost you. She slices a morsel of pale flesh from her *brie*.

–I mean to say, death must come as quite a relief to the artist – no more scrimping around for the odd crust. Leave the money to the experts, and concentrate on the *foie gras* and the trumpets. But perhaps you don't believe in an afterlife? I mean for people, you know.

–I don't believe in it or disbelieve in it. I try to keep an open mind.

–Not easy, is it? So much garbage seems to keep falling into it. So I take it you're not religious?

–Not specifically. Although I was brought up as a Christian Scientist.

–Really? You're lucky to be here then.

She gives him a wintry smile. –I'm not so sure.

As they step out into the mild night, Walter throws away his cigarette and sighs. –God, it was spifflicating in that place – spiritually, I mean.

Across the road, the Luxembourg gardens are dark and tranquil, getting ready for the next day's infant laughter and donkeys and the shout of tennis players and the importunity of lovers.

–A bit different from the dead groves of academe, eh? He take a deep breath.

Connie is silent, and there's a look of cool detachment on her face.

–Listen, he says, –shall we take a cab?

–No, let's walk. If you can manage it.

–Do me good.

–Yes.

He grins and trips on the stone border of a plane tree. –Damn.

She steadies his stagger automatically, then lets her hand drop. –You did it on purpose, didn't you?

–No I didn't – just didn't see it. I must be a bit tight.

–I don't mean that. I meant when you spilt your coffee on the carpet; it was deliberate, wasn't it?

–What makes you think that?

–I was watching you.

–Oh well – it was decaffeinated.

–She'll never get it out completely.

–Sure she will – a bit of elbow grease. Give her something useful to do for a change.

They turn into the rue de Fleurus.

–If you did that to my carpet, I'd . . .

–What? Kill me?

–I might slap you.

–Marion would never do that.

–But she wasn't even cross with you.

–She's a good hostess – and a nice woman. They're all nice.

–Yes they are. So what I don't understand is – why were you so absolutely foul to them?

–Was I? Surely you're exaggerating. I admit I got a bit hot under the collar, but –

–You *attacked* them! I've never seen you like that before.

–I can't stand all that bloody smugness.

–Who's talking? And you shouted at poor Stan.

–You mean the cross-eyed little creep drivelling on about the intertextual unconscious?

–He is not cross-eyed – and he's devoted half his life to narra- . . . narra-whatever-it-is.

–Narratology. Then he's wasted half his fucking life.

–Yes, you said that too.

–And I meant it. Bloody typical of the lot of them. All this semiotic shit.

–But they're professors – experts – they must know –

–What they know is a lot of worthless guff. They know nothing and they understand nothing. If you want the brutal truth, they're a bunch of damned smiling villains making away with our civilization – or what's left of it – and they're only nice to you because in their world you don't count. If you were a book, they'd be scooping the heart out of you, and your charming Stan would be first in with the scalpel.

They have stopped in the street in front of the shuttered fishmongers just before St Placide.

–You're jealous.

–Of Stan? Why? Do you fancy him – or what?

Connie is quite motionless, the red of her dress darkened by the streetlight, only the jet earrings tremble at her ears. And then she slaps him. He falls back against a litter bin, slips to one knee, recovers shakily.

They stand staring at each other as the traffic of the night passes them by – still and appalled.

–Hold me, I'm cold.
    –I am holding you, he says as though they were both blind.
        –Walter . . .
        –We could live in the country . . .
        –Could we – oh could we?
        –Why not? Tranquil with hackberry trees.
        –What trees?
        –Fruit trees – pear and peach and damson and fig. And tomatoes and flowers.
        –And strawberries and radishes and cucumbers.
        –And ride bicycles –
        –And keep a goat.
        –And give English lessons.
        –To the goat.

–He wasn't anything to look at, you know – Cyril – nothing special at all. But when he touched me, I was gone . . . gone – turned to water and fire. It was all blaze and desert – blaze with him, desert without him . . . I did anything he told me to do – I'd have jumped in the Seine if he'd said do it. And I did do things I oughtn't to have done . . . I remember once . . .
    –Do you really want to remember?
    –Yes, I do – I do want to remember . . .
    After a while, as she talks, through the open window come the cries of the next-door baby. Soon the light goes on and falls across their bed. But for a long time the child will not be comforted.

138

At last the light is turned off.

–And then, what – the vodka weekends?

–When it was all over, yes. I didn't care any more. I suppose I became a sort of nymphomaniac. I just did what I wanted when I wanted with whoever – I didn't care, so what did it matter? I'd lost him – lost him . . . I was completely empty like a hole, and it didn't much matter what filled it up. Anyway, I've never felt guilty about sex. But I'd nearly destroyed myself – I'd almost killed myself – for . . . for nothing.

–No, not *nothing*.

–No – I don't believe one does that sort of thing for nothing – not that utter total self-sacrifice.

–One has an inalienable right to self-sacrifice – what if it's the only thing you have to give?

–But what about love? Where was the love? I'm not romantic – I've never been romantic. I'm an animal, I know I am. But does that mean I can't love? Does it – does it?

–Connie, you –

– It does, doesn't it? I don't know how to love, do I? Tell me the *truth*! she cries out, trembling in his arms. –Oh Walter, dear God, I love *you* . . . She kisses the palms of his hands, his fingers, the soft pulse in his wrist. –I love you I love you . . . I love you . . . there my darling, there – see how I love you . . . love me, make love, oh quick quick . . .

Looking out of the window in Saturday-morning languor, the warmth of the sun moves them gently from sleep to lazy daytime. Sparrows flit among the unpruned bushes in the garden and pigeons coo on cornice and gutter. The fat old man at the dormer pokes his head out and withdraws it; the rest of the pavilion is shuttered still.

–I feel sort of purified, she says. –Shall we give up drinking?

–No fear. I'd sooner give up food.

–Smoking then?

–Why do you want to give up anything?

–I'm just asserting my right to self-sacrifice. She laughs, but there is a catch in the laugh. –Oh Walter! She hides her face against him. –What have I done? Tell me – tell me.

–I don't know . . . He touches her back, the nape of her neck where the hair grows stiff.

They stay like this, her cheek soft against his, but not weeping.

Outside, the door of the pavilion is opened by an unseen hand and the dog prances out. He halts on the top step, sniffs, glances round for something to bark at, one ear up, one down. He lollops down to the garden and begins to poke about with little grunting noises.

–Look – he's searching for something. Perhaps he's hungry.

–He won't find much in the garden. Besides, he's too fat to be hungry.

–Don't be silly – the fatter you are, the hungrier you get. Haven't we got something we could give him?

–Arsenic?

–You brute. I know! Here, dog dog – here you are.

With a quick twist she pulls off her wedding ring and tosses it into the garden.

–Connie – that's . . .

–What – what's wrong?

–It's platinum.

–Yes – I never liked it. Look's he's seen it. She leans out bare-breasted as the dog noses forward suspiciously. –He's sniffing it, she says. –Walter, I believe he's going to take it. Oh, look, look. She clutches his arm. Down below, the animal has got the ring between its teeth, growling and worrying. –He thinks it's a bone.

And with a toss of the head and a harsh cough the dog swallows the ring.

And Connie laughs and the dog barks – and after a moment Walter begins to laugh too.

–Connie, listen to this. Walter triumphantly waves the last page of *Fleur* as he steps into Amy's room.

–Hold on a moment. She is seated upright and competent at the word processor, her cigarette smoke clinging to the shining screen like an animal at the fireside. She's been at it for hours. –Damn. It's no use – I just can't get on without a dictionary.

–Maybe I could help?

–What do you know about law?

–I know a lot about divorce law.

–That's no good – this is commercial law.

–Doesn't your fat old *maître* have a legal dictionary?

–I'm not going all the way up there when there's a perfectly good one sitting at home. She stubs out her cigarette and switches off the machine. –I'm going to have to go and get it.

–Well okay, but can't you listen to this first? It won't take a minute.

–Alright then . . . She settles back with a sigh.

Walter raises the typescript page and clears his throat:

> The wind gently shifts the sand on the beach – all trace is swept away. The gulls rise with one great flap of wings. The sea is as empty as the beach. And I am alone in the abandoned car, all alone now that the gulls fly higher and higher in the sky, farther and farther away. Windows and windshield are gradually covered with a fine film of sand. I can no longer see the beach – nor the sea, nor the sky, nor the gulls. The veil before my eyes grows thicker and thicker until I can see nothing – nothing but Fleur clothed in my bridal veil in the Fairy grotto. . . .

–Wind*screen*.

–Damn. Well, what do you think?

–Is that it? Is that the end?

–Yes.

–Oh wonderful!

–Do you really think so? I thought it was a bit on the mushy side.

–Oh that – oh yes, frightful piss.

141

–I suppose it is a bit sterile, but doesn't it have a certain limpid quality – like Gerwürtz, thinnish but quite acceptable on a hot day?

–Maybe, but don't invite me into your fairy grotto to drink it.

–Perhaps it would sound better in Konkomba?

–Listen, I can't sit around all afternoon discussing literature. I've really got to move it if we're to get away by Thursday.

–What's the hurry? You've got all tomorrow.

–I have not – we're teffling tomorrow in case you'd forgotten. She stands up and shuffles the legal-looking papers into a rough pile. –I'm off. Want to come?

–To the apartment?

–Where else? Do come. There won't be anyone there.

–How do you know?

–Tom and Sarah are at school, Henri will have hobbled off to the bank and –

–You can't be sure – he might have broken the other leg. And what about the cleaning lady?

–She isn't coming any more. I told you – Marie has taken over everything. She moves close to him and slips her hand under his shirt. –Why are you making excuses – don't you want to?

–Yes – but not *there*.

–Why not? It's a gorgeous bed.

–No, Connie, I draw the line at that. Besides . . .

–God, you're stuffy sometimes. Besides what?

–All that weight of history books over my head would put me off.

She laughs and pats his cheek. –Anyway – congratulations.

–On *Fleur*? Well – thank you.

–When do you get your two thousand pounds? she says, whisking into the hall.

–Er, well – I looked it up. In fact, it's only fifteen hundred.

–Never mind. She puts on her overcoat and her red gloves and slings her bag over one shoulder. –Better than a slap in the face with a wet fish.

142

–Connie . . . he says impulsively.

–Too late, my love. She grins. –I'm off.

–We're going – we're going!

The plane begins to move like an animal purposeful after prey. Ten seconds, fifteen, twenty, twenty-five, -six, -seven, -eight – twenty-nine and it pounces and soars with a lovely surge of freedom.

–Oh! Connie beams as they're pressed back in their seats by a large gentle hand. And in a moment they are wrapped in the grey clouds that hang heavy over Roissy. –Isn't it glorious? It's years since I've flown anywhere – I'd quite forgotten.

–No vertigo?

–On a plane? Good heavens no – the opposite, if anything. It's like been lifted up in lovely strong arms. Why – are you frightened?

–Not frightened exactly – a trifle anxious.

–You poor lamb – perhaps you should have a drink.

–No, I'm okay now. Anyway, they'll be too busy dishing out the food to bother with drinks.

–Food – are we going to get food? What sort of food?

–Inedible little brown sandwiches and a plastic rum baba with a cherry on top.

–I'll have yours if you don't want it. I'm ravenous.

–Alright, but remember we've got to deal with Mrs Marryat's lunch in a couple of hours.

–Mrs Marryat – the daily?

–Margot calls her the cook-housekeeper – and she is a first-class cook. Margot's asked her to make us lunch.

–Oh. I thought we'd go to a pub. Connie looks out of the window at the cloud enclosing them, looks dubiously back again at Walter. –Will she be there every day?

–Normally, yes – but Margot has left it up to us. In any case, she won't be around over the Easter weekend.

–Well – okay . . . It's just that I don't like the idea of some old biddy spying on us all the time.

Walter laughs and unclips his seat-belt and lights a cigarette. –You'll like Mrs M.

–Shall I? She lifts the cigarette from his fingers and inhales deeply. –Did I tell you Henri is learning English?

–No, you didn't. He lights another cigarette with care. –How do you know?

–I saw the Linguaphone records in the apartment. And he's got one of those Nouvelles Frontières brochures – you know: *la langue commerciale, l'Anglais des affaires, l'Américain pour le droit commercial* . . . all that stuff the Tove was slithing on about on Tuesday.

–ESP, ETP, EBP, EOP . . . I told you we could have cut the class.

–You were right . . . useless and boring – balls, as you would say. She sighs. –It's just bloody typical, isn't it? Twelve years and he didn't make a blind bit of effort to learn English, but as soon as I'm gone, he turns round and . . .

–You've given him a nasty jolt – that always works well with the French.

–Why? I hate that. It's all power, isn't it? Well, thank God I've left it all behind. I – hey, that's our food, why are they going past us?

–Smokers get served last.

–That's not fair. Oh look!

The plane has burst through the clouds into the open sunlight, and brilliance fills the cabin. The impeccable beauty silences them. Connie takes his hand, and after a while she turns to him with a serious look.

–Walter . . . I want to have a baby.

–A baby . . .? He stares at her, bereft of speech.

–With *you* – an English baby – *made* in England.

–You mean – now, over –

–Yes. Over Easter.

–But your coil . . .

144

–I had it removed yesterday. I've always hated it – that awful *thing* inside me.

–So that's why last night you wouldn't . . .

–Yes. She gives a small strained smile. –Did you think I'd gone off you? I had to tell you first, didn't I?

Walter blinks at the brightness. –Connie . . .

–Well?

–I'm not going to live forever.

–What does that matter? I'm forty, you know. Please. It's – it's my last chance.

–Mine too, I should think.

–Then you don't mind?

–Mind? I feel as though I've been lifted up in lovely strong arms . . .

–I love you, she says as he leans over and kisses her.

–Yes.

She whispers smiling into his ear. –We'll have to do a lot of fucking.

–. . . we are now crossing the Channel at an altitude of 35,000 feet . . .

–You know what's wrong with that Birmingham most-used word list?

–No – what? Connie wipes crumbs from her lips. The cake isn't bad.

–. . . in a few moments we will be beginning our descent towards Gatwick . . .

–It just came to me. Forget 'man' and 'time' and all that – what's really the most-used word in the language? Think.

–I don't feel like thinking. Tell me.

–'Fuck', of course – as in 'fuck off', 'fuck up', 'fuck over'. Or possibly 'fucking'.

–As in, this is a fucking awful cup of tea.

–You can say that again. I wonder why they left it out – do you think the place is secretly run by the BBC?

–Perhaps they just don't do much of it in Birmingham. Aren't you going to eat anything at all?

–No. Why, do you want mine?

–Not really. I'd better not. Give me a cigarette.

–You know, he says, lighting her Gauloise, –one could make quite an interesting class out of sex.

–Thanks. How? There are only two men in our class – and I'm not sharing you.

–Poor old Fred. Come to think of it, he looks a bit shagged out. He laughs. –No, one could make a kind of game of it – Testing Sexual Lexis – like a naming of parts . . . and practices.

–Well – how would it work? Don't you even want your cake?

–No – have it, have it. It would be like that old word game we used to do with fruit or whatever – you go from 'a' to 'zee' and –

–'*Zed*'. Perhaps I'll just . . . She lifts the cake from his tray and slips it into the pocket of the seat in front.

–You take it in turns, beginning with the 'a's, and anyone starting a new letter loses a point – and at the end you –

–Arsehole.

–That's it. Arse.

–I gave you that one, didn't I? Let's – oh, anus.

–Animalism.

–What's that?

–Animal sex.

–I thought that was bestiality.

–No, bestiality's a bloke and a turkey – or a bint and a donkey. One point to me.

–You bugger.

–My turn actually. Buggery.

–Buttocks.

–Bum.

–Bottom.

–Breasts.

–Balls.

146

–Bollocks.

–Blow-job.

–B-b-b . . . I can't think.

–Be quick, you've only got five seconds.

–What do you mean, I've only got five seconds?

–It's the rule.

–Oh shit. Cock.

–Cunt.

–Copulate.

–Coitus.

–Clitoris.

–Cunnilingus.

–May I have your trays please?

–Ummm . . . here you are . . . Cocksucker! Oh, I'm sorry, I didn't mean you. She smiles ravishingly at the astonished steward. –Just a little private game.

–Right-on. He gives a tove-like snigger.

Connie gives Walter a nudge. –Come on, you've only got five seconds.

–Er . . . coprophilia.

–What's that?

–Passengers are requested to fasten their safety belts and extinguish their cigarettes.

–Love of shit.

–Oh. You know, perhaps I won't have your cake after all.

–We shall be landing at Gatwick in approximately three minutes.

The plane has plunged into the clouds and Connie grips his hand tight. –This is the part I don't like.

–. . . eleven fifteen and the ground temperature is six degrees – that's forty-three degrees Fahrenheit . . .

The rain patters soundlessly against the windows.

–Chilly England.

–How are we going to get there? She shivers convulsively.

–We'll take a minicab. Cold?

–No, it's just . . . Why not the train?

–By the time we'd got up to Victoria and all the way down again we'd have missed tea, let alone lunch.

–We should have come by car. Won't we need a car? Oh God! She shuts her eyes and squeezes his arm with all her force as the plane bumps, lifts, and bumps again.

–Oh yes, but we can use Margot's car – or even Edward's, come to that. It's alright, we're down.

–. . . until the plane comes to a complete halt. We hope you have had a pleasant flight and we look forward . . .

Already the plane is making wide waltz-like turns on the dark tarmac. Connie opens her eyes. –Will I be allowed to drive?

–I don't see why not. But no Paris antics.

–Alright – promise. She sighs as the plane glides to a stop. –We're safe!

The passengers rise like a shot-scattered clamour of rooks – cawing and flapping.

He holds her wrist as she makes to get up too. –Let them go first. We'll wait.

–Yes – why not? I'm not in a hurry, am I?

–We've got all the time in the world.

–Time – and Man . . . What bliss!

–I don't know who you people are. . . A bald-headed man in the seat in front turns a savagely scarlet face upon them. –But for sheer filth –

–What?

–I've never heard a more disgusting –

–You *people*?

–conversation in my entire life!

–Sod off, says Connie in a cold voice with a bored stare. –Go on – fuck off. Get stuffed.

Bald head blenches and hesitates, backs into the aisle. –Disgraceful, shameful, ought to be reported . . . And mutteringly retires.

Walter laughs. –England, Home and Beauty.

He throws the end of his cigar into the fire and gives the logs a gentle prod with the toe of his shoe. Then he crosses the room to stand beside Connie at the window. The rain has petered out, and now and again there is a quick thrust of sunlight. The lawn is smooth and unruffled, but the wind is keen, and laburnum and lilac and rhododrendron in premature bloom toss with dismay.

–Well, what's the verdict?

–Alright, I suppose – a bit *banlieusard*.

–If Margot heard that, she'd kill you.

–Well it's not my idea of the country. Where are the flowers?

–Flowers are in the walled garden on the other side of the house. Vegetables are in the vegetable garden. Herbs are in the knot garden. Everything has its place, you see.

–I see now why you wore a tie.

–Didn't want to shock Mrs Marryat.

–Shock Mrs Marryat indeed. You are an evil creature – she's all of twenty-five and very pretty, and you let me think she'd be an old hag.

–Margot would never put up with an old hag. Nor would Edward, I daresay – although he's quite impervious to the charm of the lower orders.

–They sound awful. Oh look, there's a dog.

A small brown and black and white animal runs skittishly across the lawn to the sundial, sniffs at the pedestal, hops on its hind legs as if to take a quick look at the time, then drops down to do some more sniffing.

–That's Butter – a bitch, actually.

–Mary wants five children.

–Mary who?

–Mary Marryat. She's going to start in two years' time when she's finished taking her degree at the Open University. Her husband's called Sam and he's a carpenter and the handyman around here. They're fantastically well organised. Mary makes all her own clothes and she's a bell-ringer at the local church and she's a member of –

–Damn!

149

—What's wrong?

—Butter's squatting — strictly forbidden on the lawn. He reaches to open the window. —Margot would have conniptions.

—So what? Margot isn't here. You piss in the teapot, why shouldn't poor Butter pee on the sundial?

—Well — why not? He laughs and lets his hand drop. —Perhaps we should take her for a walk.

—Not me. Not in this weather. Not after that lunch. She takes his arm and leads him back to the enormous sofa. —Walter . . . Margot and Edward — what do they do all day? I mean, everything seems to be done for them.

—Well, they're vaguely sporty — tennis and golf, and I think Edward still plays squash. And there's bridge, of course, and Margot does a bit of gardening, which mainly means annoying the gardener. Then they often pop up to their flat in town for the opera and ballet. And they do a fair amount of entertaining — dinner parties and weekend guests and one huge summer party every year. And they go away for the filthy weather — Jamaica, Kenya, Barbados — just so long as it's warm and they speak English. Not the States, of course — Edward disapproves of America. It's quite a busy life, really.

She looks at him pensively, then smiles. —Why don't you take off that grotty tie?

—And then what?

—We're going to have a practical demonstration of what we learned in lexis.

—A bedroom class . . .

—No, my love, right here in front of the fire.

—What a wonderful, beautiful car — you just put your foot down — and wheee!

—Less on the wheeing — these lanes are lethal if you don't look out.

—I am looking out. And I'm a very good driver. You said so

yourself . . . And she sends Margot's Jaguar scudding down the narrow winding road between the high embankments.

–Yes I know – but you've had a few, Connie.

–Only four. Do you think I'm sozzled? I'm not sozzled, I'm happy.

–Jesus, steady on – you're doing over sixty.

–Sixty-five . . . seventy . . . seventy-three . . . oh lovely! She sounds the horn in a triumphant silver blare.

Walter says quietly, –I'm going to have a heart attack.

–Oh darling, you can't do that – you're much too young. But she slows down down down to a genteel thirty-five and a prim smile.

–Thank you. I need a large Scotch.

–And I need food.

–But you had two pork pies at the pub.

–Little ones. I'm starving. There's all that cold lamb to eat – with mint sauce and mashed potatoes and I took a gooseberry tart out of the freezer this morning. How marvellous not to have to cook.

The Jaguar moves majestically down the long drive and stops with a tiny patter of gravel before the front door.

–Thank God, he mutters.

–Thank me. Why, what's the matter – you're hobbling?

–Just hit my knee on the car door, he lies, limping up the steps between the leering stone salamanders. His knees have always been vulnerable to love and in three days he's spent more time on them than in fifty years of fitful prayer. The soul soars, but the legs creak.

–I'm hungry too, he says.

The dog is full of prancing delight at finding so early a riser, and she runs and returns, eagerly inviting Walter to prance too. But even with the support of Edward's ashplant, it's a long pull up the drive and at the top he leans against an oak to get his breath. Below, a layer of smoky mist clings to the

151

dormant cottages, and only the high chimneys of the old house are touched by the Easter-yellow sun.

The dog fawns and paws at his thighs. –Down, Butter, down!

He throws a stick for her, then lights a cigarette. In a moment she is back with little barks and a coy tilt of the head. Perhaps he smells like Edward – a family scent. He laughs, and Butter pauses, puzzled. Edward is not much given to laughter – a wry smile or, *in extremis*, a judicial cackle.

He throws the stick again, further this time.

It has rained heavily in the night, and the dark strip of cloud like a ridge of faraway mountains on the horizon promises more rain. The brilliant dawn has caught the rest of the world sleeping, Connie curled in innocence in Margot's enormous bed, the Marryats in the master cottage waking now perhaps to precautionary morning love, Old Horace fast in dreams of harrowing Margot's flower beds for cabbages and carrots.

The ground is drenched and the gravelled drive is scarred with small channels where the rain ran down the hill in the night. The English put their farmhouses in the valley – concealed and cozy and damp –while the French build high on shoulder and rocky spine above marsh and miasma with a long view and a strong wind. In such a house Amy was conceived – decades ago, hundreds of miles away – with walls a metre thick, weather from all four quarters and a sight of the Alps on a clear day, and silence.

He rubs the bristles on his cheek and shivers.

–Butter – Butter, come on – we're off!

He roughs his cigarette out against the tree trunk and slips the dead end into his pocket. As he lopes off down the long hill to the village, the dog emerges with muddied muzzle and little frisks of joy.

When he comes into the kitchen she is sitting at the big deal table in Margot's green silk dressing gown, smoking a cigarette and drinking a cup of tea.

–Hello, honey, I didn't expect to find you here.

–Honey . . . She gives him a blank look. –Where did you expect to find me?

–Oh in bed, I suppose. Here, I've brought the papers. He puts them on the table and sits down opposite her.

–In bed . . . She picks up *The Times* and puts it to her nose. –Smells nice.

Against the bright green of the robe, her skin is as pale and lucid as French Asparagus. Walter smiles. –You know –

–What are you leering at me for?

–Leering? That was supposed to be a friendly grin.

–You were ogling me as though I were a page out of *Playboy*.

–You're much too beautiful to be in *Playboy*.

Her whole neck and face flush red. –God, how I hate men!

Walter takes the pack of Gauloises from his jacket pocket and lights one with a not quite steady hand. –I'm sorry, I thought you'd got over that hang-up about beauty.

–It's not my hang-up – it's yours. Beauty – that's all you ever think of. Her voice is white with scorn. –Every slimy waiter, every old fart in a wheelchair – My beauty! What a beauty! *Quels beaux yeux!* It's like a disease – like AIDS or leprosy or – or being crippled. Why are you all so stuck on beauty?

–You wouldn't want us to hate beauty, would you?

–But you do hate it – you want to crush it, own it, fuck it, screw it to death, get rid of it . . .

Walter presses his hands hard on the table to stop them trembling. –Isn't that what *you* want – to get rid of it?

–Don't fucking psychoanalyse *me*!

–Is that why you gave so much of it away?

–Bastard – *bastard*! You deserted me!

In the silence he looks up at the old-fashioned kitchen clock over the door –but it's not really old-fashioned, it's a quartz imitation and has no tick.

He says, –I should have left you a note. I didn't think you'd wake up this early . . .

–Or you thought I'd just wait in bed till you came . . . oh shit. She looks away from him.

–Connie . . .

–What's in that paper bag?

–Croissants – the village bakery's got quite a reputation for –

–Croissants – in Sussex? I suppose that's what brother Edward does every Saturday morning?

–I believe he does, actually.

–Well, I don't want croissants. I want a proper breakfast. She stands up decisively. –Bacon and eggs and sausages and toast and marmalade.

–Are there any sausages?

–Of course. Mary bought them for us, Mary's a sensible Englishwoman. You can make the coffee.

–Coffee?

–I'm fed up with tea. How many sausages?

–Two?

–Four each – they're only little ones, she says, stabbing them rapidly with a fork. –And what else does Edward do on a Saturday?

–Plays golf, I expect. A bit wet for golf today. They'd probably go to the races.

–Horse races? Can we go?

–I don't see why not. He plugs in the coffee machine. –There should be masses of meetings over Easter, let's take a look. Yes – right – there's one at Plumpton.

–Where's Plumpton? She turns the sausages with a spatula.

–Just the other side of Lewes – not far. As a matter of fact, I think Edward's a member there.

–Let's go there then. She smiles. –Plumpton – what a nice name – it sounds like a sausage. I'll drive.

–No no, don't look at the card – just look at the horses.

–Why mayn't I look at the card?

–Because you'll take a fancy to a name and that'll influence you. I want you to judge by the look of the horse.

–But I don't know anything about horses.

–That doesn't matter – nor do I. But you can tell a cripple from a beauty.

–You're a rotten sod, Walter. She laughs. –But there are hundreds of them.

–Fifteen to be exact. You don't have to make up your mind all at once – they're led round several times.

–Okay. She moves in closer and examines each animal as it passes.

In green gumboots and Margot's massive Burberry, Connie has an absurdly horsy look. All through their lunch at Lewes (Scotch eggs and sherry and pickled walnuts) the rain poured down, but ceased as they stepped out of the pub. There's a capricious sun now, but no wind – a moist and delicate air, a soft snuffling of horses, a quiet creaking of leather.

–Number four and number eight – and number nine. That's what I like. Oh, look at the jockeys.

–No, don't look at the jockeys. Keep your eyes on the gees. They've got three miles to go, remember – twenty-odd jumps and the ground'll be like glue. So which is it?

–Oh well – number nine then. He's got a sort of superior air, don't you think?

–Number nine – Halcyon Days, ummm . . . he may have a superior air, but he hasn't won for two seasons, although he did win here three years ago. Let's have a look at the odds.

–You did ask me. Though I can't think why.

–Beginner's luck. The intuition of the innocent. Let's see – Charlie Crewe is offering twenty-to-one.

–That's good, isn't it? Let's do it.

–Hold on. We have to shop around. Yes, here's twenty-five-to-one. What do you think, five quid each way?

–Fifty francs?

–A hundred actually.

–That doesn't seem much.

So they put ten pounds each way on Halcyon Days and go up to the stands to watch. Connie's eyesight is better than Walter's efforts with Edward's binoculars and she doesn't lose the quartered purple and mauve colours for an instant.

–He's almost last!

–First time round. Don't fret.

–Walter, she says huskily a few minutes later as the field comes over the hill again, –Walter, there're only six left – and he's third! Oh the beast!

–If he can stay third, we're forty quid up.

–We are? Halcyon Days! What a stupid name – how can anyone shout that? He's second now. Isn't he second? Do we get more money if – oh, the other one's tripped. Come on Number Nine!

–My God, I believe he's going to win. Number Nine, he cries, Number Nine, for God's sake!

–Come on, you bugger. He's winning, Walter – he's going to win.

–He's won, my love. He's done it!

–And us? How much have we won?

–Three hundred quid, I reckon.

–Oh Walter – it's so easy – oh Walter darling.

–Money for old rope.

–Oh beautiful Halcyon Days!

–I know it. I remember it – don't I remember it?

–I shouldn't think so. A bit before your time. Oh maybe.

–What's it called then?

–Lullaby of Birdland.

–Oh yes – I remember. This boy at Cambridge – he took me to a May ball – although it wasn't in May at all.

–May balls are in June.

–Why?

–Hallowed tradition.

–Oh. Anyway, he was always whistling this lullaby thing.

156

–*Vieux jeu.*

–That's the way he was. I mean, it was nice, but he was strange. He took me out in a punt on the river – it was lovely and hot and summery, but he sort of coughed a lot and said, 'You don't mind, do you?' – and touched my breasts as though they were made of glass and might break at any moment.

Walter half closes his eyes in the drowsy firelight; he pulls her head down and kisses her soft lips.

–It's funny, she says. –I don't particularly feel like making love.

–If you have money, you don't need love.

–You don't? He feels her smile on his cheek. –Tell me again how much we made.

–Five hundred and forty-four pounds. But we didn't make it, we won it.

–Yes. But we were clever . . . She touches his eyes, his ears, his cheeks, his chin. –Perhaps you should grow a beard.

–I'd look like the old man of the sea.

–I like the sea. I like the old man too, she says into his quiet ear. And stays silent for a while. Then, –Do you think *they* ever lie like this on the couch in front of the fire on a stormy night with the wind and –

–Good God no.

–Why not? We're perfectly decent – we're fully clothed – we're hardly even snogging . . .

–Edward is a bloke who keeps his change in a money purse and buttons the top button of his pyjama jacket – it's impossible to imagine him fully clothed in a prone position, except possibly in a coffin. It'd be like going to matins in the nude. He's a very proper person – an example to us all.

–How can you be sure? You don't really know – maybe they do strange things. People do. Don't you ever wonder?

–About Edward and Margot doing strange things?

–Not them necessarily. Anyone. Sometimes at dinner parties I listen to them babbling about their winter skiing and their summers in Turkey and I look at them and imagine all sorts of things they might get up to . . .

–Sex in the Métro?

She laughs. –My nice old badger – you're proper too, aren't you? She rolls on top of him. –I'm going to smother you . . .

–It *is* Easter, Connie.

–You don't think going to Church might be a bit hypocritical? After all, we're sinning like mad.

The sun lays a golden band across the bed where Connie reclines in a plethora of pink pillows. Walter, already washed and shaved, feels a pang of dismay as she lights a Gauloise. Smoking in bed is really spitting in the eye of the deity (Margot in this case).

–Well, this is the home of hypocrisy. He looks out of the window at the walled garden and the daffodils and the revolving summer-house. –It seems appropriate somehow.

–But is there a Catholic church around here?

–I haven't the faintest idea. I meant the local parish church – St George's I think it's called.

–I can't go there!

–Why not? It's perfectly respectable. He looks at her with amusement. In the still air of the bedroom the smoke hangs softly about her head.

–But I've never been to one of your churches – except for the odd wedding, of course.

–It's not *my* church – it's the Church of England. It won't be strange, there might even be incense – Edward's always moaning on about the vicar being High Church and calling it 'mass' instead of 'matins'. All the local boobies are bound to be there – it'll be fun.

–Mass isn't supposed to be *fun*. She drops ash into her early-morning teacup.

–If we dress up and take the Roller, somebody will probably ask us back for drinks.

–I've got nothing to dress up in.

–Borrow something of Margot's.

–Do you think I could?

–Why not? I'm going to wear one of Edward's suits.

–She does have some lovely clothes . . . Connie stubs out her cigarette in the saucer with a meditative smile. –Okay – you've bribed me! She leaps out of bed and runs across the room and pulls the towel from his waist. –And can I drive the Rolls?

–Oh sure.

She gives him a shining smile and tweaks his cock. –*Pater noster qui in caelum est . . .*

She seems to know by instinct what to do – sinks to her knees and stands and sits exactly as everyone else. But then, she is quick to pick things up – quick to catch the tune of the hymns,

> Now empty are the courts of Death,
> And crushed thy sting, Despair;
> And roses bloom in the desert tomb . . .

She sings in a true strong contralto, Margot's lilac silk scarf at her throat and her head well back. It seemed to Walter that she picked the clothes at random from the closest – purple tweed suit, mauve cashmere sweater – yet she looks better in them than Margot would, as if they'd been made for her. (Whereas there's something odd about Edward's suit – he scratches an armpit surreptitiously. A curious odour – camphor, mothballs, legal dust?) If she'd been married to Edward, she'd have picked it all up in no time – the bridge, the riding, the cocktails and flower-arranging, the . . .

She takes his hand and pulls him down to the pew beside her. The hymn is over and everyone is settling for the lesson.

–I thought you knew all about this, she whispers as a small, narrow-faced man in a dove-grey suit and waistcoat takes his place at the lectern.

–Here beginneth the second lesson! A startlingly stentorian bass bellow.

–Have you got a cold?

–No, why do –

–Then for heaven's sake stop sniffing.

–Set your affections on things above, not on things on the earth . . .

–It's this suit – it pongs. Can't you –

–Shut *up*!

–Mortify therefore your members which are upon the earth, bellows grey waistcoat. –Fornication, uncleanness, inordinate affection, evil concupiscence, and covetousness, which is idolatry: For which things the Wrath of God cometh on the children of disobedience . . .

Connie is wearing an air of strained distaste – Walter takes her hand and squeezes it gently.

–Don't take it personally, he murmurs, –it's only St Paul shooting his mouth off.

–To hell with St Paul, she says, without moving her lips, –it's your suit – I can smell it now alright.

–Here endeth the second lesson.

There's a rustle of coughs and shifting of feet. The organ groans. Walter sneezes. The huge old vicar advances menacingly.

–What happens now?

–God knows . . .

–You're Teddy Waller's brother, aren't you? Says dove-grey waistcoat, catching them at the car.

–Teddy? Oh – er, yes.

–Thought as much. Recognised the Royce. I'm Maurice Felt-Harrow – and my wife, Vicky.

–Hello – Walter, isn't it? Margot said you'd be coming down.

–Walter – right. And this is Connie, er –

–Pleased to meet you. Connie gives them each a brisk French handshake.

–Quite. Terrific. Good service, don't you think? Always a good service at Easter – none of this Alternative nonsense.

–You've got a wonderful voice, Connie says.

–Very nice of you to say so. People sometimes tell me I should have been an actor.

–You are an actor, darling, says Vicky, who is tall and blonde and as lean in the face as her husband – lean but not hungry. –You live in France, don't you? Do you live there too, Connie?

–We live in Paris.

–Do you? How exciting. You must come and tell us all about it.

Connie gives a teffle smile. –About living together?

–I see you were in the Fleet Air Arm like Teddy, says Maurice quickly, then chuckles at Walter's bewilderment. –The tie, old man – you're wearing the Fleet Air Arm tie.

–Am I? He looks down at the striped tie Connie picked from Edward's tie-drawer. –So I am.

–Maurice – they must, mustn't they?

–Must what, darling?

–Must come and have dinner, and tell us all about Paris.

–Oh absolutely. Vicky adores Paris, you know.

–Shall we say Monday then? It may be a bit scratch – the long weekend, you know.

Maurice Felt-Harrow laughs in his resonant bass. –Don't worry – she just means no caviar.

–Monday, says Connie, –would be very nice.

–Go on – what are you waiting for?

–It's his right of way.

–Not when you're driving the Roller, my dear. He's waving you on.

Connie puts the Rolls sleekly into motion, giving the other driver a dignified nod as they pass. –What's this 'my dear' business?

–What?

–You called me 'my dear'.

–Must be the influence of the car – or the suit maybe.

–I don't like it. She gives him a quick glance. –What are you doing now?

–Trying to get this damned thing off my neck. It's got . . . stuck. He gives the tie a fierce wrench and it parts with a ripping crack. –Christ – that's torn it!

–Well, it's only a tie.

–*Only* a tie? It's an authentic badge of heroism – and one I'm not entitled to at that. Trust that pompous little ass to catch me out on it. He unbuttons Edward's waistcoat and sighs. –That's better.

–You mean Maurice?

–Maurice Felt-Harrow – what a name.

–He can't help his name. I thought he was quite nice.

–Oh yes – the wonderful voice.

–Not just the voice. I rather fancy small men.

–Then why did you marry that long wet streak of a Frenchman?

–That's unfair. He's only an inch or two taller than you. Besides, you know I didn't mean to marry Henri – it just happened. And anyway, he's quite small inside.

Walter chuckles, takes a breath, laughs outright.

Connie colours a little. –Alright! I didn't like *her* much.

–Mutual, I'd say.

–I wonder why. She is driving at a serene thirty-five – no dashing down the lanes today. –Do you think she recognised Margot's suit?

–Could be. But it's more likely to be that enigmatic quality of yours.

–What do you mean? I'm not enigmatic.

–You would be to her. Who are you, what are you? You might be my kept woman – or a passing fancy I'd picked up on the plane – or –

–Charming!

–or you might be something glamorous – an actress or a

162

newscaster or . . . I don't know. The point is, she can't place you easily – so she's not sure whether to fawn or to sneer.

–You mean she's a snob?

–Naturally she's a snob. What on earth did you think?

–I thought they were just people. I detest snobs . . . Perhaps we shouldn't go.

–Of course we'll go. It'll be interesting and the food's bound to be good – she'll be all out to impress us.

–But you've made me a bit scared of her.

–He's more dangerous than she is. Little men with big voices are always untrustworthy.

–You are so ridiculous. We're nearly home. There's Butter! Walter – let's ask Sam and Mary in for a drink.

–Sam and . . . the Marryats?

–Yes. Why not? You're not a snob too, are you?

–It's just that – well, we don't know what he's like.

–I do. He was the chap I was talking to in the pub yesterday – with the beard. He's sweet. Shall I drive into the garage?

–Yes better – don't want Butter pissing on the paintwork. Okay – I'll give them a call. God, I can't wait to get out of this smelly suit of Edward's.

–Can't you?

–Do you think he's saving it to be buried in?

Connie switches off the ignition and sits for a moment upright and sedate, her hands still on the wheel. She smiles. –Walter – I've got an idea . . .

She pauses, straddling him. –It's years since I screwed in the back of a car! Her eyes are shining in the dim religious light of the garage and her face above him is wide open with joy. –And the last time was a Morris Minor . . . She laughs.

He clutches her, smelling her hair, her almond flesh, leather and wood and sweet sweat, rising in flood, pulling her down close.

–Lovely concupiscence, she whispers softly.

–Inordinate affection . . .

163

–Fornication everlasting.

–Idolatry, he mutters.

Outside, the little dog barks to hear such fun.

They all have the same look: the men as though they'd been plunged in some pinkish, vitamin-rich emollient, then zipped into moulded dinner jackets; the women, tautened in maso-chistic ritual, then tanned and brushed with wire brushes to remove all traces of lint or nap. They don't smoke and they hardly drink – Walter's third glass of champagne before dinner had been poured with a discreet curl of the lip. Even Blain, the large heavy-boned man in his late sixties on Connie's right, looks unpleasantly fit – ready to run a mile at the drop of a hat or an aitch.

Walter, wary, tries to imagine them in ridiculous positions and – unwarily – smiles.

–But I'm serious, says Kit with a frown. He's much younger than the rest – thirty-five perhaps – but is given ingratiating attention. A star player of some kind. –You can say what you like about the French, but they've got the right idea about unemployment compensation – a strict cut-off and no nonsense about supplementary benefits.

Walter glances at his empty wineglass – his three empty wineglasses. How much they all seem to know about France. –You don't put much stock in the compassionate society then? he asks mildly.

–That's just a catchword, isn't it, old boy? (At the beginning of the evening Kit had been calling him 'sir'.) –Of course I believe in compassion – we all believe in compassion. But it's hardly the business of the state, is it? When you come down to the wire, it's affluence that funds compassion, wouldn't you agree?

–Interesting idea, Walter murmurs, watching Maurice Felt-Harrow at the other end of the table, his hand hovering over a claret decanter as he expounds to Connie.

–How do you mean – interesting?

–Umm? Oh well – the notion that vice can fund virtue.

–Vice? I'm not with you. Kit leans forward, suffused with the clean glow of the changing room.

–Greed, you know – one of the Seven Deadly Sins.

–Ah, that's a bit of an old chestnut, isn't it? Greed is simply what motivates acquisition – wealth, wisdom, knowledge, health. What benefits me, benefits us all. If you call that greed – so be it. But I think you're getting it mixed up with gluttony, aren't you?

–Perhaps I am . . . Walter gives a placatory smile. Certainly none of them could be accused of gluttony. They eat almost nothing – but then there is almost nothing to eat. The first course was a small round piece of nameless white fish accompanied by four raspberries and a sprig of mint. And on the plate the maid has just put in front of him there are three minute lamb chops, a fig cut into an eight-sectioned floret and a small branch of redcurrants.

Maurice has still not taken hold of the decanter, though his discourse has switched from the wine to the wineglasses.

–Jacobite glasses – brought out in secret to toast the Young Pretender, you know. I was lucky enough to pick up half a dozen several years ago, but I had to wait a long time to find a couple more. Quite extraordinarily fine engraving – notice the arabesque medallion here enclosing . . .

Walter fights against a yawn and a strong desire to smoke. Connie has her teffle look which their host obviously mistakes for one of absorbed interest.

–I suppose you know Burgundy well? says Margery, Walter's left-hand neighbour.

–Not well, no. I know the bit around Autun a little.

–Really? How fascinating. Margery has a voice of superior boredom; she is dressed in a lemon yellow that clashes with a prominent pair of freckled breasts that sit incongruously on her emaciated body. –It wasn't far from Autun we found our porch – Cussy-en-Morvan, do you know it? No – well of course it's no more than a hamlet really. We came on it completely *par hasard* – an absolutely perfect twelfth-century porch.

–In a church?

–No, a farmhouse – of course it must have been a chapel once – but there it was, with the cows going in and out. And can you imagine, they'd painted it pink!

–Easier to keep clean, I expect – farmers aren't great ones for aesthetics. He has finished counting the redcurrants – thirteen – and turns his attention to the freckles.

–How right you are. But then all the French are peasants at heart, aren't they? Absolutely no sense of their national heritage. Of course we snapped it up at once. Blain is very clever at that sort of thing – and his French is perfect of course. But would you believe, it cost more to get the paint off the stone when we got it home than it did to buy the porch itself? I find that very hard to forgive, though it does look absolutely splendid at Wethers now – as though it had sort of come home. Do you know what I mean?

–Oh quite – quite . . . The claret has come round at last and Walter takes a mouthful from his Jacobite glass. It tastes like wine alright. If he drinks fast enough, maybe he'll get a refill. He tries to absorb himself in the food, but as he picks at the chops, they keep picking at France. It's Sylvia now, Kit's young wife, pretty in a drawn foxy way, inexorably vivacious.

–. . . it's absolutely untranslatable, isn't it? I mean, 'joy of life' sounds so – so frightfully serious somehow, do you know what I mean?

Walter raises his head. –Wordsworthian?

–Exactly – so terribly heavy and dated! But *joie de vivre* is so stylish and elegant and now-ish – it just sort of *says* Cartier and Hermès and Maxim and Dior and the Plaza-Athénée – don't you agree?

Maurice smiles indulgently. –Let's ask the expert. Connie, what does *joie de vivre* mean to you?

–Sex, she says.

There is an infinitesimal hesitation, and then a pleased

burble of laughter – after all, this is what they are paying for.

–There you are Sylvia. But tell me, my dear, says Maurice, delicately patting Connie's arm, –tell me, how do you personally get on with the Frogs?

Connie, all innocence in Margot's diaphanous pastel blue, looks down dangerously at the well-manicured hand, then smiles. –We manage to hop along together quite amicably.

The hand is removed.

Blain, who has just consumed his portion of redcurrants in one mouthful, turns his fleshy face to Walter – enough of this frivolity. –Seriously, the Frogs have got it in for us, haven't they?

–Oh I wouldn't say so, no – not particularly.

–Come on, you've got to admit they hate our guts.

–To tell you the truth, I don't think they worry about us any more than they do about – well, Bolivia.

–Why Bolivia?

–It's a far–away country – and they wear bowler hats, don't they? Or is that only the women?

Blain pauses – there's a fleck of currant juice on his underlip. – What you mean is, I take it, that they're too damnably arrogant to pay any attention to anyone else at all.

–Arrogance – ummm. They'd call it pride.

Kit says, –And what have they got to be proud about? The war? Their economy?

–I don't know about that. But their cities are clean and their trains are comfortable and run on time and their telephone system is –

Blain interrupts, –My dear fellow, Mussolini made the trains run on time – not that I've got anything against Mussolini – but anyone can make the trains run on time if you pour enough public money into it. And that's precisely what the Frogs do, of course – and the result is their tax system is crippling for business. There's no free play for the market economy at all. Take Renault – if it wasn't subsidised up to the eyebrows, it would be on the rocks tomorrow.

Walter keeps his voice cool, but he feels Edward's collar

getting hotter and tighter round his neck. –I admit the French attitude to cars is a bit unsound, but –

–What do you mean – unsound?

–I mean, once in a car, a Frenchman seems to lose any vestige of common sense in his worship of speed. They're a menace and the accident rate is appalling – they kill twice as many people on the roads as we do.

Blain laughs. –I should have said that was rather a plus factor.

–Not if you brought up your children in France, you wouldn't. Walter glances at Connie and gets back a don't-spill-the-coffee-on-the-carpet look.

–My dear chap, France is the last place on God's earth I'd dream of bringing up my children. I'd rather bring them up in Bolivia.

–Why? French education is streets ahead of yours.

–Mine? Ours? What rot. What conceivable basis in fact have you for such a statement? Oh of course, if you're talking about their capacity to produce a bunch of half-baked bloody intellectuals, I'll grant you that, but . . .

Oh, to hell with it – Walter brings out his packet of cigarettes and lights one. The room is stiflingly close with central heating, log fire, and the hot air wafting from the thin lips in that fleshy face. He looks down at the multi-coloured sorbet in front of him and longs for another glass of wine – but the decanter is empty. He remembers all this, remembers exactly the feeling of it when he came back from America and was shoved – accent and clothes and open mind and all – into that damned barbaric school. He'd survived, he'd learned how to deal with it in the end – but he can't remember the lesson . . .

Blain is ostensibly addressing Connie (well-armoured in her impassivity), but he has a general complaisant audience, a softly smiling Maurice, an admiring Sylvia, an eager Kit . . .

–They're the people we've got to watch in Europe, not the Germans or the Eyeties. The Frogs are an unstable bunch and always have been. No moral fibre. They'll always let you down when it comes to the crunch. Look at the two world wars – who saved them then? I'm not saying we were on the wrong side, but there was no good reason to be on *their* side. What do you say, Maurice?

–You may have a point, Blain, but it's all history now.

–It's no good blinking history. You may think I'm prejudiced and perhaps I am, but the Frogs have been our hereditary enemies for hundreds of years and you can't forget that. My great-great-grandfather was killed at Waterloo and I –

–Bit of a plus factor, Walter murmurs – but the murmur is pounced on like an owl on a mouse.

–*What* did you say?

–Oh sorry, I thought you meant the battle.

–I *did* mean the battle.

–Yes, that's what I thought – a bit of a supplementary benefit, what?

–That's not very amusing, you know. Kit, red-faced, is assaulting from the left flank. –You seem to have become a little too French, old man. In England, you know, we're taught manners. In England we don't smoke between courses.

–Now Kit . . . begins Vicky.

But Kit, in a nice bloody lust, leans across the table, snatches the cigarette from Walter's fingers and the blue packet from beside his plate and, standing up, flings them with athletic accuracy into the log fire.

–Now Kit really . . . Vicky Felt-Harrow pats his hand and pulls him down. –We've talked so much about France, I just haven't had the chance to tell you our latest. Maurice darling, do tell.

–Ah, well – it is rather exciting, if I do say so. His deep bass carries a hint of the coy. –I've bought a yacht. A twelve-metre Dragon class, of course it needs a lot of work –

Margery, –But I didn't know you were a sailor, darling!

–Oh, I'm not – I'm not.

Sylvia, in vixen surprise, –Then why did you buy it?

–I rather liked the shape.

–How sensible of you! Connie laughs and drains the last of her claret. –What a simply marvellous wine that was. And, turning slightly in her chair, she tosses the glass into the grate where the arabesques and medallions shatter into a thousand fragments.

–*Voilà!*

Maurice, half-risen, sinks back ashy-faced.

–I adore these old English customs. Across the table she gives Walter a brilliant smile. –Or are they Scottish?

–What a lovely, lovely evening. She twirls in front of him, the blue dress floating. –What is it – this music?

–An early Beethoven piano sonata. You can hear it from a million windows – all the children practise it.

And Phoebe used to play it, sometimes, on limpid summer nights . . . Practise your beauty, blue girl, before it fails.

–Come on, my old whisky drinker. And she holds out her hands to pull him up.

–Dance?

–No dance. There's a moon – a crescent moon.

–Last quarter – it can't be crescent.

–A whatever moon then. We're going out into the garden . . .

Into the walled garden, into the summerhouse, where the floorboards are still warm from daytime sun. And the flesh is white in the moon, but warm too. –Now, she says, –now, now . . .

And this is the moment, she will swear, when she conceived.

Walter unlatches his seat-belt. –Cigarette?

–Where are we?

–God knows. He looks out of the window at the placid expanse of cloud. –Over the Channel by now, I should think.

–In that case, no thanks. From now on, no smoking – and no drinking.

170

–You're really sure then?

–I'm really sure.

–All the same, you'd better have a rabbit test.

–A *rabbit* test? How sweet you are. I don't need a test to tell me what I already know. She smiles tranquilly – no gleaming grin, no teffle glaze, nothing brilliant or bewildered – a signal of secret repose.

–Alright, he says impulsively, –I'll give it up too.

She takes his hand. –Which – smoking or drinking?

–Both. What the hell – it'll do me good. I've gotten fat as a pig these last few days. We'll eat salads and fruit and do exercises and go to the pool . . .

–And drink verbena tea.

–Oh God – I left the tea in Sam's van at the airport.

–The Marmite too?

–Everything – the whole bloody lot. It was all in that green plastic sack. What an idiot.

–Mary will find a use for it. It's not the end of the world.

The plane jolts a little as it enters the cloud. They wave away the plastic food.

–Walter – you did like them, didn't you – Mary and Sam?

–Very much. You know, he's quite someone. Those animal sculptures in the garden . . .

–They're beautiful, aren't they? The sniffing dog and that enormous rabbit – and the Egyptian ram. I adored that ram . . .

–They're all good – really good – remarkable. I wonder what Edward and Margot make of them.

–Mary says they haven't been told about them – Sam usually keeps them in the barn.

–Sensible precaution.

–Why sensible?

–Art's alright in a gallery, but it's hardly appropriate to have it hanging about in your handyman's back yard. They might find it a bit disturbing.

–Why – because it's too real?

And they laugh together, enclosed in the bright cloud.

There's a slight grey rain as they get off the bus at the long-term carpark, but no wind. Walter is empty-handed, the airline having lost his suitcase (–Not *lost*, sir – mislaid. Probably in Stockholm or Madrid. No problem. We'll have it back to you in a few days).

–We were silly not to have carried them onto the plane, Connie said. And he'd nodded, not confessing that any weight could put out his knee after the exertions of England. It still aches now as they traipse along the grubby ranks of cars, but not enough to limp.

–Will it start?

–Of course it will start. Connie slings her bag onto the back seat and gives the little red car an affectionate pat.

Even the soft rain can't veil the alien bleakness of the airport – the budded stalk of the control tower, the terminal's round drum, inhuman as an enemy encampment. The twin cedars alongside the railway line and the autoroute, thin skeletons of a more comfortable time, are black and sad with acid and noxious fumes.

Further down the row a car door slams.

And Connie says, –It's lovely to be back.

–Yes, he answers as they get into the Renault, –it is.

And the car starts at once and she drives them smoothly into Paris.

–Do I look alright? She stands for inspection in her best black skirt and striped blouse. –Even a practice teacher should wear a skirt, don't you think?

–You'll do. Walter smiles across the kitchen counter. –But maybe you should roll down the sleeves.

–Why, what's wrong with them like this?

–Bit too down-to-earth – you could be all set for a morning's housework.

–Housework's your chore, ducky. I'm off to a real job. But

she buttons her sleeves as she sits down. —Oh you've put milk in my tea.

—You can carry this slimming business too far. Hilary shouldn't be deprived of milk. You ought to eat something too.

—I don't want anything to eat. What I really want is a cigarette.

—I threw them all away.

—I know. Noble. Alright, a peach then. Walter . . . are we really going to call him Hilary?

—Of course we're going to call her Hilary. He selects a peach and smells it.

—How much time do I have?

—We ought to leave in fifteen minutes.

—Oh no. I'm going by myself. I don't want any distractions. Do you know, I don't feel nervous at all? Just sort of excited.

—Adrenalin. He quarters the peach and removes the stone. —Shall I pick you up afterwards then?

—I don't think so. You'd just be hanging about – it'll take the Toy Mouse at least half-an-hour to pull us to pieces after the practice. I know – let's meet at the plastic café – at about half-past? We haven't been there for ages.

—Okay – great. Here – eat this. He passes over the carefully prepared peach.

—You'll make a nice father . . . It'll be your turn soon, you know. She laughs. —To teach, I mean.

—Ah, but mine will be advanced students. All I have to do is to give them something to talk about and sit back and listen. It's called 'discourse chaining'.

—Well watch out for the weak link. For all you know, they might turn out to be *false* advanced students. Why are there never any serviettes? Lend me your hanky. She wipes her hands and lips. —I must be off . . .

—You'll be okay, Connie love – you're really good.

—Am I? If you say it often enough, perhaps I'll begin to believe it. She sighs. —I just wish it wasn't Emma doing the judging this morning.

–Emma's perfectly harmless.

–To you maybe, but then you're her fair-haired boy.

–Oh come on!

–Yes you are, you know you are – she squeaks every time you speak to her.

–But I'm so goddamned rude to her.

–And doesn't she love it – if you were a cat, she'd roll over with her paws in the air and beg to be eaten. That's why she doesn't like me – she's jealous.

–But she doesn't know anything about us.

–Of course she does, everyone does. Why else do you think she gave me a C+ and you an A– on the last essay? There wasn't *that* big a difference. I must go . . . She gives back his handkerchief and stands up.

–Right . . . Got everything?

–Have I? She picks up her old red folder and shakes it. Yes, I have . . . Walter . . .

He gets up and puts his arms round her. –Good luck, my darling.

–Yes . . . Walter, I don't want Hilary to be a girl.

–Why not? He smiles. –She'd be a lovely little girl.

–Yes I know. That's what I'm afraid of. I'd be jealous.

Dearest Daddy darling – méchant Papa, why haven't you written me? How are you? What are you doing? Are you a teacher yet? *Where* are you? I called you from Acapulco all over Easter but you weren't there. Or did you unplug the phone again? Is it love? I do hope so!

Listen, Charles called me – from Bangkok! Tried to reach you but no luck. All in a rage about child prostitution, but sounded fine otherwise. He's off to China next, then to Japan (to hiss at the Oriental capitalists), then South America (the trouble spots natch). No, don't worry, Dad, he's quite (American quite) sensible (English sensible). Of course, he hasn't written to anyone but . . .

. . . all going to meet up this summer on Nantucket. Spencer (Hal's Dad) has a farmhouse (read palace) there with about forty rooms and everyone's invited from July onward – that means *you*! Daddy, do say you'll come – and bring her too (I know there is a *her*, so don't pretend) – please please please . . . They're all very sporty but you don't have to do any of that – you can just sit on the porch and drink old-fashioneds and be a wise old owl . . .

Walter looks up and out of the window. The top of the Eiffel Tower is still mauve in the morning haze, like a giant asparagus tip against the sky. Somewhere someone is practising the piano. Amy wouldn't know about Nantucket – he'd seldom mentioned other wives to his children, let alone honeymoons. Paula had worn white for that marriage (her third) – a kind of dead white, matching her albino soul – and charmed all the world, even the black waiters at the White Elephant hotel, saucily slitting her eyes and wagging her tail. Even the grey of her hair was wrong for the grey town – the grey of steel, not of weather . . . or sea . . . or cloud . . . or memory.

He skips to the end of the letter,

. . . and doesn't everyone deserve to be happy? and does my happiness diminish anyone else? Au contraire, I feel it spreading out like a lovely ripple –and may it reach you across the ocean, Dada darling . . . with huge love and a million zibous . . .

As he lets the page drop, he hears for an instant Paula's harpy laugh out of the past. He shakes his head to put her out of his mind – what was she doing there anyway? – and gets up and goes to the window. Almost at once the piano stops. The dog is not in the garden (maybe it has died of the wedding ring) and only the occasional fart of a distant bus ruffles the backwater calm. Connie will be coming to the end of her practice teach, and soon it will be time to be off.

He picks up a remaining unopened letter and holds it up to the light – but the envelope is too thick to reveal the contents.

It's the type of semi-official missive he'd have shoved under the china cat to cool off in the old days, but now he opens it with only momentary hesitation.

Dear Walter,

I have just had a very positive word on the translation from our reader. It seems unnecessary to wait for her final report which I am sure will confirm this, so I am enclosing our cheque for £1,500.00 with this letter.

One other point – *Fleur-Marie-Fleur* does not seem a very appealing title for a British readership. Do you have any suggestions for an alternative? Yrs etc . . .

Walter rubs his chin slowly. *News from the Grotto . . . On the Fairy Beach . . . Bride of Jonathan Livingstone Seagull?* He smiles and unclips the cheque from the letter; £1,500 is three months' rent – two and a half teffle courses – four round-trip tickets to Nantucket – thirty pairs of jet earrings – fifty red gloves – or . . .

He reaches for the phone and his address book and in a moment is punching the number for England.

–Sam? Walter here. Listen, are you still game to sell the Ram? Wonderful – I'm on then. No no, four hundred is fine – I'm in funds, as they say. The only thing is, can your friend with the van – Billy, yes – can he get it here before June the fourth? Connie's birthday – it's going to be a surprise. . .

–It worked! It was wonderful! I was good – even Emma said so afterwards – and I know I was, I felt it. There were only six of them, but everything worked – the role play, the happy families, even the drills! I could tell they enjoyed it, you know how people are when they're interested, all bright-eyed and bushy-tailed, you can tell, can't you? It all came together and I just knew I couldn't do anything wrong. Walter darling, it's such fun! They were eating out of my hand . . .

Her ebullience fills the empty café with life. He's caught up in her smiles with smiles of his own, and even the patron behind the counter, uncomprehending, incomprehensible, beams in the radiance.

–. . . Harriet was alright in that boring school-mistressy way of hers, but poor Molly made a mess of it – she tried to do too much and then got lost and in a thorough muddle, and afterwards when we all sat down with Emma, she was in tears. What's that, Evian? Oh-ho, you *are* being good. Give me a sip. Yes, I'll have Evian too.

–Sure you wouldn't prefer champagne?

–Champagne? I don't need champagne! Never again. Perhaps it's tempting fate, but I really think I'm going to make a teacher, after all. I feel – almost holy . . .

Ecclesiastical acoustics and the high-powered sound-system are ill matched in the great cathedral; invocations grate mechanically on the ear and the holy words carry a robotic echo like a long-distance call from Bolivia.

Watching Connie out of the corner of his eye, Walter stands and sits as the others do. No one appears to kneel. There is an astonishing quantity of young women, a smattering of widows and elderly males, and a sprinkling of kids. Only the altar is full of men – in bright green vestments or white-cowled gowns coming and going in a ritual mime under the thunder and squeak of mechanical sound.

At breakfast she'd said, –Walter, let's go to mass.

–To mass? For God's sake, why?

–I don't know. I just feel like it. It's your turn to come to my church – it's only fair.

Fair? It's not that, of course – no one goes to church in search of justice. He puzzles at it slowly as the acolytes move about up front, muttering and chanting and raising their hands and fiddling about with the sacred regalia. She crossed herself with holy water at the entrance as briskly as she delves in her purse to pay for a pound of tomatoes. Now she sits calm and attentive, as does the rest of the congregation – no bowing of heads or private devotional murmurings. No questions asked, no answers expected. There is something soothing about the lack of spontaneity and the suspension of disbelief – like a gigantic teffle class.

The students know the drill and remain tranquilly unmoved by the sermon. The jack in the pulpit presents with dramatic severity of gesture, but the message comes across now in a hoarse shout, now in an indelicate whisper.

As the incense is swayed from the thurible, rising in a slow, soft cloud into the sunlight from the rose windows, Walter slips into a kind of classroom dream. Connie's hands are folded in her lap – a characteristic stillness, but no longer watchful. Perhaps all the time she had been waiting for this – for another child, for the still, invisible burgeoning in the womb. Is this her holiness? If God were the father, there would be no need of man – no call for Walter. And if pentecostal fire bestowed the gift of tongues there'd be no demand for teffle, communion not communication, the language of love would be foreign to no one . . .

He feels her touch on his hand and opens his eyes. Everyone is standing. As he gets up, he yawns and engulfs an unexpected mouthful of incense – and coughs. People are kneeling now, at last – but not Connie. Some special moment. He coughs again and covers his mouth with his handkerchief, but even through the cotton the sickly scent catches his throat. His head swims as though he were inhaling a thousand cigarettes at once. He glances covertly at the others – but no one else seems to be affected – or is it that which has brought them to their knees, a sacred tear gas? Maybe if he were to kneel too, it would go away.

Connie whispers, –Are you alright?

He nods, straightens his shoulders, stands manfully. The service has already lasted fifty minutes, there can't be much longer to go. Like a seasick passenger hiding his shame, he switches his attention to trivialities – to the white-cowled minions coming down the aisles with golden bowls, two, four, six of them. Ah, the kneelers are the communicants – forty rows with fifty to a row and half of them at least are slipping out to eat the sacred wafer. A thousand upraised faces and protruding tongues. Can there possibly be so many without sin? Or have all the innocents of Paris gathered by accident under the one cathedral roof? No, innocence is an uncountable noun . . .

It's ending at last. The bishop is handed his crozier and puts on his golden mitre; the gilded rood is raised and the priestly procession potters off.

Walter clings to Connie's arm like a sickly bridegroom as they move down the nave and into the open air. He sits on a low concrete bollard and struggles to draw a deep breath.

–Walter darling, what is it? You're pale . . . She touches his forehead. –You're sweating. She kneels down beside him.

–Going – to – be . . . sick. And he leans forward and vomits onto the pavement – melon, boiled egg, cherry jam . . . decorative. –Sorry about that.

–Oh sweetheart. She takes his handkerchief and wipes his mouth and strokes his hair and kisses his hand. –Is that better?

–Yes, alright now. But he coughs again and when he lifts his head, the sunlight hurts his eyes.

–We'll go home. Can you stand? Put your arm round my shoulders – that's right.

–Fine – I feel fine. Want to go to the bird market.

–No birds for you today, my sweet – I'm taking you home. She raises him up gently – how strong she is! –Hold on to me. Can you manage?

–Yes. And he does hold on to her, holds hard, breathes in the almond smell of her.

–Whatever brought it on?

Salmonella – incense – abstinence . . . inordinate affection?

–Who knows?

That second Monday holiday in May, they wake early, brought out of sleep by the next-door baby, and make easy love, coming as the child's wails ceases.

While Connie sleeps again, Walter lies listening to the half-summery noises of waking up – the clack-clack of the metal shutters as the housekeeper opens up the pavilion, the pigeon coos, the preliminary growling of the dog (as acrimoniously alive as ever), the rapid chatter of the ladies in the courtyard, woken maybe, in their turn, by Connie's cries. She turns over to curl against his chest, her hair tickling his chin. He strokes her swan-white shoulder and sniffs the brackish scent of sex. He hasn't mentioned Amy's summer invitation and maybe he never will. Nantucket, silver with youth and riches once, would only be ashy with nostalgia. Paula's laugh would haunt the streets like Mary Malone's ghostly cries in Dublin; and the young honeymooner's simulacrum would mock the old man in love, not with a coy mistress, but a pregnant middle-aged runaway mother.

There is a distant sound of martial music, thin but coming closer; he traces its course by ear, along the broad street parallel, left at the corner, and suddenly louder as it enters the square.

Connie wakes up. –What's that noise?

–A band – a military band.

–What for?

–It's Victory Day – they'll be marching to the war memorial, they always do.

She sits up. –A band? A parade! Oh we must go! And she springs naked out of bed – from slumber to bustle in the twinkling of an eye. –Come on, Walter! she calls from the bathroom. –Hurry up – don't you want to come?

–Oh yes, he says, putting his foot to the floor to test the rickety knee, –I love a parade.

The memorial is in the shady corner of the great square in front of the *mairie*. Its granite soldiers strain sightlessly up at the leafy branches above. The living gathered at their feet have the slightly self-conscious air of intruders; only the civic officials, swathed in their blue, white and red sashes, are fully at ease. They speak with the slow-toned gravity which French politicians use for the simple-minded, of courage and honour and dignity, the heroic dead, our sacrificial brethren, and of Paris – glorious symbol of liberty to the world. Finally, the simplicity of bugles – the last post – and then silence . . .

Before the little crowd has time to turn away, a quick command is given, and buglers, band, veterans and officials fall into rank and march across the square to the forecourt of the *mairie* and form up in separate blocks.

The bandmaster, a small, nut-brown fellow laced with gold braid, announces in a vibrant bellow, 'La Marche du Deuxième DB', and brings down his baton. The band immediately breaks into an exultant quick march. The pigeons fly off the roof in a flutter of fright, but everyone else stands firm, the honour guard rigid, the politicians solemn, the veterans somnolent with age, the crowd transfixed, even the children quite still. One after the other, the marches stir the heart with wistful pride. And the sun glitters on the gold-tipped railings and the band's silver instruments and the bright medals of the ancient heroes on stick and crutch.

And when it is all over, Connie and Walter turn to each other. Connie sniffs. –Why do bands always make me cry?

–Patriotism.

–But we're not French.

–You don't have to be French to weep, he says, passing her his handkerchief.

It has been warm for too long – from September to May – and the students have gone beyond fatigue into stupefaction. Janet is milky-eyed and bovine, sunny Harriet has petulant lines from nose to mouth; Kathy has the fine transparent pallor of the terminally ill and Linda's freckles have the look of leprosy;

even Molly, pretty baby of the class, is spotted with pustules and white-faced with exhaustion. All the native users have the slurred mouth and slack eyes of long-term mental patients in forgotten psychiatric wards. Only Emma is on form, stimulated to mechanical liveliness by her Audio-Visual Aids – TP, OHP, TV; machine answering to machine.

Walter glances at Connie, but she has gone into her glazed teffle mode – or the prospective calm of motherhood. Will they come out of this course without permanent damage? He thinks of the strange work being wrought upon voices and minds and hearts. Every day across the world from darkest Africa to brightest Tokyo millions are chanting, not 'Our Father which art in heaven' or 'Workers of the World Unite', but 'I'm sorry I can't, I'm washing my hair tonight . . .'

– . . . I taped this last night from BBC1 News. It's easy to do if you've got cable television and it gets students interested because it's something that's happening now . . .

He opens his eyes as the tape runs soundlessly on a group of ragged soldiers with automatic weapons crouching behind an embankment; every now and again they bob up and fire across the road at an invisible enemy in a landscape of flame and smoke. On the road itself is a burned-out armoured vehicle and next to it a family collapsed in death – a man on his face, a bundled woman, a half-naked child with stick legs sprawled between them.

– . . . bringing reality into the classroom. They get really involved. What is happening? What's going on? What are these people doing? It's ever so useful in teaching lexis . . .

Walter holds his breath for a moment – mustn't be rude to the Mouse. –Don't you think, he says evenly, –that maybe the material is faintly objectionable?

She looks at him and blinks. –No. Why?

–Death and blood and devastation?

–It's the news – that's the main point, isn't it? It holds their attention.

Don't expect toy mice to have hearts; but he can't let it go. –Supposing somebody's son had been killed in a war?

–But, Walter, that was in Afghanistan!
–You mean – so it's not real, after all?

It might be high summer. The sprinklers sweep the grass in the esplanade and workmen are putting up freshly painted flagpoles for another state visitor. The glass roof of the Grand Palais gleams in the sunlight and a little breeze sways the symmetrical chestnuts in the tiny parc de Bolivar. More workmen are mowing the drained moat under the old brass cannons that guard the army museum.

–I don't know, sometimes it gets me down, says Walter as they wait for the lights to change to green.

–Yes I know – it was awful this afternoon.

–Yes, that too. But I didn't mean that. I meant all this glitz and glitter. He gestures at the newly gilt beasts guarding the pont Alexandre III. –Everything's so damned shiny. Look at this place – not a single floating sheet of newspaper, not a dead bird or a rotting mattress in sight, even the pigeons are fed birth-control pills.

–They're just getting it smartened up for the bicentenary.

–I know – but don't tell me the Revolution was like this. There was something to be said for Paris in the old days, when the buildings were black and the Métro was noisy and stinking and there were *pissoirs* on every corner.

–There wasn't any Métro in the old days.

He laughs. –I meant my old days.

They cross slowly, arm in arm; it's too hot to move fast.

–Connie . . .

–Yes, my duck?

–I don't suppose you'd fancy going to the States?

–The States? America, you mean?

–Oh not permanently – just for the summer, the summer vacation. We've been invited to Nantucket – it never gets too hot there, there's nearly always a sea breeze and –

–But, Walter –I can't go anywhere with you in the summer.

–You . . . what do you mean? Why – why not?

–Sweetie, I'm taking the children for the vacation. I told you. Don't you remember?

He stares at her aghast. –I don't know. Vaguely – I suppose I do . . . but that was when . . . that was years ago.

–Not quite three months . . . She reaches out and takes his hand in hers.

–Yes – alright. But that was then, and this is now.

–All the same, I promised, Walter. I can't go back on that.

–But that's exactly what you would be doing – going back. Going back to the old life. That's not your life now, not *our* life – yours and mine – and Hilary's. Doesn't that make a difference?

–Yes. It makes it . . . much harder. Perhaps if I'd known . . .

How light and soft her hand is. –Perhaps if you'd known – you wouldn't have promised?

–Perhaps I wouldn't . . . But I did. And I can't back out of that, can I?

Walter stops typing and looks down at Connie lying on the floor in red shorts and a turquoise tee-shirt. She is stretched full length in the square patch of afternoon sunshine from the window. Her eyes are closed and her hands are folded placidly across her stomach. There is a thin film of dark hair on her bare arms. Her breasts rise and fall slowly – already they seem a little heavier.

–Finished? she asks, without opening her eyes.

–Yes, I think so. I don't suppose you feel like having another shot at taping, do you?

–Of course – if you want me to. She sits up and stretches. –Oooh, that's good. But listen, could you go in the other room while I do it? I feel awkward with an audience.

–Right, I'll go get some iced coffee. Come and sit here, it's all set up . . .

184

In the kitchen, he stirs fresh ice into the cold coffee, nostalgic for a pitcher of martinis. Abstinence may make the brain clearer, but he knows strong drink would help him through tomorrow's teaching practice. Through the far door into the sitting room, he can hear Connie reciting into the radio-cassette player he'd bought on the cheap.

– . . . lose and leave it.

Then all the blood
Forsook the face. She was too pale for tears,
Observing the ruin of her younger years.
She went and stood

Under her father's vaunting oak
Who kept his peace in wind and rain – *no, sun, damn!*

Walter laughs and carries in the jug and glasses. –Don't worry. Have some iced coffee and try again.

–Alright, but I'm no good at this. I told you. Why can't you record it yourself?

–Because it's a poem about a woman, so I want a woman's voice. And you've got a particularly clear diction – perfect for it.

–But shouldn't I understand what I'm saying? Ugh – this coffee's bitter.

–What don't you understand? Sugar?

–No, I'll drink it as it is. Well, for instance, why is it 'the oak tree *who*' and not 'the oak tree *which*'?

–Because the oak is the personification of her father – a nice peaceful old bloke, patient and stoical with a gentle voice.

–I don't think he's so nice. Look what he's doing later on –whispering reproaches to the wan daughter. Is that the oak tree or the father?

–Well, both – the spirit of the father.

–Does that mean we never get rid of our parents even when they're dead?

–Connie – that's rather good. I can use that.

–Put it in your lesson plan then. She sips her coffee and makes a face. –Was your father like that – patient and gentle?

–No – actually he was a terrible ranter.

–You never talk about your parents, do you?

–Don't I? Oh surely I must have. He stirs uneasily on the grey couch. –Shall we get on with –

–Only about them dying – you did tell me about that.

–Well . . . to tell you the truth, I wasn't awfully keen on my parents. He swallows some of the cold coffee. –You're right – this stuff is filthy.

–Why not – because they sent you away to America?

–Good grief no. That was the best thing they ever did. I was glad to get away. You know what I mean – you were too, weren't you?

–We're not talking about me, we're talking about you.

He gives a half-laugh. –Are you trying to psychoanalyse me?

–Don't be cross – I'm just trying to understand. She looks unsmilingly at him from the chair at his worktable.

–Listen – I'm sorry. Ask anything you like. What do you want to know?

–If I knew what I wanted to know, I wouldn't have to ask, would I?

–That's wonderful! He laughs too loudly. –I'm going to get some sugar . . . But he doesn't move.

–Walter, what is it? Is it the summer? It is, isn't it?

He nods. –It's just that eight weeks . . . you – and Hilary – God knows what might happen . . .

She comes and sits beside him. –Nothing's going to happen. Eight weeks won't harm the baby – our baby, yours and mine, nestling here inside me, so –

–But . . .

–So don't you see, you'll be with me all the time – in the flesh? And I'll only be in Normandy, not so far away . . .

–Normandy? With all those awful relatives? But you'll hate it, Connie.

–No I won't – they don't matter to me now. Water off a

duck's back. No more role play – I don't have to, do I? I'm immune.

He gets up and goes over to the chimneypiece. –I could come and stay nearby –in an hotel, or rent a cottage . . .

–So we could meet on the sly for a quick poke?

–Connie!

–No, Walter. Absolutely not. I can't manage two lives.

–Alright – then we'll make it one. You don't have to go to Normandy, do you? We can take a house all together, in Devon or Tuscany or wherever – you and me and the children.

–You'd really do that?

–Yes of course. Why not?

–Because they're my children, not yours, don't you see that? I couldn't inflict another father on them.

–Inflict? You mean, I'd be some kind of a punishment?

–Yes, you would. Of course you would. You can't just trade in a father for a new model and –

–An old model, he says harshly.

–New or old, it doesn't matter – it would be a *foreign* model to them. Don't you understand? They don't need a substitute father any more than I need a substitute husband. That would be going back to square one with a vengeance! I'm free now – I'm not crazy. I love you, Walter, and I'll live with you as long as . . .

–As long as what?

–As long as I love you.

–And how long does love last?

–I don't know. But it won't die in Normandy, if that's what you're afraid of.

He smiles with difficulty. –You won't one day just write me a letter with characters venomous and hatefully curved?

–Oh – that poem. No of course I won't. Walter – come and sit down.

He moves heavily back to the sofa – why does the healthy life make him feel so appallingly unfit? –What's wrong with the poem?

–Don't you think it's a bit – complicated, for students?

–Maybe – but that's exactly what makes it interesting. It's a lot better than some chunk from the *Economist* about interest rates. Isn't it?

–I don't know, she says miserably. –I don't think they'll like it.

–But it's so very human and touching – it has a story – and the language is beautifully lucid and precise and –

–You don't say to anyone, 'Go up the serpent's track and turn left at the vaunting oak, then –'

–Is that what you object to? It's not everyday, native-user usage?

–No of course not, not if . . .

–Then what? What is your objection? It's a fine poem.

–I don't know – I don't know about poetry. It's just that . . . She hesitates. They are sitting very close on the sofa, but not quite touching.

–What is it? Tell me.

–Oh Walter, it's so full of hate! I can't think why you chose it . . . And suddenly she bursts into terrible wrenching sobs.

–Connie!

–It's hateful – hateful!

–Connie my darling . . .

They touch now – hold – cling on for dear life.

Standing on the corner waiting for her to fetch the car, Walter remembers that other earlier expectant morning seven months before. Today he whistles a different tune, but he feels the same tremor of excitement, so that when she drives up and opens the car door for him, he is grinning.

–You're chirpy.

–Yes, I am, he says, settling in. –I can't think why.

–Perhaps you're high on the prospect of teaching.

–Oh yeah – and I get drunk on mint tea. No, I guess it's because this whole damn teffle farce will soon be over.

–Not the final exam.

–Oh phoo to the final exam.

–How can you say that? It's what counts the most – and we've only got twelve days left. Tomorrow we'll have to start revising.

–Not tomorrow. Monday, if you like. Tomorrow's your birthday.

She says nothing, but sits a little straighter.

–I'll bet you thought I'd forgotten.

She smiles and darts him a glance. –Have you got me something nice?

–Wait and see – and keep your eyes on the road. Incidentally, isn't this a one-way street?

–Shit – so it is! Oh well, there's nothing coming the other way.

Walter crosses his fingers. –What would you like as your birthday treat?

–I get a treat?

–Of course you get a treat.

–Well, I don't know . . . she says, driving contemplatively past the backparts of the Ecole Militaire. –Have you got any suggestions?

–How about a day out at Longchamp?

–At the races? Tomorrow?

–Yes. Does that appeal to you?

–Will it be like Plumpton?

–Good heavens no – no mud and gumboots. Lobster and champagne.

–Shall I have to dress up?

–I think so – in a modest way.

–And will we win lots of money?

–If you bring us luck, we will.

–Well, I do bring us luck. She puts her hand on his knee. –Don't I?

At the same time as Walter rises to face the class, in Normandy an old man's jaw drops and his rasping breath finally ceases, and on the other side of the world the tanks are moving into Tiananmen Square and the massacre of the innocents has begun.

–I want you to listen to a poem. A poem . . . I shall play it again, so don't try too hard to understand it this time around. Listen – just listen . . .

Although no apprehension of catastrophe touches him, Walter senses an infinite distance in the heart of this class.

She stares for a moment as though not recognising him. –Hello. You're early.

–Yes, well, I didn't stay for the full autopsy. He puts his briefcase on the table; the blue cloth is spread with letters and cards. He clears his throat. –Mail?

–Just my post. Her hands lie on it protectively. –I picked it up from Suzy while you were teaching. And then, as if the word reminds her, but in the same dull tone, –How did it go?

–As these things go, it went. He sits down opposite her, but she's not looking at him. –Birthday cards? Can I have a dekko?

She hesitates, then pushes them towards him without a word.

Happy Birthday, With All Best Wishes, Bon Anniversaire, Many Happy Returns of the Day from Daddy, Trudy, Henri, Suzy, Marie, Mum . . . Then two that are home-made, hand-painted: a black and white dog on a green field with an idiotic kind of grin – *We lov you mumy very much, happy birthday from Sarah*; and a scarlet brontosaurus in a mauve and purple swamp – *happy birtday to the greatest mummy in the world, with love from Tom* . . .

–Oh Christ . . . He lays them down gently. –And in English yet.

–Yes. They tried . . . didn't they?

He looks at her closely – how had he missed the pallor, the swelling under the eyes? –Connie . . . He reaches out for her hand.

But she moves it away and shakes her head. –I don't want to talk about it. She smiles faintly, as if struggling back from far away. –I expect you'd like a drink, wouldn't you?

–No thanks. There's nothing to celebrate.

–No, well. Was it that bad?

–A total disaster.

–Tell me.

–Well, you know how it is sometimes when you start telling a joke and after a bit you realise your audience is not quite with you? You can't stop, you just have to plough on in the face of the blank stares and the fidgets – and in fact you go on much too long to put off getting to the punchline – and your mouth's full of cotton wool and the words have no sense or meaning . . . He laughs. –That's what it was like . . .

–But they must have understood something.

–Nothing, I think. Quite honestly – nothing. I suppose to them poetry slots into some category of useless irrelevance, like algebra. They were there, they'd paid for the lesson, so they were polite, like tourists at an archaeological site, listening obediently to the guide describing the life of the people that used to live there, but completely indifferent. What do they care about those old people? All they see is ruins. The poets are dead. So what? You were right, you see.

–I didn't say it was ruins, Walter – I just didn't like it.

–You *hated* it – that's great. But these poor fish didn't react at all – they were dead too, dead fish.

–Maybe they were a bit scared. You can rather frighten people sometimes.

–I don't frighten you, do I?

–No – but then I know you're an old softie underneath. But I really meant – scared of the language.

–That's what our Tove said: 'All those archaic words that nobody uses, I could have told you it wouldn't work. Far too academic,' he said. *Me* – academic! He laughs loudly.

–You don't seem too upset, she says, blocking the birthday cards into a neat pile. –You seem almost happy about it.

–Maybe I am; relieved, anyway. Maybe the Tove's right.

Maybe it's all too late. If the poem's archaic – if that's all they can see in it – then so am I. So be it. I tell you, I was glad to walk out of that classroom and know I was never going back. What was I ever doing there in the first place?

–But you can't just walk away from something because you don't like it.

–Why not? And it's not simply a question of not liking. It goes much deeper than that. I'm an alien there – and I don't care to be an alien in my own country.

–But you're not in your own country – you're here, in Paris.

–I'm not, you know. I'm not really in France – I never have been. Not like you. I'm not anywhere in particular. The only place I'm really at home is in my language.

–Our language.

–Our language – yes, that too.

–Walter . . . we are going to teach, aren't we?

–I'll be lucky to pass the course.

–You'll pass alright, of course you will. But do you want to teach?

–Well – no, obviously not. Who wants to do something they're lousy at? I'd rather deliver mail, lead a band, sweep the streets –

–Then why don't you?

–Because I'm too old, damnit.

–That's nonsense, that's just an excuse. You're not too old to love, you're not to old to screw, you're not too old to be a father – you're –

–But I can't make a living out of that, can I? Those aren't communicative skills – they're not *marketable*. If only they were! He laughs. –The plain fact of the matter is that I don't know anything worth tuppence.

–Then look at me – I don't know anything at all!

–You're okay – you're adaptable. You've got your feet on the ground. You can absorb new things. I can't. And I can't get rid of the old ones.

–But you will try, won't you?

–There's not much alternative, is there?

–Oh I don't know. She smiles gently. –I can think of one right now.

He looks at her eyes, dark as Guinness, bright as Marmite, and feels a shoot of lust. –Alright – I don't mind – good idea.

–Sometimes you're so bloody English! And she laughs.

Up at dawn, he has already been down to the cellar in his pyjamas to haul the ram up to the apartment with much sweat and groans from the overstrained lift. Then he went down again to buy bread and croissants *au beurre* and *chouquettes* – today is a day of indulgence, nothing spared. Standing in the square, still in slippers and robe, feeding the pigeons broken bits of baguette, he felt a kind of surprise in the greyish light of the early day.

The Egyptian ram waits patiently in the sitting room, his power reserved in animal wisdom. I am the master now, he seems to say. Walter puts out his hand to pat the head, then draws it back – one doesn't pat the head of the master.

In the kitchen he puts the water on for the tea and sets out the croissants and the *chouquettes* and the cherry jam and the willow-pattern plates to pick up the blue of the Braques on the wall. He whistles between his teeth and begins to sing under his breath, –It's a lovely day tomorrow – tomorrow is a lovely day . . .

Then he turns on the radio to catch the news.

–Will there be any English horses running?

–Umm? Oh yes – I expect so, there usually are. Let's take a look. He opens the *Paris-Turf* at the Longchamp page. Eel Bird . . . Annersely – oh no, that's French . . . Broadboy . . . Mummy's Plum . . .

–Mummy's Plum?

They are breakfasting in the sitting room so Connie can keep an eye on her ram; she is soft with delight and ready for the day in her scarlet dress and jet earrings and just a touch of eye shadow.

–That's what it says here. Let's see – four votes to win, five for a place. It looks to have a fair chance – might be worth a bet if . . .

–If what?

–Yes, he says, –yes. He licks a fleck of cherry jam from his knuckle. The child is practising the piano again, and the notes drift sweetly across the garden in the misty morning drizzle. –Sorry?

–What's wrong, Walter – there's something wrong, isn't there?

He folds the newspaper and lets his tight smile die. –It's the students – they're killing them in the streets.

She stares at him, wide-eyed. –The . . . students?

–The Chinese students. In Peking. They've sent in the tanks. I heard it on the Beeb – they're mowing them down like – like blades of grass – crushing them . . . I . . . And all at once he is trembling, his fingers, his lips.

–Oh Walter, how awful. She reaches across and catches his hand.

–It's Charles, you see. He should be in Japan by now – he *ought* to be – or Chile or . . . But he's got this instinct for trouble spots, for turmoil. If he'd have been there, he would have stayed – if . . . It's damn silly really – I'm sure he's alright, but . . .

–Surely they wouldn't hurt him – he's British. Isn't he?

–Among other things – I'm not sure which passport he's travelling on. But guns don't recognise the colour of your passport. It's a massacre and he's a white capitalist running dog – and if he was in the square . . .

–Can't you find out? Who'd know?

–Amy might, but I've called already and she's not there – and I've tried Halston's place, but she's not there either. I'll have to leave it till after the races.

–Walter darling, don't be absurd, we're not going to the races. Not now. We're not going anywhere until we know he's safe.

–I'm not ruining your birthday for –

–Screw my birthday – I've got a million more to come. Look, if she's not in Boston, she probably went away for the weekend. Where would she go? Where do Halston's parents live?

–Connecticut someplace, I believe – and they have an apartment in Manhattan of course.

–And what about that Tucket place?

–Nantucket – yes, that's possible. Well . . .

–Walter . . . you do *want* to know, don't you?

–Of course, it's just that it's early yet – it's only five o'clock in the States. I'd be waking the whole house up.

–What does that matter?

–Well, it doesn't, I suppose. Of course it doesn't.

–Right. I'm going to get out of these clothes then.

As he takes his place at the worktable he notices that it has begun to rain seriously. The drops splash heavily on the window ledge and the pretty piano music has been washed away. The Eiffel Tower is invisible. He feels a heaviness in himself and even after getting the New York City number from international information, he is filled with reluctance. It's not just that he's an old hand at putting off reality, but some half-hidden recollection gives him uneasy pause in the past. He recognises the number as an old Academy number – the Makepeaces live on Riverside Drive . . . Academy 2–8484, the figures float unsummoned from the past . . . Sheila – Sheba – no, Shona. He shakes his head and punches the buttons quickly.

–This is the Makepeace residence. There is no one available at the present. Please leave a message after the. . .

–This is Walter Waller calling from Paris. I'd like to speak to Amy – Amy Waller, my daughter, about her brother Charles . . . or if you know where she is, have her call me . . .

He stumbles on the foolishness of talking to a machine and, hanging up, wipes his damp hand on his trousers.

–Any luck?

He shakes his head. —There's nobody there — or maybe they're asleep or . . . Hello, where are you off to?

Connie has changed into jeans and trainers and an old green anorak. —I'm going to do some shopping. If we're here all day, we'll need food.

—Food — of course, yes.

—And I thought I'd get us a television so —

—No! No, I mean — we've got the radio. We know the lexis — butchery, bloodshed, carnage — we don't have to look at it to realise what it's all about. Do we?

—Well . . . no . . . She touches his head lightly, strokes it for a moment. —Just food then. And cigarettes?

—A couple of packs maybe . . .

—I shan't be long . . . you'll be alright?

—Oh sure . . . I'll try Westport next.

—Westport?

—It just came to me — that's where they live, the Makepeaces — their principal residence . . .

As the front door clicks softly shut, the memory snicks into place. Academy 2 — Moscowitz — that's it — Shona Moscowitz, black and Jewish, the Magon Dovid shiny gold between the black black boobs — Shona in the dark bar on Columbus Avenue with the piano thumping in the dark times of Paula. Shona fervid, merry, eager, who called out in love — 'Macey, Macey!'

In Westport, in Nantucket he leaves precise syllable-stressed messages, mechanically lacquered pleas — call Mr Waller, call her father, Walter, Daddy, for Christ's sake call . . .

—*Macey, my darling!* she shrieked. Macey, her brother, one of the very first grunts killed in Vietnam . . .

The Haydn trio dwindles and dies away in the middle of the melody.

—*Jean-Jacques — qu'est-ce que vous en pensez?*

–*C'est beau. Il faut dire que c'est très beau.*

–*Fernand?*

–*Oui, c'est indiscutablement beau – très très beau, mais –*
mais . . .

–Hell's teeth. Walter switches over to Radio 4 on Long
Wave.

–I really am trying to do my best, Phil, but I do think Ruth
could show a little consideration for –

God, will these bloody people never stop talking? He cuts
off 'The Archers' and looks round for his whisky glass.

–On the chimney, says Connie, calmly sewing shirts on the
sofa.

–*C'est beau, c'est très beau, c'est incroyablement beau, c'est magni-*
fiquement beau . . . I do think she should be more considerate, I
do think one should consider others, I don't think I'm being
unfair, but I really do think . . . babble babble babble . . .

–They're practising their communicative skills, sweetie.

–Communicative piss and wind.

He catches a glimpse of himself drinking in the mirror – an
alcoholic old fool with a frogged throat and eyebrows dis-
arrayed. He grimaces and comes to stand over her. –I didn't
know you could sew.

–I can sew and darn and knit and embroider – and babble.

–All the wifely arts.

She gives him a half-smiling glance. –Arts – because they're
unpaid?

–I suppose so . . . That button you've just sewed on doesn't
match the others.

–Oh shit – oh well, who's going to notice?

–I don't know. I don't know . . . He turns away to the
window and the grizzled day – Atlantic weather, Nantucket-
grey skies, Heine-green seas, birdless beaches, empty
grottoes.

–She'll ring again soon, Walter – she said she would, didn't
she?

–As soon as there's any news, and even if not – tonight.

Amy had finally called at two in the afternoon – awake,

alert, already amazingly on top of the situation. Charles had been in Peking three weeks ago, had phoned her euphorically, the line as clear as crystal. And now . . . Spencer Makepeace had contacts in Washington, with CBS, at the *New York Times*, was touching all bases, pulling all the strings. –Don't worry, Daddy, Charles has got his head together . . .

He rehearses it all again, as he has ten times already and will all afternoon, walking up and down from radio to window to kitchen and back to the radio, sitting for a minute, then up again for a light, for a refill – Connie his silent anchor.

But when the phone rings at last, it's not Amy.

–It's someone for you – a woman.

–Don't worry, she says quickly, taking the phone. I'll make it short. *Allô?* Oh hello, Suzy . . .

He listens, not to the words, but to her perfect neutrality of tone. If the sky fell in, she might say, 'What a nuisance!' And yet . . . her veil of watching calm could come unseamed at any unexpected moment ('Walter, Walter . . . oh, what have I done? . . . Macey, Macey!')

–Alright – well, thanks anyway. She puts the phone down. –Damn. Henri rang her – he wants me to call him. That's all we need.

–What about? Is it serious?

–It's supposed to be serious – those are the ground rules.

–But maybe he just wants to wish you *bon anniversaire*?

–Yes, exactly. A little manoeuvre to get me to talk to the children. She slowly skirts the room, touching the leaves of the plants – most of the flowers have long since fallen away. –Give me a cigarette.

–On the other hand, one of them might be sick. He lights her a cigarette and she stands still by the window smoking it.

–What with? Mumps, German measles, chickenpox? They've had all that – at least, Sarah has. I'm not a doctor, Walter.

–No, but . . .

The unspoken thought hangs in the air like the cigarette smoke between them – Perhaps both our sons are dying.

–I shall have to call, shan't I?

–Yes.

She makes a little helpless gesture, and picks up the telephone.

–He used to go on and on burbling about whatever it was – the banking system or the state of his bowels – and they all just sat there and listened, or pretended to listen. Nobody could get a word in – and if they tried, he'd just raise the noise level and shout them down. She sips her mint tea, the steam of it wetting her face.

–Well, he won't be shouting anyone down any more.

–I don't want to go, Walter. I hate funerals. And I hated Papi. At least, I hated what he did to them – he cowed the lot of them, wife, children, grandchildren, the Spanish cook, the daily woman, even the old gardener. Nobody loved him.

Walter reaches for a cigarette. –How do you know?

–Oh, they'll say they did. I know just what it'll be like – there'll be a sort of ghastly silence with everyone pretending to be sorry. I'd feel so false. I don't think I could bear it.

–You never know, perhaps they'll stop pretending and make merry over the funeral bake-meats.

–No chance – it's bitten too deep for that. Pretence is a way of life. Monique told me once that René had never seen her naked – and they've been married twenty-six years. She got very huffy when I laughed – but I thought she was having me on of course, who wouldn't? I never could get it right with any of them – I believed the lies and laughed at the truth. I couldn't tell which was which.

–Maybe underneath it all he was a noble old fellow.

Her tea drunk, she wipes the moisture from her cheeks.

–You think I should go, don't you?

–How old was he?

–Ninety-one.

–He had guts. Walter lights his cigarette. –When is it exactly – the funeral?

–Tuesday morning. She pours herself some more tea. –If I do go, I shall go on my own.

–Oh God, Walter, I've got it all muddled up – I thought 'temporal' meant to do with time.

–It does – or did. But we don't talk about time any more – we talk about 'aspect'.

–But aspect's something you *see*.

–Not in grammar it ain't. Aspect like an ever-rolling stream bears all its . . . He turns abruptly to the window and flicks his cigarette in a bright arc into the garden below. The evening sky has shaded from blood red to almond pink, but it is still hot and humid from yesterday's rains and breathless. He sighs. –Red sky at night, shepherds' delight.

–Walter, she says gently from the room behind him, –it'll be alright.

–Will it? He turns round, but the light is too indistinct to make out any expression on her face. –It's been thirty-six hours already – and nothing.

–That could be a good sign. She switches on the small lamp on the table next to the sofa.

–Well . . . He yawns hugely; but he isn't tired, although he's not slept at all – and feels he will never sleep again. He's talked five times to Amy and twice to Spencer Makepeace – or rather, listened to reassurances in that opulent Orson Wellesian voice. –Well . . . I suppose we'd better get on with it.

–Sit down then.

–Nope – I can never think properly on my ass. I get like that Civil War general who always dated his dispatches 'from my headquarters in the saddle'. He was a terrible general and –

–You mean because he was sitting down?

–Sure – he had his headquarters where his hindquarters should have been.

Connie's laugh rings clear and healthy on the heavy evening air. And Walter laughs too and feels unaccountably better; and for fully ten minutes, maybe even half an hour, he is sure that everything will be all right.

–You are absurd. It must be my turn to ask the questions by now.

–Absolutely. Here, take my notes. He hands her the sheaf of neatly typed yellow pages and retreats to the mantelpiece.

–Right. How many tenses are there?

–Two. The present simple and the past simple.

–What do they talk about?

–Factuality.

–What's the difference between them?

–The simple past deals with remoteness and the simple present – well, doesn't, I guess.

–What do they offer?

–Offer?

–You've got down here, 'The simple present and the simple past are offering' . . . what?

–Offering? Did I really write that? He moves across the room and lays his hand on the ram's pensive brow. –Well, let's see . . .

–Try thinking with your arse.

–Good idea. He mounts the ram and grips its curly horns.

–Terrific – I've got it now. The simple past and present are offering non-temporal statements.

–There we are again – it's all so much shit!

–That's why it's better done with the ass – or arse.

–I'll never get it right. It doesn't make any sense at all!

–Forget about sense, Connie. Just empty your mind. Think of it as a kind of ritual – What is your name? My name is M or N.

–What's that?

–It's the catechism. Didn't you have to learn the catechism?

–Yes of course. But I didn't understand that either.

The call comes at five o'clock in the morning and Walter leaps out of bed like a galvanised ram. The line is thick with a confusion of foreign voices but one of them seems to be trying to say his name.

–Valaire, he shouts into the crackling phone, –Yes – *oui. Si, si* . . . What the hell is Chinese for 'Yes'? –*Da*, he says in desperation, –*da da*.

–Hi – Walter?

–Charles! Where are you, how are you, are you all right, are you . . .?

–Sure I'm alive! And his son's boisterous laugh comes through hardly distorted by distance. –I just talked with Amy and she said to call you right away. Listen, I'm doing fine. I left Peking ten days ago. Goddamnit – if only I'd known. Right now I'm in Managua and –

–Managua?

–Nicaragua.

–Nicaragua – Christ! What the hell are you . . . The line is cut. Walter puts the phone down and begins to laugh.

–He's all right?

–Yes, he's fine. He turns to Connie, naked and hesitant in the dark room behind him. –He's alive – alive, alive alive oh!

And laughing he takes her in his arms and they twirl round the room at a tremendous pace, through the dining room, into the kitchen.

–What are we doing here?

–We're opening the champagne, he says, pulling the last of Henri's private *cru* from the fridge.

She laughs half-protestingly. –But, Walter, I've got to get up at the crack of dawn to drive up to Normandy to the funeral.

–You'll drive all the better with half a pint of champagne inside you. Get the glasses out, will you, love? Anyway, to hell with funerals.

He strips away the foil and draws the cork with one vigorous twist.

–What are we going to drink to?

–Life, he says, pouring from glass to glass. –Life, liberty, and the pursuit of happiness.

–Happiness! she says, smiling, and, later as he lies with his head in her lap on the sofa, –Walter, you know what – you're not going to sleep are you?

–No, I just shut my eyes to . . .

–To what?

–To listen better. He puts his ear to her stomach. –I can't hear anything.

–Well of course not – not yet. Did you expect to hear him practising his modals?

He smiles and, turning his head, murmurs softly to her belly, –We hold these truths to be self-evident, that all men – and women – are created equal, that they are endowed by their creator with –

–What *are* you doing?

–Teaching Hilary some fundamentals. He opens his eyes. –It's the subliminal method of learning English . . . The Thompson-Waller Approach. Best thing.

She pulls his hair gently and sighs. – I do love you.

–Ummm. Is that what you were going to say?

–When?

–Just now. You said –'Walter, you know what . . .'

–Oh. She blushes. –No. I was going to say about my ram – it's the nicest present I've ever had.

At half-past seven she leaves the house, pale-faced and serious in neat black dress, black pumps, jet earrings.

–You ought to wear a hat.

–I stopped wearing hats the day I left school – and I'm not starting again now.

He kisses her on the landing and closes the lift gate.

–What time will you be back? he asks through the grille.

–I'll get away as soon as I can – it depends on the traffic. But six at the very latest, I should think . . .

She presses the button and the cage jolts and begins its jerky cautious descent into the depths.

–Take care! he calls. As the words echo down the shaft, Monsieur Bailly opens his door, takes one look at Walter, and steps back into his apartment without any sign of recognition. As the door closes on that great white face and the dark corridor behind, Walter thinks suddenly that it's as though the man is mortally afraid. But of what? Certainly not of a dishevelled, elderly fellow in an old tiger bathrobe, coughing on the landing.

Two days of solid smoking have caught up with him; there is a large dead animal in his chest which no amount of coughing will dislodge. He squeezes half a lemon and stirs a dollop of honey into a cup of tea, but resists the impulse to add Scotch. He is already in that state of dreamily euphoric detachment induced by long lack of sleep – if it weren't for the animal under his ribs, he would be completely happy.

At ten-thirty he is still in his bathrobe, pottering – he has cleaned the kitchen windows and the glass on the lithographs and washed the paintwork around the lightswitches and several times made more tea. He is reluctant to get dressed, as though clothing would somehow return him to bachelorhood and deny the nights.

For a while he sits side-saddle on the ram, imagining the black birds of Normandy about the old boy's bier. He is filled with profound reflections. The barking of the dog disturbs him not at all.

He gathers together the classroom notes, both his and Connie's, and divides them into piles for revision on the sofa. He sits down cross-legged on the floor to examine them, but they seem extraordinarily difficult to decipher. He peers intently, leans closer. He rests his head for a moment on the sofa, coughs once, and is immediately dead asleep.

Waking up is like cycling very slowly up a long hill – in his final dozing dream, that is what he is doing; and at the top is a vast bright field of rippling daffodils – the yellow-pad notes lifting with his breath. Cross-legged and crook-backed, he is locked in an old man's parody of foetal peace. He pushes with his arms and rolls over onto his spine and slides sideways, the rigid angle of his neck forcing his cheek against the ancient moquette and a million frantic ants in each leg.

After a while he manages to creep to the bathroom. He sits for a long time in a scalding bath, his ear alert for the sound of Connie's key in the door. He dries himself with care and massages mentholated liniment into neck and shoulders and knees and thighs. Then he shaves and dresses and combs his hair. By the time he is finished, he tells himself, she will be home.

Neat and clean at last and smelling like a bag of old-fashioned humbugs, he pours himself a small Scotch on the rocks. There will of course be long tailbacks of evening traffic on the autoroute du nord – a hundred thousand drivers impatiently picking their noses, and another hundred thousand on the *périphérique* dementedly circuiting the capital trying to get in. He transfers the pile of notes to his worktable and plumps up the cushions on the sofa; then he sits on the rocking chair and rocks gently back and forth in the quietly gathering twilight. Silence counts the seconds. He longs for the dog to bark or the ram to mutter a word to the wise.

Three drinks later, he moves to the sofa, facing the mirror, facing the familiar catastrophe that haunts all those who only love and wait – from the wan mistress under the oak tree to the small girl on the roadside billboards murmuring to the shattered windscreen, '*Papa, je t'aime!*' And out of the old corners of unsummoned memory are dragged the quiet bodies laid out to die on the hard shoulder or the grassy median – the spilled handbag, the shoeless foot, the gloved hand – all that which is crept by in prurient hush. Mother, what is that mess that looks like strawberry jam? Hush, child, that is your father, run over by a tram. And Christopher Robin is saying his prayers . . .

He has no rights. If she were dying, he would have no call to be at the deathbed; if she were dead, no standing at the graveside.

Ravenous, he picks up the phone and orders a Mega Chicago pizza (tomatoes, cheese, origan, pepperoni) and a litre of California red.

At least old Monsieur Mantel, iron to the end, died in his bed, not amidst mangled metal on the ketchup-coloured pavement.

Later (having devoured the pizza, drunk the wine) – thoughts darker than death. The funeral family has turned her head with champagne and feasting, the prancing kids consumed her in greedy infant joy – Henri is nibbling her ear. She is lost . . .

He stretches out full length on the sofa.

And gone forever . . .

–Tea – wonderful . . .

–And aspirin. She stacks the pillows behind his head. I expect you need aspirin, don't you, my sweet?

–I should think. Walter sits up with a struggle that sends the brain spinning inside the skull. –Ugh!

–Here then. Connie sits beside him on the bed and feeds him sips.

–Mmm. He takes the mug in both hands and gulps down the sweet strong tea. –You look very cheerful.

–That's not surprising, is it?

–Isn't it? He blinks at her sitting here bright as the morning star, open as a bride. –Oh . . .

–You don't remember, do you?

–Well, not exactly . . .

–It seems rather a pity if you don't. She grins and pats his cheek. –I should think Hilary did a lot of subliminal learning last night.

–Ah . . . He laughs and makes a futile effort to disentangle his legs from the duvet. –Well . . . How was the funeral? When did you get back? Why didn't you phone me?

–I did phone you, cloth-head – about a million times – but you'd left the receiver off the hook . . . I suppose you've forgotten that too?

–I do sort of vaguely remember calling the pizza place. I guess I . . . God, Connie, I feel awful . . . Where are those aspirin? I think I . . . Can you untangle me from this bloody thing?

–Poof! There we are! She reaches under him and whips off the duvet. –Oh look – isn't he sweet? She tweaks his shrivelled cock. –Like a rosebud in a bush.

–Connie, don't, I think I'm –

–Look – he's flowering!

–I'm going to throw up.

–That can wait, she says, bending down to him with the feline grace of a cat to the cat-nip.

–It wasn't a bit like I'd thought – more like what you said it would be. They all wore hats – I got that part right – but the people under them were utterly different. They were solemn enough at the church of course, but when we got back to the house they were, I don't know – like children let out of school. They babbled – how they babbled! It was like a hundred years of talk all gushing out in five minutes. They laughed – they actually laughed, it was amazing. They were nice to everyone, even to poor Zabie – that's the Spanish cook they're all so foul to usually. Do you want another beer?

–Is there one?

–There's plenty – I thought you might need it after last night. Stay still – I'll get it.

–And were they nice to you?

–That was the oddest part, she says, handing him the bottle of Martin's pale ale. –They were specially charming to me. They really talked to me – and they listened and seemed interested. I told them all about teffle and . . . well, I wasn't the *quantité négligeable* sitting in the corner any more. I was suddenly a person . . .

–Did they know about the separation?

–Oh yes – anyway I wasn't going to make any bones about it. But I expect that's what made the difference – I wasn't going to be around any longer, so they could afford to be gracious – no skin off their noses.

–Could be. Walter gently pours the beer into the glass. –But they might have been envious too – because you've done what they've always secretly wanted to do, but never had the guts.

–Well perhaps – I don't know. But I'm glad Henri didn't bring the children, they might have got quite the wrong idea – they'd have thought death was some kind of celebration. I mean, the whole family was so jolly.

–Not really surprising – they'd just come in to the old man's money.

–Yes, I thought of that too. But they've all *got* plenty of money – so it can't be going to make all that difference. And they weren't gloating – they were just, well, happy. It was a wonderful summer party. Nobody wanted to leave. In fact, Monique and René decided to stay overnight – that's why I gave Henri a lift back; he'd come with them, you see.

–What time did you finally get away?

–Not till about half-past six in the end. I know I should have rung you then, darling, but I didn't want to phone from the house with all their ears flapping and –

–It's alright, Connie, I understand – I'm not blaming you.

–I know you're not – you never do. I never feel guilty with you, that's what's so . . . She turns her head away for a moment and takes a deep breath. –Anyway, I thought if we just pushed on – but the traffic just got worse and worse – so finally I pulled off and drove into a little town and found a restaurant and rang and rang, getting more and more panicked – but of course I bloody well wasn't going to show Henri that, so I had to keep smiling while all the time I knew you would be worrying and . . .

–Panicked is the word. I saw you lying lifeless on the autoroute and –

–Oh Walter – don't!

He kneels down beside her chair and they touch and hold.

–I thought you could have fallen asleep with a cigarette and the whole place was on fire and . .

They kiss each other's ears, each other's lips, eyes.

–and you'd be burning – burning . . .

–But all I was doing was eating pizza.

–Yes. Oh my love, my love. She clutches him, weeping, smiling. –And I was pecking at a mushroom omelette.

–He's going to *America*?

–I know. I can hardly believe it either – he's always been such an old stick-in-the-mud. But the bank offered him this marvellous job looking after their venture-capital business on the West Coast – and he says it's the sort of offer you can't refuse.

–How long for?

–Two years to start with, then if it's a success, well – indefinitely, I suppose. He's been to-ing and fro-ing to San Francisco for weeks, apparently – making contacts and setting things up. It really does sound good – they've given him a car and a rent-free house for the first year and all sorts of perks and a lot more money of course.

–And when does all this happen?

–He's off at the end of the month. So you see it was important that we talked. Not that there's all that much to arrange – he seems to be amazingly well organised. The only thing he hasn't done is the children's passports and visas, but I'll take care of that – they'll have to have separate British passports now.

–The children are going too?

–Yes of course – and Marie as well, at least for the first year – to look after them and run the house and well – you know – the whole business.

It seems to Walter that her face blanches a little, but her voice doesn't falter. He reaches out and takes her hand, fighting the sudden elation running strong in his blood. –Then you won't be going to Normandy for the vacation?

–Well of course not – I'll go with them to San Francisco.

–But . . . His heart sinks.

–It doesn't make any difference to my promise, does it – where we go, I mean? And it makes sense – I'll be able to settle them in; there's bound to be a lot to do – organising schools for them and their clothes. The house is furnished, but I expect it'll need a bit of fixing up. It should be fun.

–Fun . . .

She pats his hand. –Well, shouldn't it? America's your dreamland, isn't it? And you've always said San Francisco is the most beautiful city.

–Have I? And – and what about Henri?

–What about him? Oh I see . . . She laughs. –Don't worry, Henri won't be there – not in the house. He'll have a hotel room – that's all arranged. Of course he can visit, but he won't move in till I've gone.

–Oh, well . . .

–You're blushing, my love. I'm not an utter fool, you know.

–I know that – far from it. I'm the fool.

–Yes, but only sometimes, and that's alright – it gives me the chance to be sensible.

–Umm . . . 'Mechanical' . . . 'Meaningful' and – I know – 'Manipulative'!

–Nice try, but no cigar. There are five qualities of inter-active oral-grammar exercises, not three – and anyway you got two of them wrong.

–Are you sure? Who says there are five?

–W. Rivers.

–I don't remember any Rivers – who's he?

–Ole Man Rivers – very celebrated communicative chappie – he must say sumpin', he don't know nuttin', he just keeps –

–Oh Walter, do be serious – I must try and get this right. Tell me.

–Okay – here goes. 'Communicative' . . . 'Meaningful' . . . 'Limited Choice' . . . 'Expressive' . . . 'Integrated'.

Connie looks at him with the still, baffled stare of early teffledom – can this be real? She sighs. –How far have we got – are we half way through yet?

–Just about. What shall we do – celebrate with a glass of orange juice?

–Yes, I'd love a glass of orange juice – and it'll be good for Hilary. I suppose you want something stronger.

–No no!

–Don't sound so shocked. There's whisky in the cupboard.

–That's for emergencies. I only drink alone. He stands up and stretches. –Maybe milk would be better?

–Alright – milk then. Perhaps it'll sharpen my wits.

As he leaves the room, Walter touches the head of the ram; it's become a habit for both of them, a little light caress – touching for luck. And they are going to need all their Plumpton luck to pass the exam in five days' time. Five days to Bloom's day. And then two weeks, a fortnight, fourteen days till she flies away – and sixty-three days to the *rentrée*. Nine weeks without the option – Independence Day, Bastille Day, Labor Day . . .

–Oh thanks. She looks up from the notes and takes the glass. –I think I'm beginning to get it now.

–Connie, he says, placing his milk on the lighter patch on the mantelpiece where the china cat once sat, –I wonder if it was such a good idea to tell Henri you were pregnant.

–Why ever not? It's going to be obvious before very long – Monique spotted it right away at the funeral.

–I don't know. It's just that I'm kind of – uneasy. I mean, nothing's really settled yet, is it?

–Between Henri and me, you mean? But there's nothing *to* settle – we both know exactly where we are. And if there is anything to sort out – well, we're communicating now – for the first time for years – so there shouldn't be any problem. Really.

–Maybe, but in my experience with separation and divorce and –

–Oh *your* experience! But that's not a very good model, is it? Your wives were just out for what they could get and –

–Not Maddy. But the point is –

–the point is, my sweet, that I'm *not* trying to get anything. I don't want anything. I wouldn't take anything if it were offered on a silver platter. I don't *need* anything.

Walter drinks half the glass of milk. –All the same, I'd feel happier if you knew something about your rights. You could pop in and see your Maître Bizien, couldn't you?

–Walter, I'm not claiming any rights. I don't *have* any rights. How could I? Besides, Maître Bizien doesn't know anything about divorce. And anyway, Henri's going to take care of all the legal side of things.

–Oh is he? Walter finishes the milk and burps gently. –That's very trusting of you.

–I am trusting, yes. She considers it for a moment, then nods. –I do trust Henri on this – after all, he's got absolutely nothing to lose. I admit he's sometimes been a bit devious in the past – about money and investments . . . and the marriage contract, of course. But that's all finished. There's no reason to play games any more – it's all out in the open now. Do you understand?

–Well . . .

She gets up and comes over to him and lays her hands on his shoulders. –What is it?

–I'm not sure . . . nothing, I suppose . . . I don't know.

She smooths his forehead with her thumb. –Why shouldn't I be trusting? I'm free and independent now. You've no idea how wonderful it is not to have to hide anything any more . . . Your lips are all milky, did you know?

He moves to brush his mouth, but she catches his hand and turning it, kisses the palm, kisses his lips with little licks.

–In September, she murmurs into his ear, –I'm going to start paying my share of the rent.

–Rushing about getting everything together, then an hour and a half in the queue – for nothing! Why didn't they tell me in the first place the photos had to be signed on the back?

–They *are* bureaucrats, you know.

–But they're British!

–Well, they're only observing the local norms of bloody-mindedness – highly diplomatic.

–I nearly told them to stuff it, but I'm feeling too good-natured to shout at the moment. And I got all smartened up to impress them – I might just as well have dressed as a tramp.

–You impress me . . . And she does – all milky white and summer and bare arms and great shining eyes.

–When I said, 'But I've known them all their lives not just two years', they said, 'Oh but that doesn't count, you're the mother'!

–Look, I'll sign the photos. I'm British.

–But you're never even seen my children.

–The bureaucrats can't know that.

–Oh . . . Then she laughs. –Alright – why not? Oh but you're not a magistrate or a solicitor or a schoolteacher.

–You never can tell – all things are possible. Come on, hand them over.

–Well – okay . . . there. Marie had them done at the photo-maton, but all the same they're rather sweet, aren't they?

–Yes, he says, –yes, and takes up his pen to write lies on the back of them.

–Walter . . .

–What?

–I think you'll be a wonderful teacher.

–We must get up, sweetie.

–Why? You don't have to go anywhere, do you?

–No, but tomorrow's The Day – in case you'd forgotten.

–Worried?

–I should be, shouldn't I? she says in a surprised voice. –But I'm not – not at all.

So they linger late into the amorous morning, making soft love, chuckling dove-like, reaping their happiness. They doze and wake again to stroking and murmuring. There is an amplitude about her body now, a rounder confidence of breast and belly, laughter more deep and lasting.

–And you are definitely thinner, my love – look at that, hardly any flab at all! I can't think how you've done it.

–Teffle-training. You don't just lose your mind, you lose weight as well. Highly recommended.

–Cutting down on the alcohol more likely . . . Walter . . . this summer, when I'm not here, you will be sensible, won't you – about drinking, I mean?

–I'll try . . . He smiles as though smiles might stay her flight. –But I can't promise.

–I'm not asking for promises, just common sense.

–That's not exactly my strong suit, you know.

–I know. You wretch. And now we really are going to get up. She leans into him. –But first I'm going to tickle you.

–I'm not sitting near you, Connie had said as they came in, –the sight of you scribbling away would put me right off.

The examination room is windowless – airtight and silent. No smoking, no talking. Not much scribbling either – not for Walter. Something seems to have gone wrong with his hand, his wrist has stiffened, and the ancient fountain pen stains his fingers with much ink but makes only spider traces on the page.

Across from him Kathy is filling sheet after sheet with lovely Irish fluency.

In what way are the following words connected: unknown, careful, helpless, disabled, economical? Walter stares dully at his jottings: *A careful government, in preferring the Unknown Soldier to the helpless hero, is guided by the economical consideration – better dead than disabled.*

This won't do. He is losing his way in the maze of communicative English – but surely at the centre of it there is an open sunlit space sportive with nymphs and sylphs. He sighs (sighing is permitted) and looks surreptitiously round at the others – Kathy is still racing away, Connie is sucking the tip of her pen, Phyllis is crying . . . crying? No doubt about it. Somehow the sight of this perfect student in tears rouses Walter from the sweet lethargy of negative panic. He blows his nose, bends his mind, and reads another question: *Give six different ways of apologising* . . .

He flexes his fingers: *Miss Otis regrets she's unable to lunch today . . . I'm sorry, she's washing my hair . . . You'll never believe me . . . I'm such a fool about love . . . I didn't mean to do it, You made me do it . . . Can you ever forgive me?*

Outside the washroom he stops for a moment to light a cigarette. The foyer is empty, all the birds have flown – except for Linda, last out, coming down the stairs alone.

–Hello.

–Oh hi. Linda in a dark green Paisley pattern, hunched shoulders, holding back – never one of the crowd. –Hey, can I have one of those?

–Sure. What did you think of the exam? he says, lighting her cigarette.

–Thanks. Yeah, well . . . the same old crap. There is a rash of freckles across her sharp pale face like a bitter curse. –I've failed this course anyhow. I haven't learned one lousy thing about teaching I didn't know better already. How about you?

–Well no – but then I didn't know anything about teaching in the first place. Maybe it was a mistake to take it too seriously.

–You don't take a thousand dollars seriously?

–Oh yes I do – I take a thousand dollars with the utmost seriousness.

He smiles, but Linda does not smile back – she smokes with

angry puffs as though she had it in for the cigarette. –And what for? A bunch of creepy teachers putting you down the whole time – who needs it? Boy, they really hate Americans, don't they?

–Well, I shouldn't take it personally, it's a kind of cultural tic. The English are never really happy without someone to patronise. But they'll all be talking American in the end.

She looks at him. –Yeah . . . Anyway, I guess *you* found what you were looking for okay. And then she does smile.

Walter laughs and touches her arm. –Are you coming to the Chinese restaurant with us?

–With who?

–The whole class – we're having a kind of farewell lunch.

–Nobody asked me.

–Well I'm asking you now.

–Thanks, but no thanks. She shakes her head. –I'm going downstairs for a cup of coffee.

He watches her, a thin wan figure crossing the marble foyer, and then he goes down the front steps to fall in with the rout of ladies on the street.

–We're thirteen at table, have you noticed?

–Well who cares? says Harriet, demurely commonsensical. –We're not superstitious, are we?

–Oh I am – at least for me. Phyllis, dry-eyed now, long-necked with an awkward ugly elegance as though at any moment – pfff! – she will turn into a swan. I'm sure I've failed – I thought it was terrible.

–Not you, Phyllis – you're the star of the show, you know you are.

Phyllis shakes her head in inconsolable modesty.

–If anyone's going to fail, it will be Linda.

–Poor Linda, she didn't seem to understand anything.

–Well it was hard for her – being American.

–You think she was *incapable* of understanding?

–She didn't even try, Harriet says decisively. –She just sat there, sneering.

–Perhaps she should have gone back to America. Walter drinks some *sake* and winks at Connie. They smile in secret complicity, remembering their lunch here after their first trip to England so many joys ago. She is as shining and merry, but quieter now; and Walter has an odd pang of nostalgia for the early anguish of the plastic café – not far away, just down the road. As the *dim sum* arrives in round wooden boxes, he has an urge to call out, 'How lovely you are!'

And they are all lovely! Rid of teffle at last, they have momentarily put off the frowns of family life, and their hearts shine with decent glee – even Fred is benign with smiles (how could he ever have been jealous of Fred?). Lovely, loving, lovable, beloved . . . *agape* at the Pékin de St Dominique . . .

Walter fills his cup with *sake* and eats a steamed parcel of shrimp and listens to their talk of vacations.

–Well, as I say to him, we're not going down to Aurillac, are we, my darling? So we'll be off home where the children can be happy with the horses . . . All fine bone and Irish pride, Kathy rules the table as she must rule her spouse. –Oh he doesn't like it, that's sure, but I tell him if we can't go to Ireland, I shan't stay in Paris. It's the same argument every year, but they all give up in the end when you dig your heels in – and I can be stubborn as a mule.

Walter says, –As a bull, surely, not a mule?

–Oh, and why a bull?

–Because you're a Taurus, aren't you – when were you born?

–May the tenth. And what does that mean?

–It accounts for the stubbornness. All Taureans can be mulish when they want to – not to say bloody-minded.

–And that's true – you've said a mouthful there, Walter. She gives him an entrancing grin. –And I thought it was just the Irish in me.

Walter smiles and empties his cup. Perhaps, he thinks, Ireland is the real answer to everything.

And Janet says, —But goodness — astrology, that's all nonsense, isn't it?

—Not *all* nonsense. It can be a useful guide to, not character exactly — to temperament. Sometimes it sticks out a mile.

—What am I then?

He looks at her, gentle-voiced, but dark-browed, fierce and mysterious. —That's easy, he hazards, —you're Scorpio.

—You're right . . . Janet blushes as though caught out in some foolish teffle error. —But how —

—And me — what am I? Harriet, who surely never blushes, has had her hair cut in a short cap that makes her seem even more round-faced and self-possessed than usual.

—You? Let's see — I'd say you're probably Cancer.

—You must have been looking at our files!

—Harriet, if I could have got past those dragons at the gate, I'd have gone after the examination papers, not your files.

—Well, how can you possibly have guessed?

—It's just a party trick, you know.

—What does it mean to be Cancer then?

—Sensitive, tender, imaginative, sensual, dreamy, artistic . . . those are the good things.

—And the bad?

—Secretive, proud, assertive . . .

Phyllis says. —And what are you, Walter?

—Me? Oh I'm Cancer too.

And everybody bursts out laughing.

—Goodbye Phyllis . . . Goodbye Harriet . . . 'bye Kathy . . . 'bye Janet . . . 'bye Fred . . . goodbye . . . good luck . . . have a good summer . . . goodbye goodbye . . . see you . . . *ciao* . . .

Waving, they shake off the last of them and turn down the boulevard.

Connie takes his arm. —I wonder if we shall see any of them again.

–I doubt it. It's like those shipboard romances in a storm – once you set foot on shore, all promises are off.

–You first fell in love with me on a ship.

–No, it was before that. Besides, cross-Channel ferries don't count.

–Why not?

–Because you're never out of sight of land for one thing, and for another –

–We were. Don't you remember that lovely milky mist? We couldn't see a thing.

–We could see each other.

And they smile as they stroll down the boulevard in the balmy afternoon, sedate as any married couple. In the garden of the Rodin Museum a few children are cautiously at play, and through the railings comes the musty summer smell of box.

–Oh Walter, do look – they've taken the plaster cast off the dome.

–Christ! Walter stops dead and stares at the glittering Baroque horror. –What have they done?

–It *is* a bit shiny.

–A bit! They've turned it into a great gold bottom. What's it supposed to represent – the Emperor's haemorrhoids? Homage to Benny Hill? Oh Lord . . . and all those lovely twilight mauves and greys . . .

–Perhaps they're planning to sell it to Disneyland.

–Paris already *is* Disneyland – or damn nearly. Just look at it – no, don't look at it. I can't bear it.

–We'll cross over, then we shan't see it.

–I'm shutting my eyes. Lead me, Connie – I'm blind.

–Alright. She laughs and slips an arm round his waist. –Step down – now. That's it. Steady, we're nearly – shit! The bastard!

–What happened?

–A sod in a Jag trying to run us down. Step up coming – now. Left a bit – straight. One more. Hold on, stop. Got to wait for the lights.

−Whatever you say . . . He smiles, happy in the orange world behind his eyelids, the sun warming his cheek, the guiding hand at his hip, a flash of Vivaldi from a passing car, the smell of hot pavement . . . −Connie, let's get out of this. Let's go to the country for a few days.

−Step down. Oh I couldn't do that. Quickly now.

−Why not? It's all over and done with and −

−Step coming . . . up−now! There we are. Sweetie, I've got a million things to do in the next ten days, I'll be running around like a mad dog.

−*Ten* days? Walter opens his eyes and immediately trips over the iron grille round a plane tree and falls to his knees with a cracking jar. −Hell.

−Are you alright? Walter?

−Eh? He stays on all fours for a moment, dazed, foolish; then she puts her hands under his armpits and he struggles to his feet. −Connie −

−Are you hurt?

−No no, it's nothing. Connie, what's this about ten days? I thought you only left on the fourth?

−We do but . . . oh look at your hands! Give me your hanky.

−But what? I don't understand.

−Well, school breaks up the week before, you see. She spits on the linen and wipes away the little prickles of blood on his grazed palms. −And I have to be there for that.

−Why do you have to be there?

−Because that's when the vacation begins. And Sarah's ballet class is giving a performance of something or other and Tom has a part in a −

−Can't Henri attend to all that?

−Darling, he'll have flown on ahead by that time.

−Oh.

−There . . . She tucks the handkerchief back in his trouser pocket and gives him a quick little smile.

−Why didn't you tell me all this before?

−Because I . . . because I didn't want to think about it.

–And what else haven't you told me? What are all these millions of things you have to do in the next ten days?

–There's the passports for one thing and –

–I thought that was all taken care of.

–I applied for them, but I haven't got them yet. And there's the American visas – and the airline tickets to pick up. And the appointment with my gynaecologist and –

–The gynaecologist? Why – there's nothing wrong, is there?

–Of course there's nothing wrong, it's just something one does when one's pregnant, surely you remember that? And I really must buy some clothes. And I should get my teeth looked at, it's been ages since I –

–But your teeth are fine – shining white and razor sharp.

–Oh Walter, please . . . Her smile fails and her chin trembles. –Please don't be difficult.

He draws her close and holds her. –I'm sorry, love – it's just that –I . . .

–I know. Don't you think I don't know . . . ? Her body is smitten with small shudders and her cheek is moist against his. –I don't want to go – I don't I don't.

–Hush, my love my honey-dove . . . it will be alright. Her hair smells of spring, of cherry blossom.

–I'm going to be so lonely again . . .

–You'll have Hilary to keep you company – wherever you are, you'll have her growing in health and strength every day.

She draws her head back to look at him, her dark eyes glistening with tears. –We'll be happy, won't we?

–Yes – we'll be happy. He smiles and, turning her gently, points to the preposterously gilded dome – Christmas bauble, tinsel toy. –And when you get back, we'll buy that for Hilary to play with in her crib.

–Cot.

–Cot . . .

–*His* cot.

221

–Don't you want to know where I'm off to this morning?

Walter smiles at her across the table. The day is already hot enough to have brought prickles of sweat to his upper lip, yet Connie is as fresh and innocent as the morning dew.

–Let's see . . . You're going to school.

–To *school*? She stands up to clear away her cup and plate, brisk and efficient in her new white blouse and black skirt.

–All you need is a hat and a satchel and you'd be the perfect schoolgirl.

–When I was a schoolgirl I had long hair in a pigtail.

–You did? How long?

–Long long long – when it was brushed out, I could sit on it.

Walter stands and catches her as she comes round the end of the kitchen counter. –Down as far as this? He slides his hands under her buttocks and, with a little grunt, lifts her bodily.

–Walter . . . She clutches him with her raised legs, the skirt hitching back above her thighs, and holds him hard as they kiss quickly, slowly. Then, –No, sweetie, no. I have to run.

–Why? Where?

–The gynaecologist – I've got a rendezvous in half an hour . . . oh shit, twenty minutes now. Put me down.

–Put him off – go late. Doctors always keep you hanging around.

–I daren't risk it – I'd never get another appointment in time. She wriggles free of him. –Besides, I couldn't go to Dr Fabian full of sperm.

–I expect he knows the facts of life.

–I expect so too, darling. She picks up her bag, smooths her skirt, runs her fingers through her springing hair. –But it might give him ideas. He thinks pregnant women are terribly sexy – that's what he's in it for. He'd probably try to seduce me.

–Seduce you? Connie, I –

–I'm only teasing, sweetie. Now, how do I look?

–Highly respectable.

–No seriously?

–Beautiful.

–Am I really?

–Yes you are – you're quite lovely.

–Quite?

–Absolutely beautiful.

She's shy. –I like that. I like you to say that.

–I'll come down with you, he says impulsively, –see you to the car.

He's not averse to leaving the house. Now that his phone number is out in the world, he's faintly uneasy in the apartment alone. He has a dread of answering and hearing childish voices on the line; although this, she assures him, will not happen. –They know the rules, darling. Besides, it wouldn't be the end of the world, would it? (But people do break rules, and sometimes it is the end of the world.)

Yet, once she has driven off, he is not entirely at ease outside either, despite the brilliance of the day. In the square two workmen are stripping down the caryatids on the Wallace fountain preparatory to repainting. Even here the municipal administration is relentlessly winning the battle for beautification. Reminded that he needs filler for the hole the burglars had drilled in the door, he walks up a diagonal street to the hardware store. But it is no longer there – the wave of the wicked fairy's wand has replaced it with a fashionably flashy grocers *de luxe*.

–*Mais oui, c'est beaucoup changé*, says Madame Mouchet, suddenly at his side.

–You are reading my thoughts, Madame. Where do we buy our nails now?

–People no longer have need of nails – these days everything is stuck together with money.

–But who on earth would buy any of that muck? He waves a hand at the window full of tinsel and publicity – chocolates and *foie gras* and plastic patisseries and plump bottles of mauve and rose and golden liquid like cheap toilet water or last night's piss.

–The world is full of fools, Monsieur, she says with a brusque nod of her tight dyed curls, –even in the *quinzième*.

The energy of her disapproval sweeps him up and carries him along at her side, brisk with acerbic chatter, until they come to a standing halt in the foyer as the descending lift creaks gently down. After a long moment, the gates open and Monsieur Laigle shuffles out, clutching his ancient dog in his arms.

–*Bonjour, Monsieur*, says Madame Mouchet, sharpish.

The old man looks vaguely round but makes no reply. He moves slowly across the hall, as though the dog were an immense weight. His normally pallid face is bright red and he mutters as he goes.

–He doesn't look well, Walter says.

–Have you ever known Monsieur Laigle to look well?

–No – but that colour. He must have a fever – or have caught the sun badly.

–The sun that is found at the bottom of a bottle.

–Surely not – not Monsieur Laigle.

–Why not? All men of a certain age need consolation. Is that not so, Monsieur?

He looks at her, then laughs – and is answered by a quick cackle.

–Don't you feel a sort of gap without teffle?

–Christ no – do you?

–Yes I do in a way – it's funny, as though something was missing. Of course, I'm filling in the time with all this running about. It's much worse for you, poor love – with nothing to do at all.

–Oh I wouldn't say that – I'm quite good at doing nothing.

Connie thoughtfully rinses her breasts with the sponge. Outside, it's in the nineties, but the bathroom is pleasantly cool and perfumed with passion-fruit bath oil. Walter sits on the toilet seat, his sleeves rolled up from washing her back, and tries to imagine her adolescent and languorous with long black hair.

–But seriously, I can't wait to get my teeth into teaching.

Walter smiles. Her teeth gleam from the dentist's polishing – teeth, hair, and womb in prime condition, and half a closet full of new clothes to put on her back. All dressed up and nowhere to go. But of course she *has* somewhere to go. As he fishes a cigarette from his shirt pocket and lights it with the bathroom matches, his fingers tremble.

–You're not listening, are you?

–Yes I am – I just didn't hear what you said.

–I'm going to teach you how to use the word processor.

Walter slips the dead match back into the box. –Is that my summer assignment?

–It won't take you all summer, lovey. It's easy, really, it is.

–That's what you said about the exam, remember?

–Well, it *was* easy . . . comparatively speaking.

–What were the ladies on about then? They moaned all through lunch.

–No they didn't – not really. They just didn't want to boast about being clever . . . Connie unhooks the shower head and turns on the tap. –Anyway, that's beside the point – it's got nothing to do with the word processor.

–Hasn't it – are you sure? Don't you remember Adam's ecstasies about the computer as a tool for teaching? He practically had an orgasm.

–I don't believe Toves have orgasms. She douses her head with cold water and rubs it vigorously. –But why shouldn't he be right?

–Because computers don't have orgasms either.

–Ooof – that's better! She turns off the shower and shakes her head like a damp dog, spraying Walter with droplets.

–Watch it – you almost put my cigarette out.

–You shouldn't be smoking.

–I found them in the kitchen drawer.

–A likely story . . . She slides down into the tub. –I don't really see what you've got against word processors.

–I just instinctively distrust them. Processing is what goes on in food factories or what happens to people at government offices – they get *processed* and come out the other end as statistics with identity cards or identical little squares of cheese made out of petroleum products. It's like joining the army or being sent to prison – you're processed then, put into uniform, *made* uniform . . . the idea being to make you shut up and do what you're told – to forget who you are or what you were or where you came from. The less human you are, the easier you are to manipulate – it's called 'man management' . . . and that seems to me what the word processor is all about – ease of handling, regardless. Word management.

–What's wrong with that? What's wrong with making things easier?

–Things . . . well, I've nothing against making *things* easier – washing machines, dishwashers, vacuum cleaners – terrific! But words aren't things any more than people are – the easier they are to handle, the more lifeless they become. In the end you wind up with a corpse or a dead language . . . He taps a long ash into the washbasin. –It's a question of love, really . . .

–Of *love*? Connie sits up in the bath. –How do you mean?

–Well, I don't know exactly . . . The smoke catches his throat and he coughs. –I think I mean that writing should be like – like making love – maybe teaching too and –

–But, Walter, that's easy!

–No it isn't – it's not easy at all. Screwing – fucking – is easy – but that's just because it's a process, a fucking function, like communicating or, what's it called? – discourse-chaining . . . I mean, teffle is a fucking-up of the English language, but –

–Walter . . .

–Hold on! He coughs again, hawks, spits into the basin, is wracked with more gasping coughs. –Jesus . . .

226

Connie puts her hand on his knee. —Walter, darling . . .

He turns to her, struggling to draw a clear breath, blink away the water flowing from his eyes – but he can't speak.

—It's all right, my sweetheart – it really is. It's only for a few weeks – they'll be gone in a flash. And she smiles with the tenderness of all madonnas.

—Yes – yes . . . He hiccoughs. —I think I'm going to throw up.

The midday swimmers are less fanatic than the early morning risers and don't ignore the right of way of others with such arrogant brutality. *Stenos* and *dactylos* maintaining their figures and a few recent mothers recapturing theirs smoothly compile length after length before going off to gobble yoghurt in the gardens or sip unsweetened coffee in the café.

After half a mile of crablike breaststroke, Walter feels virtuous and purified – and hungry. He has a brief altercation with the cashier who refuses him change for the hairdryer on the grounds that she is out of one-franc pieces.

—But there is a whole roll of them lying there.

—*Oui – mais pas pour vous.*

—Who are you saving them for then – the President of the Republic?

And he laughs. Of course she is saving her francs for nothing – she is simply guarding the State against unruly elements (to wit, an alien in a tracksuit and tousled hair). '*Pas pour vous – pas vous*' . . . from a thousand French throats daily fall the disdainful syllables like a national hymn. '*Liberté, égalité, fraternité – mais pas pour vous – pas vous – pas vous*' . . . not for you, not you, not you . . . tra-la-la, tra-la, tra-la . . .

On his way he buys a bottle of Chinon, a baguette and half a Reblochon, and jogs home happily. Connie is lunching with her friend Suzy, and on swimming days he allows himself half a bottle of wine.

He is too hungry to do more than towel his hair into a flying mane before he sets the table, tosses the salad, unwraps the cheese and slices the bread. It's as he's in the act of pouring the wine that the bell rings. He pauses. The meter reader? Monsieur Bailly seeking refuge from his termagant spouse? Monsieur Laigle after a firearm – or a bottle – to cure his misery? Madame Mouchet with a lecture on discipline?

He goes barefoot to the door and bends to the peephole, but sees nothing but a slice of white shirt and blue lapel. Policeman – bailiff– a telegram? He hesitates, but then when the bell rings again, opens the door.

–*Oui?* He says, but knows at once who this is – elegantly suited now, but no mistaking that pointed nose and sour mouth.

–Mistair Vallair?

–Yes?

–Mantel.

–Well, you'd better come in. And Walter steps back quickly to avoid the danger of a handshake.

But Henri isn't offering a hand – a cup of poison more likely, or a quick kick in the balls. His gleaming black shoes are slightly pointed as though for the deed, and Walter is uncomfortably conscious of his own unshod feet. At least they are clean – he represses the urge to explain that it is not they, but the cheese that is responsible for the ripe odour.

–I am afraid I am interromping your lunch.

–Interrupting.

–Interrupting? Thank you. I try to improve my English.

–Come for a spot of teffling, have you?

–I do not understand.

–Have a glass of wine?

–Thank you, no. But do not let me prevent you from eating.

–Don't worry, that can wait. We'll go in the other room.

Walter takes his glass with him and, on second thoughts, the bottle as well. He waves Henri to the sofa and seats himself on the rocking chair. Neither of them speaks.

228

Silence, he remembers, is part of the game (for he has done all this before, with Maddy's first husband, Larry or Harry – no, Barry).

He sips his wine and rocks gently. Henri sits still, just moving his head slightly from side to side, taking it all in like a large snake, with the occasional flick of a greyish tongue between the tight lips.

–I 'ave 'eard about you.

–I've heard about you too.

–Of course. I am a monster – no?

–Are you a monster?

–I am a banker.

–That rather begs the question.

Henri frowns. –I am not a beggar. He pauses to lick his lips. –Tell me, this apartment – it is yours?

–I don't own it, if that's what you mean.

–I do mean. And do you 'ave a work – a job?

Functions of the Interview – apologising and explaining. –No, he says and drains his glass. –I don't have a job. I haven't had a job for years.

–You have a heritage perhaps?

–I did have an inheritance, but there's not much of it left now.

–Then 'ow do you live?

–I do a bit of this and a bit of that. I get by. In two years I can collect my social security.

–I understand.

Walter laughs and refills his glass. –Do you?

–Why do you laugh?

–You sound remarkably like a prospective father-in-law – *un beau-père prospectif.*

–Perhaps . . . He shrugs – a tiny movement, but the first hint that he's alive. He sighs. –Poor Connie . . . Yes, you are right.

–Right about what?

–It is true that she needs a father – she is so much like a child. Do you not think so?

229

–Except you become as little children, you shall not enter into the kingdom of heaven.

–I do not –

–You do not understand. Yes, I know.

Walter tilts the rocker too quickly and wine slops over his hand and onto the tracksuit.

–Mistair Vallair, perhaps it is you who does not very well understand the nature of my wife. Connie 'as always been –

–I am not prepared to discuss Connie with you.

–Very well – as you wish. Henri looks down at his hands flat on his knees; they are long and pale and, except that they're hairless, not unlike Walter's own. –All the same, perhaps I can ask what you intend? He looks up abruptly.

Walter sucks the wine from the soft skin between thumb and forefinger. –It's Connie's intentions that concern you, not mine. And for that, you must ask her.

Henri nods. He surveys the room once more. Although it is kept clean and well polished, in the summer light it shows shabby; not only the china cat was destroyed in the robbery, but something of its coziness was stolen away too.

Outside, the dog barks. Walter stiffens momentarily – but it is much too early to be Connie. His stomach rumbles.

Henri is gazing at the ram.

–It's an Egyptian ram – *un bélier*.

Henri nods again, as though adding one more charge to the indictment, and looks directly at Walter. –We 'ave two children.

–Yes.

–Children 'ave need of a mother.

They stare silently at each other. Walter won't easily forget this face – the hooded stillness, the sleepy superiority, the native discontent that turns the mouth down in a grim reptilian curve: '*pas vous*', it says.

–You 'ave nothing to say?

Walter puts down his glass of wine. –You've made your point.

–Good. Very well.

They rise at the same moment.

At the door, Henri says, –'ave you thought of the name of the baby who comes?

–The name? Yes, if you must know. We thought of Hilary.

–No, I mean – 'ow do you say? – the name of the family?

–The surname – the last name, where you're going. No . . . I think we'll leave that to take care of itself.

–But, Mistair Vallair, such things do not take care of themselves. . . . He smiles with nice white teeth. –Goodbye . . .

–Is it a nice place?

–Ummm? He looks up from the menu. Where?

–Berkeley.

–Not 'bark' – 'berk'. It's not full of dogs – or nightingales, come to that. *Berk*eley.

–Full of berks?

Walter makes an effort and smiles. –I was only ever there for a couple of days – signing up a psychoanalyst to do a book on astrology. I didn't see much apart from around the campus.

–The house is at somewhere called Eden Grove – do you think that's a street or a district?

–Sounds like a cemetery to me.

–I thought it seemed rather poetic – it has eucalyptus trees in the garden.

–I'm sorry – I'm not being good company, am I?

–Just a bit contrary, but that's alright, sweetie. And she touches his hand with the tips of her fingers.

Contrary . . . yes. She had suggested a stroll in the Champ de Mars and dinner outside at the *brasserie* on the corner, but instead he'd dragged her up to Montparnasse and the Dôme and a quiet table at the back with bright lights and red plush and white napery, where it might be any season of the year. He wanted somewhere they hadn't been before, without memories or hauntings, somewhere anonymously cozy so that one could imagine winter outside and walking forth afterwards into a healing cold air.

–You'll like it, I'm sure you will.

–You say that, but why? Just because it's America?

–There's always that, of course. He laughs. –People smile at you. They say: 'Hi there . . . how you doing? . . . how are you? . . . good to see you . . . glad to know you . . . what can I do for you today? . . . sure, no problem . . . coming right along . . . come right on over . . .' There's an ease and openness that makes life smoother, simpler – bland and superficial it may be, okay, but I'll take blandness any day over the endless petty sadisms of this tightassed city. They say it's all changed now, but I don't believe it – nothing's going to destroy their natural courtesy.

–Like Linda, you mean?

Walter laughs. –Linda's been here too long. Besides, she's not from the West Coast.

–What difference does that make?

–A helluva lot. The West Coast is a different country – it's where you go to escape the East Coast hassles or the dreariness of small-town America. California is as far as you can get – the next stop after that is a high jump from the Golden Gate bridge. It's the American Dream pushed to its furthest limit, which is only a half step away from an American Tragedy. So there's a kind of nuttiness to it . . . but also a freedom, a peacefulness, a sort of anonymous calm. And Northern California is beautiful . . . an hour's drive from where you'll be you get into a vast untouched country with a strange, lonely beauty to it . . . Maybe we should think about ordering?

–If it's such a paradise, don't you want to go and live there?

He hesitates, looks down at the menu. —Jesus, what prices! He feels a small *frisson*, a goose running lightly over his grave. –I seem to be talking myself into it, don't I? But it's most likely all in my head; besides, I'm too old for paradise . . . What do you fancy?

–Oysters – the Belons, and then the *pot-au-feu de poisson*.

–Great idea – and a Sancerre.

–Well . . . alright – but you'll have to drink most of it.

They have dressed up for the evening in a summery way – Walter in his ice-cream suit and Connie in a sleeveless dress of natural linen, only a little too tight about the middle. She looks ravishing; more than that – smooth and blooming, bright of eye, light of touch, graceful as gulls.

–You make it sound like a cure for everything – America.

–Not old age – not poverty.

–I suppose not. But you were young and rich . . . She smiles.

–Not rich, no. I was doing okay, but I wasn't rich . . . might have been one day; if we'd gotten big enough and I'd agreed to sell out – we'd be sitting in La Tour d'Argent. But I wasn't in it for the money – at least, I didn't think I was. . .

–Do you remember that old ad for Pelmanism – 'Have You Got a Grasshopper Mind?' Well, that's what you need in publishing – or did in the old days, of course it's all ruined now . . . publishing, I mean. Luckily for me I had one – a grasshopper mind – still have actually . . . a nice superficial intelligence, a shortish span of concentration, a certain amount of native taste . . . that's about it. You have to stay ordinary of course, because the market is made up of ordinary people – it's up to the authors to be extraordinary; but most of the time that's fun, even when they're extraordinarily awful. Walter pulls the bottle out of the ice bucket and fills their glasses. –The publisher is the straight man, you see.

–Your astrology man at Berkeley – was he awful?

–Not a man – a woman. Hattie Plaice Birnbaum . . . He holds the bottle up to the light, then pushes it neck down into the ice. –That's dead. She was awful physically; about the fattest woman I've ever clapped eyes on – four foot nine, over two hundred pounds – a kind of dwarf swaddled in flesh. Our offices were in a brownstone on West 12th Street – God, that house is worth millions today – and Hattie simply couldn't manage the steps. So whenever she came to New York we used to meet in the Penguin and she'd easily put down half a dozen Manhattans before lunch – and three or four Brandy Alexanders afterward. But it didn't affect her at all – she stayed sharp as a needle. She told me once she'd never had a hangover in her life. In those days it was kind of oddball to be an analyst and an astrologer – commonplace now, I guess. She was definitely out of the ordinary – a remarkable woman.

–Was it her that taught you about the signs? It must have been.

–Yes, that's right. He laughs and drinks some wine. –We'd sit there on the barstools facing into the entrance – it was an extraordinary sight to see Hattie on a barstool – and when anyone came in, she'd say, 'Okay, what's he – or she?' Of course, I hadn't a clue, but Hattie never had a moment's doubt – and later, after the guy had settled in, she'd say, 'Go check'. It always struck me as a curious thing that nobody minded being asked, mostly they got a kick out of it . . . and we got quite a few free drinks that way. And she was always right, you know – always.

–Well, so were you.

–I was just lucky – and I knew when to stop.

–Would you have guessed me? I mean, when you didn't know me. Right at the beginning. At the mingle.

–Maybe not. Gemini's an air sign, that's always hard to pin down.

–Air? Oh . . . And what are you?

–Cancer's a water sign.

–Water? Oh sweetie, that doesn't seem very appropriate! She laughs, richly, deeply, almost to tears. –Oh – oh dear – perhaps we should have some more wine.

He grins. –I've got a better idea – let's have Brandy Alexanders.

–Tea? No I don't want tea. I'd like – whisky. Have we got any whisky?

–Yes, but I'm not sure that's such a good idea after the brandy.

–Good for who? You mean Hilary, don't you? Oh he won't mind just this once . . . She slews her chair round and pats her stomach. –There – he doesn't mind.

–Right on. The Famous Grouse coming up.

–And a cigarette – there must be some cigarettes in that magic drawer of yours.

–There you go . . . He tosses a half-full pack of Gauloises and the kitchen matches onto the blue table.

–Thanks. Famous Grouse – what a ridiculous name. Why not the Famous Toad?

Smiling, he pours the Scotch. –The Miraculous Mouse?

–The Rampant Ram.

–The Fucking Frog.

–The Damned Dog.

–The Snake in the Grass.

–You don't like him much, do you?

–Not much. Do you want some ice? I haven't put any ice in this.

–Yes, give me some ice. Why?

–I don't like what he's like. *Un glaçon – ou deux?*

–Oh stop being so fucking French – fill it up. Alright, so you don't like him – you wouldn't, would you? *I* don't like him. And I particularly don't like him sneaking up here to see you. But that's the way he's always done things. All the same, I understand why he came – it's rather sweet in a way. He just wanted to look you over and make sure you weren't – well, you know . . .

–An adventurer – after your money – *his* money.

–Not money – property. *His* property. As long as we're married, I'm his property – that's the way he thinks. Like a banker with an investment, it's his duty to protect it – however rotten the investment might be. But once he's – what do you do with an investment when you want to get rid of it?

–You liquidate it.

–Shit, I don't like the sound of that.

–Dispose of it, then.

–That's not much better. She drinks quickly, the ice

235

clinking against her teeth and a trickle of Scotch running down her chin. −Anyway, he's just being careful − what do you call it? − prudent. Doing his duty − he's a great one for doing his duty, too scared to do anything else. As soon as it's all over − the divorce, I mean, and everything − he'll have done it, his duty, and he'll be able to wash his hands of me . . . I need an ashtray.

Walter brings over the china ashtray stamped *Jules Verne, Tour Eiffel* − one of the few the burglars missed (maybe they recognised it as already stolen property) − and sits down at the blue table.

−There may be a bit more to it than that.

−Oh yes − he was curious, wanted to see what you were like. And you must have been a sight . . . She laughs, pleased.

−I wasn't at my most impressive, certainly. But that's not what I was getting at.

−What then? You don't trust him?

−I've known men − husbands − in that situation before.

−And?

−They can turn vindictive.

−Not Henri. Walter, he doesn't *want* me. Hasn't really wanted me for ages − not since Sarah was born . . .

−I'll take your word for it. All the same . . . when someone else suddenly wants what you don't, it all at once gets a kind of enhanced value − and you begin to want it again.

She shakes her head. −I know what you mean. It's happened to me − of course it has. You can spend months dropping hints, pushing someone away, even telling him to go − but then when he does go, you wonder whether you've done the right thing. And I've had it done to me too . . .

−Cyril?

−Yes. And Goran.

−Goran? You never mentioned him.

−Oh well, he wasn't very interesting − he was just a crazy Swede. But Henri isn't like that. He *really* doesn't want me − he doesn't want anybody. A quick poke with *une pute* perhaps, but that'd be about it. You know what he said to me coming back from the funeral? He said, 'I should have been *un vieux garçon!*' And he meant it, you know – a poor bloody old childless bachelor. There's nothing but ice in this glass.

–Right. Walter stands up – his head swims for a second, then steadies.

–I think that's rather sad. Don't you think that's rather sad?

It's not a question that requires an answer. He empties another icetray into a bowl and brings bowl and bottle back to the table.

–Henri speaks English rather well – I was surprised.

–Does he? How typical. Ten years of marriage without the slightest effort, couldn't even ask the time of day – 'eeze a vairy nize die' – and wouldn't have begun to understand the answer, and then when it's all over, off he rushes to English classes!

–But this is business – English for Special Purposes.

–And isn't love a special purpose? She crushes her cigarette with rapid jabs, obliterating the *Tour Eiffel* in the ashtray, and the tears roll down her cheeks. –Oh shit. I'm crying – how stupid . . .

–Walter, wake up.

–Eh?

–Come on – wake up. She's gently shaking his shoulder.

He opens his eyes; across the quilt there is a long white patch of summer moonlight. –What is it? Not burglars again?

–I want to ask you something. Are you awake?

–Is that what you woke me up to ask me?

–I've been thinking. I think I should be psychoanalysed. Don't you?

–Not right now.

–I'm serious.

He comes fully awake. –Alright. Why now particularly?

–Because I want to know the truth.

–Well, yes, but . . .

–I want to be completely and absolutely honest.

–That's rather a tall order.

–I know. That's why I'll need help. Don't you think I can manage it?

–Hell, Connie, it could take years.

–I realise that – I'm not completely brainless.

–No one said you were, but –

–Henri thinks I am – the nuns thought I was.

–That's because husbands and nuns don't want brains – they want obedience.

–I couldn't have managed the course if I'd been brainless, could I?

–I'm not so sure about that one – you'd have probably done even better. But –

–Another but?

–It'll be expensive.

–Then we'll have to eat noodles.

–Connie, are you asleep?

–No. I'm thinking.

–What about this crazy Swede?

–Goran? She laughs. –Are you trying to analyse me?

–I just wanted to know. I can't sleep either.

–Well, he was every woman's dream Swede – you know, big and blond and strong with faraway grey eyes, and incredibly fit. He was some sort of international swimmer, or had been. I went and stayed with him in Sweden – he had a little flat in a place called Malmö. It was summer and there was a heatwave, which was a big surprise to me. For the first week it was wonderful, and then he started ringing up his girlfriends as though it was a perfectly normal thing to do – and going *out* with them. And when I protested he just looked at me with those grey eyes, right through me, as if he were seeing some marvellous vision in the distance and I was just getting in the way, blocking the view. And then it began to get cold and I was getting fed up and finally I said, 'Right, I'm off!' 'Okay,'

he said. He was always saying 'okay' – 'Let's go to bed . . .'
'*Okay.*' 'Let's not go to bed . . .' '*Okay.*' Anyway, so I went
back to England, feeling pretty pissed off, and immediately he
started writing to me – almost every day and very often in
Swedish. And when that didn't work, he began ringing me up
– I must come back, I had to come back, how could I leave
him? He wanted me – needed me – was desperate without me
. . . all that.

It's dark now in the bedroom – the moon has moved round
or gone out. And quiet – no baby, no dog, no siren.

–I can understand that. He must have been crazy – to let you
go, I mean.

–I wasn't like I am now, you know. I wanted love so much
and I searched for it and ran after it – and then when I got it, I
didn't want it any more. I think I thought that anyone who
loved me – well, there must be something wrong with them.

–I wouldn't want to belong to any club that would take me
as a member.

–Exactly – that's exactly what I felt, I'm sure – deep down. I
couldn't let myself be loved. They were stupid to love me
because I was unlovable – or lovable for the wrong reasons.
There was something wrong with *me* – not them. But I didn't
see it like that – I didn't work it out that way. I thought, well –
it must be Englishmen . . . Walter, I'd like a cigarette – do you
mind – in bed?

–Of course not. Hold tight – I'll get you one.

In the kitchen he drinks a glass of water, fills the glass again
and brings it back with a lit cigarette and sits on the bed. He
says, –So it had to be foreigners?

–Yes. It's strange. They weren't nearly as good.

–As lovers?

–As anything – not just the sex. But they were . . . mysterious . . . I think that was it.

In the quick glow of the cigarette her eyes are as black and
unfathomable as holes in a ballroom mask.

–Mysterious . . . in what way?

–Well, it's the great romantic thing about foreigners, isn't

239

it? You think somehow they must have the secret, they must know the answer. So you learn their language – though they don't learn yours, they keep writing to you in Swedish or speaking in French – and you immerse yourself . . . but in the end you're lonely. Which only serves you right because that's what you really wanted in the first place – although you didn't know it. What you deserved. Anything else was always impossible, so you come to terms with it finally and wind up as . . .

–As the dummy auxiliary.

She laughs softly. –Until a Walter comes along. What shall I do with the cigarette?

–Here . . . He guides her hand and the cigarette end hisses in the water glass.

They hold hands. Then she says, –Goran committed suicide. I heard about it six months later quite accidentally from a friend. He swam out to sea and never came back . . .

He slides in beside her, then over her, covering her body, close, entwined.

There is a gentle pre-dawn light in the room when she wakes him next.

–Walter, did you ever make love to your fat Hattie?

–Er? Yeah – once – I did.

–Did you really? How was it?

–Well, I tell you, it wasn't easy . . .

And he sleeps again to the sound of laughter.

–Shall I bring us some croissants on the way back from the pool?

–Alright – lovely . . .

–*Beurre* or *ordinaire*?

–Umm – *ordinaire*, I suppose.

—One or two?

—God – one.

—Or would you prefer a *pain au chocolat*?

—Oh Walter!

—Right – you go back to sleep.

Connie shuts her eyes, then opens them for an instant.
—Why aren't you wearing your tracksuit?

—I spilled wine all over it when Henri was here. You
wouldn't like a cup of tea before I go?

—No! Oh God – go, go, go . . .

Carrying his swimsuit and towel in a plastic bag, he quietly
shuts the front door and presses the button for the lift. From
the Bailly apartment across the landing the children's early
morning clamour sounds less shrill, softer somehow since
Monsieur Bailly moved out.

In the street, Walter turns left, away from the pool, and
hurries towards the bus stop.

He is early enough to have a quick café-cognac at the plastic
café and a few minutes' incomprehensible conversation with
the *patron*. He buys a pack of Gauloises and walks slowly to
Connie's square, favouring his right knee, which has begun to
ache again (it would not have been a good day for a swim). In
the gardens he leans against a tree with a clear view of the
house and lights a cigarette with the casual care of someone
who has all the time in the world.

He is nearly at the end of his second cigarette when they
come out, all four together – the two children, one fair, one
dark, laden with satchels. Henri kisses the boy and releases
him to the buxom young woman – of course, the indispen-
sable Marie. Walter moves a little further behind the tree, but
Henri is not sensitive to others' stares; he takes his daughter's
hand and they walk off together – Sarah, light-haired, light-
skinned with an almost American smoothness, is as solemn as
her father. They don't speak or smile.

241

Walter turns out of the gardens and, keeping his distance, follows Marie and Tom. The boy is bright-eyed and full of chatter and pulls at her hand with eager dancing steps so that she laughs out loud. Soon, other children with mothers or *au pairs* merge into a small convoy of maternality.

Walter, singular male presence among them, remembers his own children. '*Tu sais, Papa*, today we're going to . . .' Amy confiding in the odd family muddle of French and English. And Charles, even at four a doubter. 'But why? How do you know? Why? How can you be sure?' And Walter, impatient at last, 'Because . . . *parce que . . . je suis le grand maître!*' And Charles, cocking his head, 'Oh sure – *le grand maître de rien de tout!*' And laughing – laughing.

At the school, delivered of infants, the flock of summery mothers dissolves and separates and off they fly to swimming pools, shopping, aerobics, lovers . . . Walter, limping away from the fashionable precincts, soon loses them, hastens home to Connie, forgetting the croissants, home to Hilary.

–A *birthday* present – not to be opened before the day. Promise?

–Promise . . . He smiles, tentatively holding the white package tied with scarlet ribbon as though judging the weight of a cake at a vicarage fête. But it's not nearly as heavy as a cake. –Thank you, my darling.

–I don't suppose you'll be able to resist opening it as soon as my back's turned, will you? She laughs from her sidesaddle perch on the ram. –But that's alright, I forgive you in advance.

She is wearing one of her white striped shirts and a new pale blue skirt – with adjustable waist, to accommodate the growing child. Yet today she looks too elfin to conceivably be a mother. As Walter puts the package in the place of honour on the mantelpiece, he sees his face in the mirror swollen with unspilled tears.

He goes to her and kneels down, quick with the pain in his

knees, and puts his arms round her and his head on her breast.
–I love you – God, how I love you . . .

After a while she raises his chin to look at him. –Why, Walter, why do you love me? I've never really understood.

–Because you gleam . . .

–Like the dome of the Invalides, you mean?

–Like a precious jewel in a silver sea.

–Oh Walter . . . She slides down from the ram and, kneeling, they hold fast together for a long time, until gradually their quiescent flesh quickens with little kisses, touches, murmurs.

–What shall we do? I feel energetic – let's go for a walk.

–Well . . . we could . . . it's a nice day . . .

But he has no desire at all to walk about Paris in the beautiful afternoon where everything touches on nostalgia. He hasn't the heart for it on this their last day. Maybe a brisk trot in some faceless suburb . . . but, better still, to lie close and guard her in the bed forever. –Haven't you still got things to do?

–Nope – the slate is clean, I'm free as a bird.

–What about packing?

–I'm all packed.

–Oh . . . He looks round the bedroom.

–I put the cases under the bed. She laughs. –Listen, if you don't fancy a walk, we could go for a drive.

–Where to?

–Compiègne?

–No! I mean – let's go somewhere we haven't been before, like . . . Chartres.

–Okay, fine – Chartres it is. Come on then, wake up, sleeping beauty. She leans over and kisses him on the mouth, then slips out of bed. –Let's get dressed. And, Walter . . .

–What?

–Bring your driving licence, she calls from the bathroom.

–What's the point of that?

—Because you're going to drive, my sweet – I got you put on the insurance cover so you'll have wheels for the summer. She pokes her head round the bathroom door. –But just remember it's not the Roller and this isn't England.

—Are you sure you're alright? Maybe we walked too much.

—I'm okay. It's just the heat . . .

They are sitting at a small café close to the river from which only the tops of the cathedral towers are visible. Even in the shade of the umbrella, the heat is intense and the single pathetic ice cube in Connie's Perrier has instantly melted. Her eyes are closed and her head is resting against the back of the wicker chair and there's a glisten of sweat along her upper lip.

Walter sips his drink distastefully. –I'd forgotten just how filthy Dubonnet could be.

—Why did you order it then?

—Because I remember drinking it the first time I ever came here and thinking how delicious it was – before you were born.

—I can't really believe you were alive and grown up before I was even born. What was it like then?

—Miserable.

She opens her eyes and smiles. –I mean Chartres . . .

—Shabby. All France was . . . shabby, stripped. There was no one in the cathedral then – no Japs, no Krauts, no coaches, no cameras . . . just the odd verger and the workmen re-assembling the rose windows – the stained glass had been in storage for the duration, you see, and it took them a while to get around to putting it back.

—It must have been a bit bleak without all that marvellous colour.

—Bleak? Maybe, but I don't recall thinking that. Una-dorned, yes. The plain glass let the sunlight in . . . it was silent, of course . . . you could still believe it was a serious place . . . He picks up his Dubonnet, sniffs it and puts it down.

−In a strange way it reminded me of the old Meeting House in Mount Kisco . . .

−What was that like?

−Ummm? Oh – quiet, you know . . . sitting still. I can't stand this awful muck – let's have a real drink. Do you want a cognac? I'm going to have a cognac.

−Not for me. Someone has to drive us home. But don't let that stop you.

All the same, it is he who drives them back, whistling softly in the light traffic and the late sunshine.

−You like it, don't you?

−The car? I admit, she's a handy little thing.

−And you will use it, won't you? If you're here . . .

−I'll be here. I'm not going anywhere. He begins to whistle again.

−What's that you're whistling?

−I miss my Swiss, my Swiss miss misses me . . . ta-da, ta-da, ta-da-da-da-da-da-da . . . What the thunder said.

She puts her hand on his knee. −Walter – why shouldn't you go and see Amy and Charles? Don't you want to?

−I'd like to see them alright but . . . oh I don't know – they've got their own lives to lead.

−But you wouldn't be intruding on their lives.

−It's not that exactly. I wouldn't be an intrusion, no. But I'd be peripheral, part of the furniture – the old guy with an old fashioned, rocking on the porch in the twilight . . . Hello – a Long Vehicle. Give him a wave, he's a Brit.

−But they want to see you.

−They know where to find me, Connie. What's he look like?

−Who?

−The truck driver.

−*He* is a *she* – and *it* is a *lorry*. Aren't you being a bit . . . hard?

–I don't think so. What I represent in their lives is the past
. . . and however fond you are of it, you don't want the past
hanging round your neck day in, day out.

–God no!

–Well then . . . He raises his voice. –In Dublin's fair city,
where maids are so pretty, there was . . . As they plunge into
the tunnel, he suddenly sees the ghost of Paula sashaying out
of the sea mist, and he puts his foot down hard.

–Hey! You're supposed to slow down, not speed up.

–Sorry – wasn't thinking. She's got gumption, hasn't she –
your old rattle-trap? Light me a cigarette, honey?

He feels her hand like a small bird in his shirt pocket, hears
the scrape of the match.

–Walter . . . She gives him the cigarette. –It was . . . I mean
I . . . oh – nothing.

–Look, he says as they come out of the tunnel into the
startling sunlight, all Paris spread before them. –Isn't it wonderful? I always love this moment. Journey's end – home,
safe-keeping.

–Yes, she says. –Walter?

–What?

–I think you're wonderful . . .

They park the car in a sidestreet, and Connie gives it a quick
farewell pat as they walk away, hand in hand. There is an
unusual amount of hooting and honking and they can see two
or three people standing on the chairs outside the Floréal and
staring.

–What's all the fuss about, I wonder.

–Perhaps it's a brass band, Connie says hopefully.

–I don't hear any music, he says as they turn into the square.
–Oh Jesus . . .

Parked higgledy-piggledy in front of the house there's an
ambulance, two fire trucks and a police van, and a small crowd
at the door.

–A fire . . . oh God. Walter halts abruptly, a cold clutch at his heart; and for a long moment the whole scene is held motionless – a mouth open, a hand raised, a pigeon pinned in flight. –Too much, he murmurs, –too much . . .

–It's alright, he hears her say, –it's alright, darling, it's not a fire – there are no hoses out . . . it must be some kind of an accident.

As she takes his arm and threads her way through the voyeurs – *Pardon, Excusez-moi, Pardon Madame* – the ambulance moves slowly off with a muted moan.

In the flowered courtyard there's a group of policemen and firemen in gleaming brass helmets and with axes at their hips. A policeman steps forward.

–Do you live here, Monsieur?

Walter nods. –Waller – fifth floor left. What's going on?

The policeman looks at his notebook. –Vallaire – *bien*. You are acquainted with Monsieur Laigle, Edmond?

–Yes of course. What has happened? Is he dead?

–Yes, Monsieur, he is dead. I will accompany you to your apartment, if you have no objection. There are one or two questions . . .

They cross the hall where Madame Fontaine and Madame Mouchet are gossiping. As they enter the lift, Madame Fontaine raises her painted eyebrows. –*Oh, là-là!* And as the three of them ride up in silence, other words float round the stairwell. –Scandalous. . . inevitable. . . unhealthy. . . disgraceful . . .

When they get out, Walter notices Madame Bailly's door is open a crack. From the floor above comes the heavy tread of official feet, and a fireman descends the narrow stairs, carrying in his arms Monsieur Laigle's ancient grey dog. It has a white plastic label tied to a hind leg.

Walter bursts out absurdly, –The dog too?

–The dog too, agrees the fireman. And they stand staring at the dead animal.

Walter says, –I never heard him bark.

Fireman and policeman nod gravely. Silence – an excellent thing in dogs.

247

—May I have Mr Fox, please?

—Yes – there you are.

—And Master Fox?

—No, I'm sorry . . . Walter wipes the back of his neck with his handkerchief. Although the sun has gone down, it is still oppressively hot.

—Your turn, sweetie.

—Oh. Er, can I have Miss Shrew?

—You asked for her last time – the answer's still no. She smiles at him across the table, and he wonders how she manages to look so cool and serene. – Come on then – take a card.

—A card . . .

—Walter . . . it's not your fault, you know.

—I know – not directly. But I should have put two and two together when I saw him in the hall last week. I've seen that cherry-red look before – carbon-monoxide poisoning – it's obvious when you know.

—May I have Mr Badger? When did you see it before?

—Mr Badger – no, too early for badgers. Just after I moved out from Leonore – there was a little old lady lived above me. She was a drunk and I used to hear her falling about – then one day she fell down the stairs. She was just a tiny creature, but God what a noise she made falling! And she had that look.

—What do you want?

—Er – how about Mr Shrew?

—Sorry, not today. You're not having much luck are you? Did she die?

—No, they caught her in time – before she went into a coma. But it was the same thing – a defective gas water-heater. One of those bloody stupid accidents . . .

—Maybe with Monsieur Laigle – maybe it wasn't an accident. The *flic* didn't seem too sure. And you said, if he wanted to die anyway . . .

—He wanted to die alright – but not like that, not hole-in-corner till the smell annoyed the neighbours and firemen came and smashed down the door with axes and then bundled him off down the lift in a black plastic sack . . .

–Well – how then?

–He might have shot himself – if he'd had a gun. Got up one morning, shaved, dressed, breakfasted, unlocked the door, shot the dog, shot himself – bang bang! That's how he'd have liked it.

–Mrs Owl, please. Aren't you being a bit – melodramatic?

–Mrs Owl, yes. No, not at all.

–How can you be so certain then? Mr Owl?

–Because he told me. He wasn't very talkative – but he told me that. Yes, here you go – Mr Owl.

–Thank you. And Miss Owl by any chance?

–And Miss Owl, you wretch – you've stolen my owls.

–Isn't she beautiful? Family!

–No honestly, I'd prefer to take a taxi.

–Well, if you're sure – but it seems so ridiculous with the car just up the road . . .

–The car's for you now. And by the way, I've put the keys and the papers on the mantelpiece. You'll take care of it, won't you?

–I'll guard it with my life.

–I'm not asking for that – just don't dent it, if possible.

Walter cuts a small square of smoked salmon and puts it in his mouth, where it immediately turns to leather and has to be washed down with wine.

It's a cool, dismal day – the kind of day in which everything is hard to swallow.

–You won't just let it sit there, will you?

–No. I promise. Have a drop more Montagny?

–Perhaps I'd better. She holds out her glass. –Walter, I . . . that's enough.

–Yes?

–I don't want to think of you being here by yourself just – well, you know what I mean . . .

–Moping . . . all alone by the telephone?

–Something like that.

–There wouldn't be much point, would there, as we've agreed not to call each other? But I just thought – about writing, I mean – shouldn't I send you your teffle results? They'll be up on the board next week.

–That's all taken care of – they're posting it to me in Berkeley. Walter, please – you do understand, don't you? I can't do it any other way.

–Yes – yes, I think I do. And even if I don't, I accept your word for it. You just have to forget me for a couple of months.

–Oh you don't understand at all – I won't forget you for a minute of the day! But I've got to get on with it, haven't I? I can't live for phone calls and letters – how could I make any ordinary peace with the days? If I'd known – if only I'd known – I'd never have promised away the whole summer like this – but I did, I have . . .

–And you'll do it, my darling.

–I shall do it – I will do it! Goddamn these modals! She breaks out half-laughing, -crying. –I *will* be happy – I will, I shall, I must, I can!

–Of course you can – and should.

–You'll try too, won't you? You'll go to concerts and to the races and to see your friends and –

–Don't worry, I shan't die of inanition.

–I know you won't really . . . And you'll look into the job market, won't you?

–A bit premature, isn't it?

–Not at all – they'll be looking for teachers for the new school year right now. Do try, sweetie – don't leave it till the last moment before I'm back.

–Alright – I'll compile a dossier for you.

–For *us*.

–Yes of course, for us – the Thompson-Waller Language School.

–Do you think I'll come back with an American accent?

–I don't care if you come back speaking Konkomba.

She looks down into her glass, pushes it away and stands up.

–It's time, Walter.

–It's not half-past yet.

–I want to get organised before I pick Tom up. Call me a taxi, will you? I'll just go and clean my teeth – I don't want them smelling wine on my breath.

–Connie . . . He catches her hand. –These next few days – can't we phone each other – while you're still here?

She looks at him, then shakes her head. –No, Walter – no.

–Right. I'll get the bags then.

–Taxi first? she says as she turns away.

–Yes of course.

As he goes over to the phone, he almost calls out to her, – Have a last look round to see you've left nothing behind: keys, purse, perfume, comb, me . . . But he keeps quiet, and when she returns, she has even remembered her toothbrush. –Well? she says, slipping it into her handbag.

–Eight minutes – in front of the door.

–I should go then.

–No hurry. They always say eight minutes – it could just as well be twenty-eight.

–Yes, but all the same . . . Come down with me?

–You don't think I'd let you lug it all down by yourself, do you? He lifts the anonymous grey suitcases with a grunt. –How are you going to manage the other end?

–Marie will give me a hand if I need it. She slings her bag over her shoulder, pauses for a moment to give the ram's head a quick caress. Then, –Okay. Ready?

–Ready.

The lift is there waiting. The foyer and the courtyard are empty, no neighbours to impede her departure. It's the still moment of the afternoon – even the dog is quiet.

They stand awkwardly in the street, grey and quiet too.

–It looks like rain, he says.

–Yes. She is white-faced, alert, impassible, in her jeans and striped shirt exactly as she had been the first time he saw her.

–I haven't bought you anything for the trip.

–There's nothing I need – I've got everything.

–I suppose you have, yes . . . But he is overwhelmed with a sense of terrible neglect; he should have something to give her – a bottle of perfume, a chocolate bar, a packet of pins, a flower.

–Where is this taxi?

–It'll come. Connie . . .

–Yes? she says, but the look in her eye is – No, don't say you love me, don't tell me I'm beautiful, don't . . . don't . . .

–I was thinking – I'll have a go at the word processor.

–You will? A flash of a smile. –But be careful – don't wipe out its memory.

–Has it got anything to remember?

–Of course – it's full of teffle.

–Bully for it. He laughs. –Here comes the cab.

–At last.

As the driver stows the luggage, they kiss – quick French pecks, then suddenly cling. –Oh God! She pushes away, steps into the taxi.

–Connie – I'll meet you at the airport.

–Yes.

–September the fourth?

–Yes.

–You'll call me if there's any change?

–Yes. Goodbye.

–Goodbye, my . . . But the cab accelerates fast to catch the green light, and Connie and the words are whisked away in the vortex, –. . . love.

He takes his walking stick in case of treachery from his knees and walks briskly up to Montparnasse to have a haircut.

Elodie, vivacious and bandbox pretty, has no need of instructions; she's been cutting his hair for a decade and used to cut Charles's too. She asks after him, as she always does, a little wistfully.

–Everything's fine, he says, –*tout va bien, Madame la Mar-
quise, tout va très bien* . . . But all is not well with Elodie – she
has moved to a smaller apartment, is divorcing and has no
plans for the summer. Walter remembers when she was in
love, engaged, married . . . even now she seems hardly more
than twenty-one. –You get over it, he tells her. –I've been
divorced three times.

–*Oh, là-là*, she says, with charming smile.

He buys *The Times* and reads it, eating shish-kebabs at a
new Japanese restaurant down the street. He goes to the
movies at the Rotonde and sits through the programme twice
and comes out into the mauve twilight and walks home
gently, stopping here and there for a Gerwürtztraminer and an
occasional hard-boiled egg. In the distance the Eiffel Tower,
glimpsed from street end to street end, is as brittle gold as the
tinsel hair on a Christmas tree. In the apartment he stares at the
visible tip of it for a long time, drinking cognac out of a
tumbler, trying to recollect even a single moment of the film.
All he remembers is that somewhere along the line of the day,
he has lost his walking stick.

–Our Sunday Service today comes from the church of St
Michael and All Angels, Little Beddlington in . . .

Ten-thirty – fifty hours exactly to Connie's flight-time.

The housekeeper is standing in her usual pose on the top
step of the pavilion, cigarette in the corner of her mouth, eyes
wrinkled against the smoke – but today she is wearing a dress,
a curious long-sleeved garment of dried blood-coloured linen,
but definitely a dress.

–Now thank we all our God, sings the radio, –with heart
and hands and voices . . .

The dog is seated at her feet, his head cocked a little to the
side, attending to the hymn maybe. As Walter looks down,
the housekeeper raises her head and their eyes meet, and both
give a small nod.

–. . . Who from our mother's arms hath blessed us on our way with countless gifts of love, and still is ours today . . .

Walter steps back and switches off the radio. He goes over to the fireplace and picks up his birthday present. The card is in a small envelope under the ribbon; he slips it out and opens it: *For Walter, who loves me, with love from his love, C.* He glances at the mirror, as though expecting to find her reflected sitting on the sofa.

–I can't wait now, can I, my darling?

He slides the red ribbon off, undoes the box, and folds back the tissue wrapping like the wings of a dove. Of course – a china cat! He lifts it out tenderly – a placid, dozing white cat, the exact duplicate of its shattered brother. How brilliant of Connie to have found one from the same mould; he turns it over – yes, *Keramos, Made in Austria* and an indented number, *79*. Seventy-nine? He holds it quite still. Seventy-nine was the number of the original . . . no replica this, but the real thing – Phoebe's piano cat mended, repaired – restored. He places it carefully in its rightful position on the mantelpiece – guardian of the mail, master of the pending.

–Thank you, he says to the empty room.

He looks at his watch. Forty-nine and three-quarter hours to go.

He has spent hours searching for the missing stick, retracing his course as far as memory goes – and further, to all possible places fugue might have carried him. In the end, without conscious intention, he has come to the plastic café. He sits alone in their usual place, sweating slightly over his sixth beer, in the delicate stasis between thought and exhaustion. Outside there is still a little daylight; inside, the orange globes make the emptiness more gloomy. The *patron* is doing the accounts. Walter lights his forty-seventh cigarette of the day; he is the last customer. In fifteen hours she'll be gone – but, now, she lives and breathes not five minutes away. Several times he has been down the narrow stairs to the *toilettes* and telephones for a piss, to comb his hair, wash his hands, but he hasn't touched the phone. Fifteen hours, love thieving time, and soon they'll be closing. Honour beats him back and keeps him clear – honour among thieves, honour between lovers . . .

   –Yes, please – another beer, and a pack of Gauloises.

O such a little word is Honour.

He drops a lump of sugar into the bitter canteen coffee, rattling the cup as he stirs it. A long white night of silence insulates him against the jolly daytime banter of the counter lady and the general cafeteria prattle. He is indifferent, fragile, weightless. If he weren't in the basement with the whole concrete mass of the English Language School above him, he might easily float up and over the city – like the balloons at the siege of Paris rising free on the winds of the secret night to be swept o'er land or sea where no man wist and lost forever.

   –Hello, Walter, what are you doing here – looking for a job?

It's the Mechanical Mouse with a cup of coffee, teetering, her breasts barricaded with briefcase and papers.

   –Oh hello – er, Emma. No, as a matter of fact I'm just returning a couple of books. Aren't you on vacation?

   –Tomorrow. Congratulations, by the way.

   –Congratulations?

   –You passed. The results should be up on the board this afternoon. Don't look so surprised.

   –But I am surprised. Here, sit down – I mean, won't you sit down for a moment?

   –Well, just for a minute . . . The mechanical smile flickers bright. –You'd have got a credit if you'd done just a bit better on your peer teaching.

   –You've got to be joking.

   –Oh no. She sips her coffee delicately. –In fact, everyone did well – there was only one failure.

   –Oh well, that's no great surprise. Poor Linda.

–No, Linda just scraped through. There were three distinctions and seven credits, that's really very good.

–Who failed then?

–Connie – she –

–Connie Mantel? He laughs. –That's ridiculous – she was one of the best of our lot.

–She was quite good, yes, but she made a complete mess of the exam – we could hardly give her any marks at all. I expect it was nerves – she's rather a nervy person, isn't she? There's usually one of them. Of course, she can always retake the exam next year, if she –

Walter stands up. –Excuse me, I'm sorry, but . . .

–. . . cares to. You've left your books – aren't you going to take your –

But he's already in the corridor. Ten past eleven – there's still a chance, an outside chance, if the flight's delayed . . . or a child is ill . . . or . . . He runs past the notice board – Course Offerings, Job Listings, Sales Items – and picks up the phone.

It rings, again and again, on and on in the long emptiness at the other end. He dials again . . . there is someone waiting behind him now. He hangs up slowly. He could call the airport . . . information, first. He picks up the phone again . . . and then what? The loudspeakers blaring all over Roissy: 'Madame Mantel to the phone, please . . . Hear this, hear this, a message for Madame Mantel – you've failed the course, you messed it up, you'll never be a teacher now . . . fly for your life . . .'

–Are you 'aving a problem?

–Eh – what? *Comment?*

–You 'ave a difficulty maybe?

Petite, blonde, blue-eyed, heavy-breasted, shyly smiling.

–Don't I know you?

–Oh yes – we meet always at the telephone. She laughs.

–I remember. Well, it's alright really – thanks anyway. He hangs up finally. –Another time maybe. See you around. Have a nice day.

–And you also – you 'ave a nice day.

Walter nods and, without looking back, goes up the stairs, across the marble hall and out into the open air.

From the second storey of the Eiffel Tower the air is clear of fumes and haze and the city glints with gold and glass. There is enough of a breeze to ripple the river and lazily loll the flags of innumerable nations. The cries of the children at play on the Champ de Mars are as thin as a shepherd's pipes on the other side of the mountain. Away to the south a rising plane catches a flash of sunlight. Ladybird, ladybird, fly away home, your house is on fire, your children are . . .

–Excuse me, sir, maybe you could help me?

A tall, silver-headed man with a bow tie and a blazer and a soft-spoken American tranquillity. Not a panhandler – no placard round his neck: *J'ai faim.*

–Yes, sure – if I can. What's the problem?

–I'm having a little trouble getting oriented here. These domes now . . . that one on the hill – I guess that's the Panthéon, but this one down here by the river I don't seem to recollect at all.

–That's the Bibliothèque Mazarine.

–The Bibliothèque Mazarine. Right. He nods slowly.

Walter thinks of his own books pushed randomly into the shelves after the burglary, for months neglected, waiting to be reordered – maybe even to be reread.

–Then this one here must be the Hôtel des Invalides?

–I'm afraid so.

The old man gives him a steady look. –Shined up for the celebrations, huh? Guess everybody is getting pretty excited about that?

–I wouldn't say so. Not excited, no. The French don't get excited.

–They don't? He smiles. –That's rather an unusual point of view, isn't it?

–Based on experience. You wouldn't say in French, 'He's excited' – *excité* –meaning enthusiastic; it would have more the sense of being irritated, nervous, out of control – or sexually aroused.

The American laughs softly –You've been here quite a while then?

–Getting on for twenty years.

–Twenty years – is that so? That's very interesting. The last time I was in Paris – the only time – was exactly forty years ago.

–It's changed a bit.

–It certainly has. I'm happy to hear you say that – I was starting to wonder if it wasn't just me, the memory getting up to its old tricks . . . But you've reassured me.

They gaze out together over the vaunting city and the years that wind up the hill forever. In a week or ten days the teffle letter will arrive in Berkeley, and there will be no one to lose or leave that missive – or mitigate it.

–It was my honeymoon, you know. We had a month – a week each way across the ocean in the old *France* and two weeks in Paris. By golly, I'll never forget the look on Agnes's face when we got off the train and the smell hit us. I don't know what we'd expected exactly, but we sure weren't pre-pared for that smell, and the dirt, and those johns that were no more than a hole in the floor. It all seemed so darned foreign. And then Agnes was properly put out that no one understood a word she said – back home she was a schoolteacher in those days and *taught* French. She didn't show it, though. As for me, I couldn't see what all the noise was about. I recall wondering what good American – dead or alive – would want to spend much time in Paris.

He chuckles reminiscently. – I'm not saying we didn't have a swell time – we did, but that was on account of what we were discovering in each other. And we'd had that blessed week on the boat. So we didn't say too much about what we felt about the city. I guess neither one of us wanted to disappoint the other. And we were shy. In those days it was okay to be shy . . .

Walter's offer of a cigarette is politely refused. As he lights

258

his own, cupping his hand over the match, he notices the raised ridges on his thumbnail. He slides the dead match back into the box. Batches of trippers released from the lift lap and eddy around them – two old guys chewing the fat – with extravagant exclamations, then ebb away until succeeded by another wave.

–But you did talk about it eventually?

–Oh sure – sure we did – it kind of came out little by little. In the end, years later, it got to be a family joke – Mom and Dad's Horrible Honeymoon . . . But then somewhere along the line we began to get the feeling we'd been kind of dumb – well, you know, naive. Our friends would go to Paris, and then all of our kids went – our two girls for their junior year abroad – and everybody loved it . . . So what had we missed – and how come we'd missed it? I don't say it exactly riled us, but it kind of niggled . . . until slowly we got this idea of going back, not just for two weeks, but for two months, six months maybe, maybe a year – and that became our retirement project . . . I don't know why I'm telling you all this . . .

–It's a fine day, a wonderful view – a good place for listening.

–That's true. You feel if it weren't for this wire mesh, you could reach out and put your hand on the whole city . . . Maybe I'll take one of those cigarettes after all, if I may?

Lighting the cigarette, Walter looks straight at the stranger for the first time – a large, heavy face, handsome in an old-fashioned senatorial style, yet fresh, like the map of some ancient unspoiled territory.

–Go on – about your project.

–You sure you want to hear?

–Sure. I've nothing else to do.

–Well . . . so this time we determined to know what we were getting into. Ignorance is excusable when you're full of buck and beans, but at our age . . . So anyways, we started to read up on France – and Paris in particular – history, architecture, the artists, the culture, literature . . . There weren't too many folk around us who'd turn off the television after dinner and sit down and read aloud to each other – but we did just that. We couldn't settle to Balzac somehow, but we got on fine with Emile Zola – seemed to have more pith – and Maupassant, of course, and . . . well, I can tell you, we got through a lot of books – in English, to be sure. I took a course in the French language and at the end of it I could read a menu just fine, but that's about as far as it went. Agnes attended classes at a *cordon bleu* cookery school and . . .

Is that what Connie would be doing – courses in American English, the Joy of Vegetarian Cooking, Great Books of America – evenings with Emerson and Melville and Walt Whitman? She was a great one for course-taking – Elevating your Self-Esteem, Creative Commitment, Mature Motherhood, Doing Your Own Thing . . . Walter tightens his fingers on the wire netting that prevents suicide, prevents reaching forth, touching, clutching, calling out – Come back, Connie, come back, my love – come back, come back . . .

All of Paris shifts slightly in a shimmer of intense heat – a great bright painting curling to invisible flame. The tower sways like a weakening web of chocolate in the sun. Walter closes his eyes and clings, trembling in her first-told dream of falling – spouse spinning silently surprised to the hard ground and the attendant ambulances and firetrucks . . . another man's vertigo.

–'Well, George,' she said, 'it looks like I'm not going to see Paris again, after all.'

Walter opens his eyes, withdraws his hand – there's a trace of blood on the inside of his fingers and he wipes it away quickly on his trousers. But the old American is not looking at him.

–'But *you* go, George,' she said, 'promise me you'll go – just like we planned . . .'

And Connie will be walking in the cool of the evening under the eucalyptus trees in Eden Grove. –So you did?

–Yes I did. That's why I'm here right now.

What had happened to Agnes – he'd missed it – dead, sick, crippled, mad? –And your wife . . .?

–She passed away one month exactly before the day I retired. It happened so fast she hadn't even the time to lose weight. She came back from the hospital on Monday and on Saturday afternoon she was gone. She just sat up there on the pillows and died. Saturday was our day for speaking French, you know – or trying to.

–And did you – speak French, I mean – that day?

–No sir, we did not. And yet . . . He looks at Walter, a mild frown on his broad forehead.

–Yes?

–That morning, you know what she asked me? She wanted me to read to her from the poet Rimbaud . . . Do you care for Rimbaud?

–I can't say he's one of my favourites, no.

–No. Well that's just about the way we felt about him too. And that's the curious thing . . . Of course, I read it to her in English – that must make a big difference. I can't imagine poetry translating too well from one language into another – wouldn't you agree?

–Yes . . . and to me Rimbaud's often fairly obscure even in the French.

–He is? Well – maybe that's not so surprising. Poor guy, from what I understand, he didn't have much of a life, did he? He sighs and brushes his face with his hand. –But it still bothers me a little – I just can't figure out why she chose *him*.

–Maybe the dying have some wonderful final clarity of mind when all things are made plain.

The American looks at him solemnly. –That seems kind of a high price to pay for clarity of mind.

And they smile at each other – and laugh.

–Well, sir, it's been good talking with you – and I thank you for your courtesy in listening.

They shake hands, and the old man moves away, then stops and turns back, a little hesitant.

–Pardon me, but would you think it an impertinence if I asked you what you do in life?

–Do? Oh well . . . I guess you could say I'm a teacher.

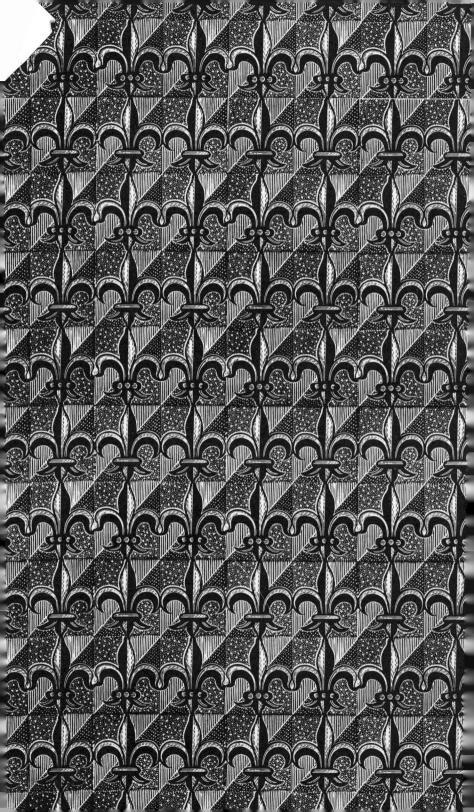